MAHMOOD AND MRS WYNWORTH

MAHMOOD AND MRS WYNWORTH

SIMON LENNON

Pine Hill Books

Mahmood and Mrs Wynworth

Fiction (Political, Thriller)

Published by Pine Hill Books

ISBN 978-1-925446-30-2 (electronic)

ISBN 978-1-925446-31-9 (paperback)

73,000 words

The characters in this novel are fictitious. Any similarity to specific real people, alive or dead, is coincidental.

Cover image: Parliament House, Canberra, 2006

To my youngest daughter

THE MEMBER FOR SEIDLER

Images of Rohingya refugees suffering in squalor strafed Carole Wynworth's mind, sitting with her cup of cappuccino coffee more than five thousand miles away. At her desk in her parliamentary office, Carole's regularly re-tinted hair was groomed high from her head, although it had become a little ruffled reading that Amnesty International report. A tiny, warm tear waited patiently behind her watery blue eyes.

Hanging from a stand were the dark woollen coat and complementing hat she had worn outside that Tuesday morning. Winter had persisted stubbornly that year, at least in Canberra, but the sprawling hilltop universe of Parliament House provided comfortably regulated temperature without humidity. Carole's deep green jacket and long dark skirt were for the House of Representatives sitting later that day.

Carole's office door pushed open, revealing her young staffer. "Oh," gasped Heidi Moore.

Around Parliament House were twenty-seven hundred synchronised clocks, positioned so at least one was visible from anywhere anybody stood. The time was past nine o'clock. "My God!" gasped Carole.

"You're supposed to be in the party room." Heidi hadn't needed to remind her.

Carole rushed up from her chair, her stockinged feet slipping from the leather shoes in which they had been resting, half wearing. She slipped her feet back in her shoes as the telephone on her desk rang. "You answer that," said Carole, moistening her lips with her tongue and hurrying to the chair on which her smallish handbag lay, carrying just enough make-up and credit cards to get her through each day, along with her mobile telephone. She had tried but never mastered the more complicated communications device allocated to her since her election, which lay neglected in a drawer until Heidi tried again to guide her through it.

Heidi reached across Carole's desk to pick up the telephone handset. "Carole Wynworth's office," she said.

Reflected in the wall mirror, thin clouds of powder tinted Carole's pale complexion pink. A fifty-year lifetime beneath green trees, back home in Sydney, had shaded her soft skin from the sun. On her jacket lapel was a silver Amnesty International badge, of barbed wire encircling a lighted candle. Carole quickly brushed her hair back to its grooming.

"Emmet would like a word," said Heidi, with her hand across the telephone mouthpiece.

"I'll call him back," said Carole, although she rarely did.

Holding her handbag close to her side, Carole bustled through her open office door, past the waiting area of sleek clean sofas and public-property paintings on the walls, into the mint-green carpeted corridor. Within the private parliamentarians' half of Parliament House, corridors were wide but ceilings not particularly high.

Built into Capital Hill, more or less replacing the hill, Parliament House was an under-hill city, most of which remained hidden from tourist cameras and view. Parliamentarians and their staff shed their days and nights there in the three floors of offices and chambers, without venturing further below ground to where golf carts carried workers around the network of tunnels and spaces servicing them. The governing party room was still several corridors and a floor away from Carole's office.

The Prime Minister was in Washington. Party room meetings

with him away were unusual, but the previous day seventeen Rohingya refugees had entered the Australian High Commission in Dhaka, demanding resettlement in Australia. Once numbering a million, the predominantly Muslim Rohingya had demanded self-determination in Burma, known also as Myanmar, which refused them the privileges enjoyed by indigenous Burmese because they were Bengali illegal immigrants. The Burmese military response to Rohingya terrorism had led many Rohingya to flee to Bangladesh and elsewhere.

Carole knocked before pushing open the party room door. Bright lights sprawled across the ceiling, leaving no shadows among the seats of well-groomed men and women in their ornamental suits and styles. The voice speaking from the front of the room stopped, as a hundred or so Liberal Party parliamentarians turned to their colleague clamouring into the room, clutching her handbag, closing the door behind her.

Standing tall at the long table at the front of the room was the Attorney General, his squarish jaw giving Leighton Ingles credibility his forty-four years of youth denied him. "The Member for Seidler," he smiled at Carole. "I wondered where you were."

"Constituents," explained Carole. Parliamentarians excused anything upon constituents, although Carole's constituents were people who cared deeply about refugees rather than refugees themselves.

Leighton waited while Carole looked around for the nearest empty chair, quickly spotting it. Members drew their legs closer as Carole slipped before them to sit there, resting her handbag on the floor and trying to become comfortable. The eyes that had turned towards her soon turned back to Leighton.

Sitting beside Leighton, facing Carole and the rest of their colleagues from the table at the front of the room, was the youthful Minister for Immigration and Ethnic Affairs. Andrea Gidley's fine blonde hair bobbed neatly on the deep padded shoulders of her modest blue blouse, while her gently rounded face tried its best to seem earnest and sincere.

"We must respect sovereign countries enforcing their laws

of sedition, public order, and morality," Leighton told his audience, drawing his already deep voice deeper. "We will not allow malcontents, opportunists, and petty criminals to claim refugee status in this country."

Carole's right hand moved towards the lapel of her jacket. She began fidgeting with the sturdy silver badge.

"I propose that we amend Australian law to restrict refugee status to citizens of those countries the Australian government declares to be dangerous or oppressive," continued Leighton. "We would closely examine the situation in Burma before deciding whether to gazette that country at this time, and thereafter keep the situation under constant review."

Carole shook her head. Human rights organisations like Amnesty International had often criticised Australia for not sufficiently accommodating asylum seekers.

"Our successful multicultural Australia will only unite," continued Leighton, "if we involve all ethnic and religious groups in these decisions, along with our friends overseas and human rights groups."

Carole laughed. If people didn't look at her then it was because they were not surprised.

"We shouldn't pre-empt a decision about the seventeen asylum seekers from Burma," Leighton cautioned them, "but our friends should not suffer the indignity to their nations our courts might cast by granting refuge to their criminals."

"We could talk to them," called out Carole. "They would understand."

Members groaned. Others laughed.

"Other countries aren't as tolerant of Islamic terrorism as we are, Carole," answered Leighton.

"I don't pander to Islamophobia," Carole insisted, "while condemning it."

"Will you gazette Afghanistan?" someone called out to Leighton.

"Iraq?" asked another.

"Sweden?"

People laughed, but not Carole. "Any more years of this government in Stockholm...," smiled Leighton.

"France?"

People laughed louder. "Not France," said Leighton, his smile broadening to a grin, "not yet."

"Principle does not change," called out Carole, rising to her feet. "Principle that changes has perished." Leighton rested back in his chair, while Carole's weak fists held the air before her. "Our party once ended the White Australia Policy, welcoming those wanting refuge, when other parties wouldn't."

She looked around her. One man studied the patterns on his black leather shoes, arching his foot below his crossed legs. A woman read a letter.

"Asylum seekers aren't criminals," continued Carole.

Andrea Gidley leant forward. "Criminals don't stop being criminals because they claim asylum," she responded, her voice dragging as she spoke. The members who looked elsewhere when Carole spoke looked up at Andrea. "We all welcome refugees, Carole, but we need to manage each situation."

"Helping people isn't a situation," pleaded Carole. "We don't want any more impediments to people coming to this country. They've come so far, overcome so much. Can't we let them share their dreams with us?"

Andrea sighed. "Aspiring immigrants want better lives for themselves and their children," she said, "but that doesn't make them heroes and it doesn't make them victims."

"They're frightened," insisted Carole, with fear in her eyes reflecting the fear she imagined in the eyes of strangers. "Asylum seekers don't understand passports and visas."

"They understand refugee status."

Members laughed. Leighton smiled.

"Would you deny seventeen refugees seeking resettlement from a camp in Africa," asked Andrea, "for seventeen people not deserving of our sympathy?"

"We should welcome them all," Carole persisted. "Is it not better that we accept a thousand men and women unworthy of refugee status, than refuse just one refugee from a homeland we don't want to offend?"

"No," replied Andrea.

"What if you were that refugee?"

Andrea placed her hands on her European face. "Tell me the Asian or African country that would take me."

"That's more reason to welcome them," scoffed Carole, looking around the room at too few faces looking back at her. "What is happening in this country?" she asked, unable to recognise the party she once lauded at garden parties in her home. Damning those around her for their indifference, Carole slumped back in her chair.

"Put the vote," a member called out.

"Is there more debate?" asked Leighton, again standing up; party rooms were normally fora for debate as the floor of Parliament no longer was. Leighton was politically astute enough to have already secured the Prime Minister's approval to so provocative a proposal, while involving his colleagues who might one day decide the next prime minister.

"Put the vote," cried another member.

"Those in favour...."

"Aye, aye, aye," the room resounded with forthright expressions of a will.

"Those against?" asked Leighton.

"No!" yelled Carole. Her conviction only accentuated the silence around her.

"We'll proceed."

Almost all the parliamentarians rose from their chairs, talking with each other. Someone opened the doors and they streamed out of the room into the corridors.

Carole remained slumped in her chair, while space emptied around her. The decades since Her Majesty opened the blandly grand Parliament House were not enough for the antiseptic rooms to become soulful. Far from her life at home in Sydney two hundred miles away, she sat in an uncomfortably thin-cushioned chair in the mellow dust-free air, her neck too taut from words unsaid to move.

Only one other person remained in the party room, watching her from the front row of chairs. Standing in the threads of his dark silk suit was the government chief whip, Rodney Bayne. The ceiling lights shone from the cream in his black hair, and from the gold pin holding tight his navy-blue tie, but not from his thin nose and lips. His clothes had kept ahead of his career since overcoming his government school education to study politics at Adelaide University, not quite fifteen years earlier. "You argued well, Carole," smiled Rodney, his long fingers dancing about the end of his long hands.

"Not well enough."

"Cicero could not have won your case."

"I don't watch television," she told him, "apart from the ABC." The ABC was the government-owned Australian Broadcasting Corporation.

Rodney began walking around the rows of chairs towards her. "I know you'll support the party decision today," he told her, tilting his long head towards the long windows admitting light from the private members' gardens and cold Canberra winter, "out there."

By one window, a tall wooden lectern stood idle. Lining one short wall to the side of the room were framed photographs of every Liberal Party leader since the party formed in 1945, from the sepia-toned serious to the colourful smiling predecessors of the current prime minister. Beyond his photograph was space for more photographs to come. If Rodney feared Carole's dissent, she was less certain of her courage than perhaps he was.

"The Senate won't pass our bill into law anyway," Rodney continued. "This is something we can use to remind the voters that we're the party willing to enforce our borders, even if we don't."

No place had felt more calculating than Canberra. "While you're playing politics," said Carole, "refugees feel unwelcome."

"If we don't present unity," Rodney repeated his oft-repeated words, "giving voters clear choices as against our opponents, then voters will punish us on polling day."

Carole looked back at him. "Welcoming refugees is a matter of principle."

"You're not the only person here with principles," said Rodney, almost sympathetically. He reached the row in which Carole sat and leant on the back of a chair to face her. "You are the only person assuming the rest of us are without them."

"I have my mandate."

"Mandate?" responded Rodney. "You're here because stronger candidates for party selection in Seidler battled each other, leaving you the only candidate nobody knew so nobody hated."

The former member for Seidler's sudden retirement one year earlier had led to a hurried selection contest for the safest Liberal Party seat in New South Wales, in which party factions fought to keep each other from prevailing. Curious twists of circumstance overcame years of secret planning as unambitious local party members conversing among themselves voted quietly for their friend and conversationalist from the Killara branch, allowing Carole to slip into selection.

The election proper followed. "A hundred thousand constituents who knew nothing about you voted for this government," Rodney continued. "The party could have selected a one-legged wallaby to be our candidate and still retained Seidler, albeit with a reduced majority."

Drawing the last air around her into her chest, Carole collected her handbag from the floor. She rose from her chair.

"You should not assume the outcome of any inquiry into the situation in Burma," Rodney told her.

"Governments only convene inquiries when they already know the results," replied Carole. "I've learnt *that* these past eight months."

"This is not about you, Carole," Rodney explained, strangely reassuringly in his voice. "This is about the Government keeping faith with the people who placed us here: the people who look up and out at this big little world and want a government willing to say this country still exists, that they still count for something, that we're doing all we can to protect them. Would you betray them for vagrants in a diplomatic confine, or jetsam in the wide-open sea?"

Carole turned and walked away from him towards the door until, before leaving, she turned back to face him. "People say, Rodney, that I won party selection with a story of my late father, who lost the sight from his right eye fighting Nazis at El Alamein. Too many nights he bounced his little girl on his weak failing knees, begging my generation, your parents' generation, not to repeat the wars he saw."

She continued staring at Rodney, as pleased with herself for her retort as she was angry with him for compelling her to make it. "Was your story true?" he asked.

Carole turned and stepped through the open door. In the corridor, she drew a long breath. Carole's skin cooled beneath the powders on her face.

Her handbag at her side, Carole trekked back along the white-walled corridors, past people too busy to notice her. She passed office doors open and closed, with blinds shielding the offices beyond glass panes beside each door. Most panes were conspicuously neat, although some city members displayed posters promoting their causes and some country members displayed posters promoting their electorates. The posters weren't there to persuade anybody bothering to read them, but to please the few visitors that security guards admitted to the corridors and staffers escorted to the offices.

Australian art adorned the higher walls and Australian sculptures interrupted the higher ceilings of lounge areas by the stairwells and beside the glass walls overlooking well-watered lawns and ambient secluded gardens. Being public property, although the public never saw it, every item was carefully catalogued.

Small plaques identified the timbers of benches: eucalypts, wattles, and other Australian woods. It was all a big museum.

The lift carried Carole slowly upwards to her distant office floor. Ahead of her as she stepped from the open lift, leaning against a wall by the window and with his hands in the pockets of his unbuttoned white jacket, was a large round man, belching with the force of too much breakfast. Carole recognised the aging Xavier Talbot from the *Sydney Morning Herald* newspaper not just from the Parliament House cafeteria but from the press gallery high in the chambers and the broadcasts of press conferences she had watched from monitors.

"Carole," he said, heaving himself away from the wall, keeping his hands in his pockets.

"You know who I am?"

"Everybody here has some reputation."

"I'm more accustomed to the attentions of the *North Shore Times*," admitted Carole. Metropolitan newspapers like the *Sydney Morning Herald* rarely troubled backbenchers, and more rarely those in their first terms.

"Leighton Ingles and Andrea Gidley called a press conference for ten o'clock this morning," explained Xavier, "but all their offices are saying is that it concerns the Rohingya in Dhaka. Do you support what they will say, Carole?"

Commentators who approved of the Government would approve of their proposal. Those opposed would oppose. Carole turned and walked along the corridor towards her office.

"This prime minister runs the tightest government I've seen," observed Xavier, following her. "Voices that once roared now won't as much as whisper in a dead man's ear."

She continued walking. Her office had never before been so far away.

"With other governments," continued Xavier, "I had to shut out the noise there were so many people with so much to say. Today, I watch the corpses in parliamentary coffins and your name keeps coming up in the obituaries."

Carole reached her office door. There, she stopped.

Xavier soon stood beside her. "I can be your friend, Carole."

"The party room unanimously welcomes refugees, Xavier."

"Friends talk with each other," he persisted.

"We're talking!" cried Carole, raising her hands in the air.

"Are you a solitary voice of political dissent, here to change the ethos of the unethical, the morals of the immoral? Lying in the flow will leave you another minor footnote in old editions of the parliamentary Hansard."

Xavier drew his hand from his pocket and, concealing what he held, forced a card into her hand. Carole crushed the card in her fingers before anyone saw it.

"What frightens you, Carole? Is it having no influence, or is it having too much?"

A young man suddenly raced from an office and along the corridor beside them. People running through the office corridors were unusual, but a young woman rushed from the same office and ran after him. "What's happening?" asked Xavier, stepping in her way.

"You better switch on the television," she said, rushing around him.

Carole glanced at Xavier before hurrying into her office, past the empty reception area. She pushed open the door to her private office, where Heidi stood before the television set, broadcasting the sight of plumes of swirling smoke from the blue of Sydney Harbour. Slowly Carole moved towards it, her heart uncertain whether to race away or stop beating in her chest.

The telephone rang. Heidi answered it.

Carole stood affixed by the images too much like war at home. Xavier Talbot's crumpled business card fell from her opening hands to the otherwise clean carpet floor, while history in a present tense shone from the television screen.

Among arrays of stumbling motorboats, a ferry burnt amidst streaks of debris: seats, and suitcases, strangers trying to swim. Bouncing in the waves of turmoil was a flotilla of bright orange buoys to some of which people were holding fast. "We have unconfirmed reports of an explosion at Queens Park," said the television news commentator.

Heidi replaced the telephone handset. "Emmet called to say he and Tessa are safe," she told Carole.

Again, Xavier stood beside Carole; the office was supposed to be Carole's private space. "You can stop thinking about the Rohingya," Xavier told her as they watched.

"Don't leap to any conclusions about the events you're seeing," responded Carole.

"Don't leap to any about me."

"They might be accidents," insisted Carole. "There could be anyone at fault."

"Leighton Ingles won't be talking today about accepting more Muslim refugees."

Carole turned to Xavier. "Crime and terrorism have nothing to do with immigration," she told him. "They have nothing to do with refugees, nothing to do with Islam. If anybody uses this tragedy to say anything else, then the police will be onto him, very fast."

"Every time something like this happens," said Xavier, "or when police arrest the would-be terrorists before it happens, the prime minister and every other major political party figure in this country say the same thing. They'll say it again soon enough today and we'll faithfully repeat it, but I report news, Carole, and you saying it isn't news. If you feed me something extra to say, I'll say it. I'll quote you, and I'm sure it will be something that sits very well with a lot of our readers: people like you, Carole."

Carole remained silent. The business of government was too private, too sensitive.

"You must know something."

She shook her head. Carole looked back at the television screen.

"No," he muttered, "maybe you don't."

"This is precisely the time we should affirm our support for immigrants and refugees," said Carole, watching the television. "You quote me saying this country should welcome the Rohingya and everybody else wanting to come here, especially poor Muslims."

Xavier stepped to where Carole couldn't help but see him. "If you're so willing to accept refugees into your country, people will say you should accept them into your home. I know enough about you and your electorate to know you live in a very lovely home."

There was room enough in the country for Carole and her family not to need to accommodate anyone, but politics and public opinion weren't well-suited to nuances. "We have a spare room," she told him, "or two." Policemen on one boat pulled aboard a body.

2

MAHMOOD

For as long as Carole remembered, all entrants to the public and private areas of Parliament House, including parliamentarians, passed through grey rectangular gates scanning them for metal objects. Any bags they carried were conveyed along black leather belts under x-ray machines.

Political conflict gave way to statesmanship, of sorts, that wintry Tuesday. Leighton Ingles briefed Parliament and so the country on the attack in Sydney. Snug within their security, political leaders repeated their condolences from previous terrorist attacks. Heroic in their doggedness, they expressed their obstinate determination not to let terrorism affect them or change government policy. Speaking from Washington, the Prime Minister also refused to flinch.

In their private offices, parliamentarians continued their customary business. Resting in their private lounges, fine wines in their hands, they said how awful terrorism was.

By early Wednesday morning, news services reported that fourteen people died, including the bomber Ojala Kassab, and more than fifty were injured on the ferry *Lady Penrhyn*: disparate lives linked forever in a moment on the water. Tayab Senussi killed only himself when police surrounded him near a bus stop at Queens Park. Witnesses reported several suspicious figures at

City Circle railway stations, all of whom fled before police could apprehend them.

Television stations broadcast montages of magnified photographs from above of three faces in blurs: three people carrying black plastic shopping bags emblazoned with the white logo of Myer department stores. "Police report," said a commentator, "that closed circuit cameras observed Kassab, Senussi, and another person together outside Lidcombe railway station at seven o'clock the morning of the bombing."

Watching the television set in her Canberra apartment, Carole cringed, gripping her mug of coffee a little tighter. Fearing that people would assume the terrorists' backgrounds and religions from the names they bore, Carole knew that many Europeans took names from other ethnic origins. Kassab and Senussi were Australian born; Carole would only refer to them as Australians, if she mentioned them at all.

"Police have not yet identified the third person," continued the commentator, "whose face remained obscured from the camera by a blue cap marked for the Canterbury-Bankstown rugby league team. The person also wore a Canterbury-Bankstown jersey and denim jeans." By Tuesday evening, Sydney public transport had resumed normal services, such as they were.

In the private world of Parliament House, Canberra, the largest open space was the arcade of shops and trades, including a bank and automatic teller machine, travel agency, and gymnasium. At the hairdressing salon, parliamentarians cut and styled their hair frequently enough for people never to notice they'd been cut and styled.

Conversations at the café were public fare, made in fear of an opposing political ear or, worse still, a journalistic ear. There, having arrived at Parliament House, stood Carole waiting in the queue; a single mug of coffee in her apartment was rarely enough to start her days in Canberra. Only when she turned around did she see the wide frame of Xavier Talbot standing a few places behind her, his hands in his jacket pockets. "Xavier," she said.

"Carole," he answered.

She stepped aside to allow the people between her and Xavier to step forward in the queue, until she stood facing him. "Must the media mention religion when reporting terrorism?" Carole asked him.

"Experts suspect Islamic..."

"Leave policing to the police," Carole told him. "People might be too proud to admit it, but they believe what they read and hear, when they read and hear it often enough."

The queue stepped another place forward. "We report what the police are telling us, Carole."

"Do you know how it's affecting Muslim people?"

"Do you know any Muslims?"

"Our gardener, at home, he's been tending to our gardens for years now, is Muslim; I dread to think how he must be feeling now." The queue stepped another place forward. "Do you know any refugees?"

"An African, his face as black as a bottle brim-full of tar, threatened me with a knife."

"It wasn't his fault," countered Carole. "They've suffered so much."

"I gave him my wallet."

"You should be trying to prevent prejudice."

"We are, Carole. You have no idea how much reputable media, like the *Sydney Morning Herald*, try. I think we do well."

"Any prejudice is too much," Carole told him, as the queue again moved forward. She turned to the man behind the café counter. "One cappuccino, please," she asked.

Xavier stood beside her. He collected a tray on which he loaded two Danish pastries and a single long black coffee.

Carole normally returned to her office to sip her hot cappuccino alone, where no one would see the froth if it collected on her lips. That Wednesday morning, she sat at the nearest empty table.

Xavier soon swaggered towards her and sat down before her. Several flakes of sugary pastry adhered to the side of his mouth as he ate.

Carole sipped from her cup. She licked her lips and then

touched her lips with her fingers, satisfied that only red lipstick was on them.

"I'm a journalist, Carole," said Xavier, swilling his coffee. "If it's news, I'll report it." The coffee swept the pastry from his lips.

"What if that news causes prejudice," she asked, before relaxing her tone, "Xavier?"

"Look, Carole," he answered, slinging forward in his chair causing Carole to jar backwards in hers. "We weren't the newspaper reporting Lebanese boys picking Australian girls to rape. We don't identify criminals' religions unless they're Christian, we don't identify the religions of victims unless they're not, but newspaper readers realise the rules and infer what we omit, no matter how often we chastise them or they chastise themselves. We report Muslim police officers, but the public still presume terrorists are Muslim and people saving us aren't."

"I don't," Carole insisted. "All the people I know don't. Where do you find these people you call the public?"

"Opinion pollsters find them," answered Xavier, taking a half-eaten pastry in his hand. "Politicians find them."

His reply slowed Carole from her passion. "What about television?" she asked.

Xavier laughed. "Your Prime Minister already complains that television programmes make news instead of reporting it."

Carole looked around. She tried to think of something to proffer or something to ask.

"What can you tell me to help me stop prejudice?" asked Xavier.

Carole looked back at him. "How can I change anything?" she asked. "How can I make people see only the good in everyone?"

Xavier chewed and finally swallowed a broad mouthful of pastry. "Tomorrow," he said, "Andrea Gidley will table in Parliament her bill restricting the granting of refugee status to countries the government considers oppressive or dangerous."

"That is quick."

"With your welcome to refugees, the Labor Party will call a spill on the vote to see if you vote against the Government, before they and the Greens kill the bill in the Senate."

Divisions in the House of Representatives, which the Government in coalition comfortably controlled, were unusual. The rare parliamentarians who cast their lot against their party's positions in recent years, representing their electorate's peculiar concerns, had vetted doing so with their leaders beforehand, but they'd not been for anything as important to other electorates as the changes Andrea Gidley proposed. If Carole were absent from the chamber or silently abstained in a vote on the voices, two Opposition members would challenge the Speaker's call of those voices. The Speaker would call a division, when the bells would ring throughout Parliament House, bringing members to account. Members would move to the chamber right or left. Carole could not hide without being seen to have hidden.

"Give me news Carole and I will report it," said Xavier, in that audible a place. "They don't need to be facts as long as they're news."

Carole was almost amused, as Xavier removed another business card from his wallet and laid it on the table before her. She took his card in her hand. Without news for Carole to accord him, Xavier left.

She licked her lips and wiped them with her fingers a final time, assuring herself no cappuccino froth had collected there, before standing up. Carole walked slowly back along the corridors and up the stairs to her office.

There stood Rodney Bayne, seeming taller with still longer dark suits every time she saw him, in conversation with Heidi. "Carole," he smiled; he was most unsettling when he smiled.

"Rodney," responded Carole in kind, "to what I am indebted for this honour?"

He looked back at Heidi. "Please excuse me, Heidi," he smiled again, before again facing Carole.

In that moment of silence, Carole proceeded into her private office. She opened the top drawer of her desk to leave Xavier's business card.

Without invitation, Rodney followed her. "Xavier Talbot does like his breakfasts, doesn't he?" said Rodney, as he closed the door behind them.

Carole feared Rodney guessing what she said to the journalist, when the truth couldn't hurt her. "I want him to do more to stop prejudice," she told Rodney.

"We all do, Carole." Rodney glanced around him before proceeding to the far end of the sofa from Carole. He reclined with his long legs stretched over the fabrics so his shining black leather shoes hung over the edges, pointed tips upright.

"Do you sit like that at home, Rodney?"

He looked at his legs. "Yes, Carole," he said, before again smiling. He pulled his legs from the sofa and sat upright, glancing briefly at her as if expecting her to mark her approval.

Carole began to walk to her far side of the desk, before deciding that might encourage him to stay. She sat facing Rodney in the chair at the front side of the desk, the chair for visitors, as she might if she soon needed to leave.

Rodney again spoke. "I want to know we have your support for the clarifications to refugee law we discussed yesterday, Carole."

"This party proudly gives its parliamentarians the right of conscience, Rodney," she reminded him, although she knew he didn't need reminding. "Haven't I always voted with the Government on the floor of Parliament?"

"You can't change the outcome," said Rodney, "but you can embarrass the Government and be forever tainted by not supporting us."

"What if I'd feel more tainted voting for the bill?"

"The Third World is rife with people ready to grab the next excuse to enter the West by claiming refugee status," Rodney told her. "Would you admit them all?"

"Yes."

Rodney sat back in the sofa, although his great height kept his head still higher than hers. "We're not taking fewer refugees, Carole. Crikey, we might even take more; the United Nations are always on our backs to take more. A thirty-year-old Pakistani can travel first class into Europe where he claims to be a fifteen-year-old Rohingya, and the Europeans don't have the will to refuse him, or even to question him. We're giving the voters in this country a message that we're not accepting everyone who wants to come here, so they don't notice it when we do."

"That message makes Muslims feel unwelcome."

"Carole, Carole, Carole, that message keeps us in our jobs. It wins us elections, so we can do the important things."

"This is important."

"Why are you trying to change people, Carole, instead of representing them?"

"I am representing people," Carole insisted, "but not the people I'm trying to change."

Rodney leant forward towards her, his hands resting on his knees. "Do you want to enter the next election as our candidate for Seidler, Carole?"

Her gaze fell more disbelieving towards him. The party leadership could not immediately evict her from Parliament, but could move enough selection votes to strip her of party endorsement for the next election. "Almost everything I value, we all value," pleaded Carole, "our liberty, country, and liberal traditions. I could be here for ten years and we never again face an issue upon which we diverge."

"Six times in eight months, Carole," Rodney contradicted her. "With your unending indulgence for people who care nothing for you, you wear your black armband like a flag, a white flag. This country and this government aren't so willing to surrender."

"Please don't deny all that unites us," Carole implored him, "for the issues that distinguish us." Since long before joining the Liberal Party with her husband more than twenty years earlier, Carole had never voted for any other party. Throughout her young years of balls and tailor-made white dresses, she had been a Liberal. Through her maturity when thoughts and conversations about politics were impolite, she quietly voted for the party without question. Through mothers' morning teas and art exhibits at which people complained the party should do more to help refugees, her vote remained resolute. Complaining no less vehemently with her parliamentary colleagues in the party room, she had always ultimately sided with her party in the chamber.

"We like you, Carole," said Rodney, "but not enough people share your idealism, not anymore."

She studied his dark, long pervasive eyes. With every moment she did, Carole felt weaker.

Rodney slowly stood up. His jaw and mouth flexed with the words he seemed to prepare, his lips rubbing together, before he turned and walked towards the office door. His hand on the handle, he paused, and turned around to face her. The smile in his face might have been kind, the smile a gentle tutor might bestow on a wayward well-meaning first-year student, or might have taunted her with the presumption he understood her. "Maybe you can change public opinion," Rodney told her, "I don't know, but I know you can achieve something within this government but nothing outside it."

The door to her office made no sound as Rodney closed it. Carole remained alone in her visitor's chair, in that suddenly cool air of Parliament House. If her parliamentary colleagues made voting against Andrea Gidley and Leighton Ingles' bill unpalatable, then the Rohingya refugees made voting for it untenable.

A timid little knock came through the door. Rodney Bayne did not knock so softly. Rodney Bayne did not knock.

"You can come in," called out Carole, assuming she had no power to stop anything.

The door slowly opened. In stepped Heidi, her young face settling on Carole in the chair.

"If I speak too loud," said Carole, "if I so much as breathe what I know to be right, then my party will punish me for disunity." Her eyes flickered around the room for evidence of Rodney Bayne hearing her. "If I remain silent, being seen to agree, then my heart will punish me no less."

Heidi closed the door behind her. "You can breathe freely with me."

Carole grinned, uneasily, but grinned. "I'm not sure I want to be here."

"Mummy wishes she could do what you do," said Heidi.

"The entire terrorism threat is pumped out of all sensible proportion," said Carole. "More people died in Sydney car accidents yesterday than on ferries."

"Two," said Heidi.

"Two?"

"An ABC radio commentator made the same point as you made, but Leighton Ingles told her only two people died in car accidents in Sydney yesterday."

Carole tossed the back of her hand at the air. "More people died in Sydney cars last *month* than on ferries."

"That's what the commentator replied," smiled Heidi. "The last of the libertarians, believing in compassion to all and tolerance, rely upon you."

Carole laughed. "Rely upon me to resign," she asked, "or to let this battle pass and try to win a smaller skirmish before I go?"

"Please try," smiled Heidi. "I'll get you a cappuccino."

She left Carole alone, when feeling sorry for herself felt like wasting time. The business of government and her electorate remained, and Carole climbed from her chair back to her side of her desk, where the papers and computer screen made a little more sense.

Heidi brought her another cup of cappuccino. The only feature of her life common to Canberra and her home in Sydney was cappuccino coffee, even if those cups in Parliament House were never quite as luscious as those from the cafeterias in the North Shore of Sydney. They were probably just as good as any others in Canberra, or anywhere else away from home.

Without committees or other meetings of whom she was a part, Carole's next commitment that day was Question Time commencing at two o'clock. Leighton Ingles would again brief Parliament on the terrorist attack in Sydney and police search for the man in the Canterbury-Bankstown cap. She'd not been given any questions to ask ministers after that; the day was not her turn. Besides, the matter of most interest to Carole and her constituents remained the fate of the seventeen Rohingya holed up in the Australian High Commission in Dhaka. They were receiving food and medical care, along with books to read and films to watch in their native language, but weren't headed to Australia.

When her back became sore, Carole flexed her taut shoulder muscles. She rolled them forward through circles to loosen them, as she'd never needed to do at home.

Amidst her review of a letter responding to a constituent Heidi had drafted, soon after midday, Heidi popped her head through the open door. "A Mister Mahmood is waiting for you at the public entrance," said Heidi.

As well as exhibitions, Magna Carta, and portrait galleries, along with the customary shop and restaurant, the public precinct at the front of Parliament House offered tourists views of the House of Representatives and Senate chambers. When parliamentarians met school groups or other visitors from their electorates, their offices had normally been informed beforehand. "Who?" asked Carole.

"He said he saw your words in the newspaper this morning, welcoming Muslims. He wants to know if you meant it."

A visitor was a distraction, when Carole wanted distraction. She stood up from her chair.

"Would you like me to meet him and bring him through?" asked Heidi.

"I'll go," answered Carole. "I'd like to be where nobody recognises me."

Carole trekked along more corridors under lights and down stairs, beyond the regime of parliamentary offices and suites. In a wide-open doorway stood two guards, their white-shirt and dark-trouser uniforms shining as much as the parliamentary security labels on their shoulders. Beyond them, the passageway turned, obscuring Carole's view of anybody there.

Turning into the next stretch of passageway, where the last daylight from the distant forecourt windows reached, she saw a man not in security guard detail. He was young, probably twenty-something years of age, wearing a long white woollen coat and beige scarf trailed leisurely around his neck and down one side of his chest. Beneath the coat, his lucid deep blue tie dominated his pale jacket and shirt; his clothes were as much dressed by him as they dressed him. He was the same height as Carole, not tall for a man, with deep brown eyes and black hair groomed close to his pale, shaven skin.

He smiled; his red lips arced across his seamless white teeth neatly set in charm. "Mrs Wynworth?" he asked. His voice was without accent, smooth and lilting with new inflexions in her name. He must have sensed her nodding without her needing to do so, for he stepped towards her and reached out his long right arm. "My name is Mahmood."

"Delighted," said Carole, offering her hand.

He shook her hand. "Most Australians aren't as delighted to see a Muslim today as you are, Mrs Wynworth."

"I am sorry," she said, "so sorry. They don't understand."

"The security guards wouldn't let me come to your office."

"Security guards don't let anybody through without a pass," Carole explained. "My husband can't enter without his."

Mahmood turned to walk back along the passageway towards the public areas. Carole walked with him. "Australia has been good to me," he said, "but your government is prejudiced against Muslims."

They walked into the Great Hall foyer, where daylight was again bright from the forecourt windows. Scores of tourists carried their travel satchels and Parliament House maps, traversing the long grand staircases to the higher floor. Some pointed their telephone cameras at the high cornices and ceilings. Most pointed them at their faces to photograph themselves.

"My girlfriend, Samina Quresh, is a good girl, cleverer than I am: a metallurgist qualified in Jordan. My MP, a good man, there are a few, asked your Andrea Gidley to let her stay a little longer in this country to be with me. I think we could marry, Mrs Wynworth, but Andrea Gidley is forcing her to leave before we can know if we should. If Samina were English, Mrs Wynworth, if she were Christian, your government would let her stay."

"This is no longer a Christian country," said Carole.

Mahmood laughed. "Only the Christians say that."

"We don't think of ourselves like that, Mahmood. We are multicultural now."

Again he laughed, leading Carole towards the exit. "Why would I assume good things about you, Mrs Wynworth?"

"I think I can help your girlfriend to stay," Carole answered. "I have something Andrea Gidley wants, which I have to give her anyway, but if I can only get some of the things I want, then so can she."

3

PRINCIPLE AND PREJUDICE

That chilly Thursday morning without a breeze, Carole in her coat walked with Xavier Talbot in his coat along a path in the private members' garden at Parliament House. There, they were visible but inaudible to anybody watching from the windows around them, which in Parliament House people assumed was everybody.

"People want hope more than fear," Carole told him. "I've met a Muslim who can show them that refugees' children are no different to their children. There must be thousands of innocent men and women suffering because of our prejudice. If you tell their stories, make people understand, then Andrea Gidley will have to admit all the Rohingya."

"We already tell their stories, Carole, but you don't notice because you think we should tell more. We report the plights of Muslims blaming only ourselves, and give them full credit for their successes. We treat good Muslims as typical and bad ones as anomalous, until finally people believe journalists even less than they believe politicians. Muslim sportsmen and actresses don't make people forget terrorism."

"This man is special," insisted Carole. "He's charming, debonair even. People won't need to like sports or films to like him."

"You're wanting too much of him," said Xavier.

"Shouldn't we start to have more confidence in Muslims," asked Carole, "instead of so little?"

"He's one man."

"Mahmood can introduce us to his family, girlfriend, and other friends. If I can help him, I think he can help us."

When neither of them spoke, the air felt coldest. "Are you certain that he wants to be a newspaper story?" asked Xavier. "Not everybody does."

"I've arranged to meet him in the lounge bar at the Hotel Canberra at noon," said Carole. "All I ask is that you join us."

"What's the story, Carole? What's the news? I'm a political reporter. My columns aren't for the community pages."

"What's more political than prejudice?"

"Does erasing prejudice mean more to you than it does to him?" asked Xavier, as they neared a door back inside the Parliament building. "The Hotel Canberra is a pricey place to drink."

"I'll buy the drinks," said Carole, "and coffee."

"If there's real news elsewhere at noon," Xavier told her, "I won't be with you. If you want to give me news to report, then tell me you'll vote against Andrea Gidley's refugee bill later today, or you'll abstain, or you'll pointedly be absent from the House."

Her coat in her office, Carole hurried along the box labyrinth corridors to Andrea Gidley's ministerial office, much larger than Carole's backbencher office but decorated much the same, in as much as any office in Parliament House was decorated. If their styles differed, then Carole couldn't see the difference. Offices were places for people passing through, even if Parliament House was not.

Waiting in the reception area, the arguments Carole would make tussled inside her head, impatient to be spoken. As unlikely as those arguments were to prevail was the certainty Carole would ultimately get what she wanted. The blue sofa in which she sat became increasingly uncomfortable, until her attention turned to the Aboriginal painting on the wall and the numbered caption explaining it.

All that changed between unadorned parliamentary offices were the staffers' faces, if not their ages. Strangely, thought Carole, in the office of an immigration minister, all the young men and women around her were Anglo-Saxon, including the receptionist who finally brought her a cup of cappuccino.

Before Carole could sip it, a private office door beyond the short hallway opened. "Carole," smiled Andrea Gidley. "With everyone trying to speak to me about our new refugee law, I can only give you a few minutes."

Carefully holding her cup, Carole rose from the sofa and walked briskly towards her. When she was close enough to Andrea to speak without the minister's staff hearing her, Carole paused to ask: "Aren't any of your staff immigrants?"

"God no!" laughed Andrea, guiding Carole into her private office. "Not since a Turk complained my Armenian was biased because of a genocide the Turk denied happened anyway."

"They could just talk about it."

Andrea closed her office door behind them. "You really do see the world through champagne crystal glasses, don't you?"

"I prefer cappuccinos."

"You can't see anything through the froth."

Carole smiled. "But the taste and aroma are lovely."

Andrea proceeded past the sofas to the far side of her desk, less cluttered than Carole's desk, behind which she sat in her large chair. "Surrounding myself with tenth-generational Australians makes all the immigrants feel equally important and equally neglected," she explained. "They all have my ear and my department's ear, without worrying about races they dislike being involved."

Around most walls were shelves housing hordes of ceremonial artefacts. Among the chrome silver statuettes were framed photographs of Andrea posed with foreign ambassadors and ethnic community leaders across Australia, including a few Sydney residents Carole recognised from Ethnic Community Council gatherings.

"Do you know Mahmood?" asked Carole, standing close to the photographs, trying to find his face among the many.

"Mahmood who?" asked Andrea.

"His girlfriend is Samina Quresh."

"You said she was the reason you wanted to see me," said Andrea, as Carole turned towards her. "The department refused to extend her visa because her application contained untruths."

Careful not to reveal her surprise, Carole sat in a chair on her side of Andrea's long desk, her cappuccino cup undrunk in her hand. Carole leant forward, her knees high and heels raised from the floor.

"Samina Quresh is not a qualified metallurgist," Andrea explained, reading a sheet of paper on her desk. "She studied engineering for one year and failed two of her subjects at the Hashemite University, Zarqa."

"A simple misunderstanding, I'm sure. Her boyfriend is Australian: a fine boy."

Andrea pushed the sheet of paper away from her. "Samina Quresh can apply for residence as his partner."

"They need more time together," said Carole. "Muslims want to be seen to be intimate unless they're married."

Taking a cup from her desk, Andrea leant back in her chair. "There wouldn't be a person here who doesn't try time and again to extend somebody's visa or avert a deportation, but they do it for friends and donors. They do it for constituents and the votes they think happy ones bring and unhappy ones cost. Samina Quresh lives nowhere near your electorate. Why do you care so much about her?"

"Why do you care so little?"

"I care, Carole, but I won't be another weak-willed immigration minister with nothing more than a long history of cuisines she's tasted and a few babies she'll never meet apparently named after her." Andrea sipped from her cup. "I'm giving the Australian people what they want: that's democracy."

"Democracy is not the rule of the majority," Carole corrected her, "but respect for the minority."

"That's white-people talk," answered Andrea. "The minorities claiming rights for minorities stop wherever they become the majority."

Carole pulled back in her chair, her heels slipping slowly to the floor. Turning her face away, her gaze passed from that room to images of boxcars crowded with prisoners bustling through her mind she was unwilling to foist away. The face of a man who died decades earlier pressed against those images, while his guttural German English voice whispered words she could not quite discern. Carole's mind alone in memory succumbed to stories of chambers filled not with talking but with gas and human screams.

"Mister Schimmelmann," explained Carole, softened to a schoolgirl's voice in a classroom too big, with soul on which no one alive could intrude. "We weren't Jewish but he became my parents' friend, after coming to Sydney after the Second World War. Tattooed on his wrist were blue letters and numbers I can still recite, if you want to hear them."

The silence in the room might have been Andrea's indulgence. They might have been her sensitivity. "Carole," she said gently, as if to free her, "no one comes from Auschwitz anymore. The Holocaust was a long, long time ago."

Carole's eyes refocussed on the moment. She faced Andrea again, still holding her cup in her hand. "Not for me."

"The only people killing Jews today are Muslim."

"That's an awful thing to say!" snapped Carole. "I can find you exceptions."

"Exceptions merely make rules into generalisations."

"Don't make generalisations."

"You know, Carole, privately all the ethnic community leaders who've called me since Tuesday support our new refugee law, even if they want countries from which their people come gazetted as dangerous or oppressive. Publicly they oppose it, as do the usual twinkly-dee sideline of churches and other refugee advocacy groups for whom no number of arrivals to this country is enough, for whom this country and her people, you and me included, mean nothing."

"I don't believe you."

Their eyes trained upon the other's eyes, without acknowledging their stares. "Politics are problems, Carole," lamented Andrea, her voice curiously amicable. "I don't like needing these sorts of laws any more than you do, but responsible government ought to be responsible. Ideals are easily pronounced but uneasily implemented, like the cavalier crusades of opposition or the tea parties of people who would rather die thinking that everything is apples than live dealing with reality. With the burden of knowing what we say can be implemented, we refine our ideals for the facts. Don't spoil the party for people without your luxuries."

Nobody should suggest that a member's vote could affect the exercise of a minister's discretion. "I want to keep quiet through debates on your bill before the Parliament and then to vote with you, if it comes to that," said Carole. "I want Samina Quresh's visa renewed each time she wants it."

"Her relationship with your friend Mahmood mightn't last."

"It might."

Andrea smiled. "We all need allies, Carole, but will I have to allow another Muslim to immigrate to this country every time I want your silence and vote?"

Carole laughed. "Only when I'm silent about something about which I should scream and voting for something I should oppose."

Andrea nodded. "If I don't extend her visa," she admitted, "she might claim asylum. That will cost us a fortune and she'll never go home, except for holidays."

The remark was not worth refuting. More relieved than pleased with what she had done, Carole departed.

With more reason than she normally had to be distracted, Carole struggled to concentrate upon her parliamentary business through the rest of that morning. What might have excited others could be very mundane with everything else Carole was trying to do, even if other members considered her interests mundane.

Among the hotels built for the new national capital in the 1920s, the Hotel Canberra was the accommodation for Members of Parliament and even a prime minister. When Mahmood had mentioned staying there, Carole hadn't wanted to sound so condescending as to mention it was her favourite hotel in Canberra, although many of her friends were equally fond of the Kurrajong. Since becoming a parliamentarian, Carole and Emmet had bought a lakefront apartment in Kingston, so each time she sat again in the lounge bar of the Hotel Canberra could feel nostalgic.

Carole arrived shortly before noon. At one of four armchairs around an otherwise empty table, Mahmood sat without a coat in a pale suit as fashionable as had been the suit he'd worn the previous day. On the table was a margarita glass, partly drunk. "Always my pleasure, Mrs Wynworth," he smiled, standing up and stepping forward to kiss Carole's cheek.

"Samina can stay in this country for as long as she wants."

"Thank you so, so very much, Mrs Wynworth," grinned Mahmood, rolling out his long arms towards her before refraining.

"Please, call me Carole," she said, remembering her manners. She sat in a chair adjoining his.

Mahmood sat down again. "With the opportunity you have afforded us...." His voice began to waver as his free hand conjured chance in the air. "Well," he said, his eyes sparkling, "we shall see."

"Is Samina with you?" asked Carole, looking around the lounge in expectation of seeing the stranger she imagined already knowing.

"She's in her room, a little tired; we have separate rooms, naturally. We've been to the art gallery this morning and are visiting the arboretum this afternoon."

"You should visit Old Parliament House, now a museum, without politicians anymore. I think I prefer it to the new."

"We will, tomorrow. Thank you."

"You *can* help me," said Carole. "I'm trying to soothe the prejudice across this country, the one that locks out refugees, the one that treats Muslims as terrorists. You can prove to people that we're all the same."

"Am I not different?"

"You are," she assured him, reaching forward and placing her hand on his forearm. "If the newspapers, television, and radio can see and hear Muslims like you, we won't have this prejudice. The Government will admit more refugees. People like Samina can some and stay here forever."

Mahmood shook his head. "I'm sorry, Carole," he said, his

eyes without their sparkle. "Samina and I, we prefer our privacy." He drank the last of his margarita and stood up. "Thank you again, Carole," he smiled, offering her his hand to shake. "Goodbye."

She shook his hand. "Goodbye, Mahmood."

Her arms and shoulders fell flatly to her sides. Carole watched him turn and walk away, through the lobby towards the corridor to the rooms at the front of the hotel. Before he left the lobby, a tall man in a commonplace suit stepped in front of him.

Mahmood stopped, his back to Carole. The men appeared to speak, although Carole couldn't hear them from so far away. Both men stood still, without movements that gave anything away.

Xavier Talbot came through the entrance door from the front car park, as Carole had, past Mahmood and the other man talking. He came into the lounge, looked around until he saw Carole, and came towards her. "Is your friend here?" he asked Carole.

"He's behind you," she said, tilting her head towards Mahmood. "He's the shorter man in the pale suit, with his back to us, talking to the taller man. Do you know who the taller man is?"

Xavier sat in a chair at the table with Carole, away from Mahmood's empty glass. "If I were the sort of person who guessed, I'd say he was federal police," answered Xavier. "He's tall, fit, and healthy, wearing a suit that's adequate but uninspiring, like a uniform he knows isn't really a uniform. He's standing tall, chest out by habit, without bending down a little as most tall men do talking to someone so much shorter than they are."

A waiter swiftly removed Mahmood's empty glass and coaster from the table. A waitress then spoke. "May I bring you anything?" she asked. Carole ordered a cup of cappuccino coffee, Xavier a glass of beer. They resumed watching Mahmood and the taller man.

The tall man left, leaving Mahmood standing alone, his back still to Carole. For several moments he stood there, before turning around. He walked slowly back to Carole, until he stood before her. "I've already lost something of my privacy," he told her. "I must surrender the last of it to recover the rest of it."

Mahmood glanced at Xavier. He looked back at Carole.

"The police wanted to know how I knew you," continued Mahmood, "and where I was Tuesday morning. I said I'd seen your kind words to Muslims in the newspaper and on Tuesday morning, I was nowhere near a ferry terminal."

Carole shook her head. "I mentioned you to Andrea Gidley," she answered. "I never thought she'd harass you."

"This is the life of a Muslim in this country, Carole," lamented Mahmood, "no matter how good we are."

"Let me introduce you to the journalist I think can help," said Carole.

"Xavier Talbot," he said, with all the confidence of a man expecting the name to mean more than it did. "Have you a name?"

"Mahmood," he replied, sitting down in the same chair in which he'd previously sat.

"Is that a first name or family name?" asked Xavier. "Have you a full name?"

"I should assume everything I tell you will appear in the newspaper. Let me keep something to myself."

"I can keep your full name confidential," Xavier persisted.

Mahmood smiled. "I can save you from that responsibility."

The waitress brought Carole her cappuccino and Xavier his glass of beer. Mahmood ordered another margarita.

Xavier drew from his pocket some photographs he gave to Mahmood. "Is there anything you'd like to tell the Australian people about these?" asked Xavier. "They're passengers aboard the *Lady Penrhyn* on Tuesday."

"Must the media dwell upon terrorism?" interrupted Carole. "Can't we move onto something pleasant?"

"That's still our story, Carole," answered Xavier, "this week."

"You wouldn't mention it if Mahmood was Christian."

"If Mahmood was Christian, we wouldn't be with him now."

Mahmood examined the pictures. "The murdered and maimed are often Muslims," he said, drawing Carole's gaze back towards him. "All Muslims are victims of prejudice." Carole dipped her head, embarrassed by her countrymen and women.

Taking her attention again, Mahmood showed the photographs to Carole. Previously clean skin had been stripped to red and black. Eyes once glowing for a day coming at office jobs hung half open in their battered, jagged sockets. Carole returned the pictures to Xavier.

"Do you own a Canterbury-Bankstown cap?" Xavier asked Mahmood.

"Why would a Muslim wear a football cap?" interrupted Carole.

"Muslims can dress as badly as anyone else," smiled Mahmood, "and if a Muslim were to wear a football cap, then it would be Canterbury-Bankstown."

"Could a Christian have worn that cap so police think he's a Muslim?" asked Carole.

The waitress brought Mahmood his margarita. Around the rim of the glass were speckles of sugar and a wedge of lime.

Xavier resumed his questions of Mahmood. "What would you say to the man in the Canterbury-Bankstown cap?" he asked.

Mahmood sipped his drink. "Please present yourself to the police," he said.

Xavier removed a notepad and pen from his pocket. He began writing.

"Be honest," continued Mahmood, watching Xavier write. "If you, or someone you know, have done something wrong, tell the police. Muslims are hurting."

Carole nodded. Her cup in her hand, she reclined in her comfortable chair.

"Tell me about you, Mahmood," said Xavier.

Mahmood grinned, almost boyishly, without looking at Carole as she looked at him. "I'm not used to being asked," he admitted. "I am Australian, I was born here."

Xavier took a mouthful of beer, as he did before most of the questions he asked. They were his moments without Mahmood speaking and so with nothing to write. "Are you studying?" asked Xavier. "Do you work?"

"The University of Sydney recently conferred on me my

engineering degree," Mahmood answered, "but not the second-class honours I thought I might get." He spoke as he would speak to the family of the girl he was wooing, who needed to know he was suitable to escort their daughter and sister. "I live at Thornleigh, with my parents, brothers, and sisters." Thornleigh was a comfortable tree-spoiled suburb in north-western Sydney, close to Carole's electorate. "My time with Samina is my last long holiday before settling down to forty-five years of work." His eyes rolled high to mention so long a time.

Xavier wrote in his notepad. When he wasn't writing, his pen poised ready to do so.

"My parents came here from Lebanon during the civil war," Mahmood continued, "although to speak of war in Lebanon can be to speak of any number of years; the Christians don't respect Islam." He turned to Carole. "Your new refugee law might have kept my parents away," he said as much to her as Xavier, before turning back to him. "My parents came here, without education, but the government taught them to speak English, taught my father a trade, and they worked hard for their family. They encouraged their children to study, while we taught them all we could of football and barbecues."

Carole wondered if her daughter spoke as proudly of her parents as Mahmood spoke of his. She felt certain she didn't.

"What more would you like to know?" Mahmood asked Xavier.

"What would you like to tell me?"

Mahmood looked at Carole watching him. "Mrs Wynworth," he started to say, before the expression on Carole's face corrected him. "Carole would have mentioned I have a girlfriend, but please let her keep her privacy by not mentioning her name. She is the most beautiful woman I have met, with skin white and pure. She is a better Muslim than I am." He smiled, again taking his margarita glass in his hand, acknowledging his vice.

"I know it isn't true," said Carole, returning her empty cup to the table and placing her hand on Mahmood's knee nearest her, "and I hate having to mention it so please don't feel offended, but Andrea Gidley tried to tell me Samina isn't a qualified metallurgist."

Mahmood shook his head. "The authorities in Jordan might have made a mistake in what they told the Australian government," he explained, "but I have to say that the Australian government, or the immigration department officials handling Samina's application, might simply have lied. It happens more than you know, but they're always trying to keep Muslims out of the country and think lying is acceptable. Muslims might make mistakes, as they might in Jordan, but we never lie."

Carole withdrew her hand from his knee. She leant back in her chair, never more relaxed.

"Being a Muslim," sighed Mahmood, leaning back in his chair, "I don't expect your security services to believe anything I say."

4

THE LAKE

Canberra radiated around and out from Capital Hill. From the Parliament House forecourt, evergreen trees neatly enveloped the white motif of Old Parliament House along a line across Lake Burley Griffin to the stone War Memorial and pyramidal Mount Ainslie.

Xavier Talbot's article, published Friday morning in the *Sydney Morning Herald*, *Canberra Times*, and other newspapers, focused upon Mahmood's plea to the man in the Canterbury-Bankstown cap to reveal himself to police. Perhaps that was the best approach, thought Carole, reading it again and again in her apartment, after she'd needed to flick through too many pages to find it. She still thought the media dwelt too much upon the ferry bombing in Sydney, by then three days ago.

Parliament rarely sat or did very much on Fridays, allowing members from electorates and senators from states far from Canberra time to return home before the weekend. Sydney wasn't so far, leaving Carole plenty of time to meet Andrea Gidley that morning. Their meeting was Andrea's idea, after she'd read the article about Mahmood. She also suggested they meet not in Parliament House, the private parts of which were eerily quiet and unsettling the days that Parliament didn't sit, but around the lakeside shores.

Water lapped the concrete banks. Along wide paths, methodical joggers in long grey tracksuits ran through any weather. Rhythmic cyclists rolled to work or study, their silent earpieces wired to pods in their pockets or on their waists. Indifferently they passed the profusely sweating power-walkers no less than they passed the slow strollers with their disciplined white dogs, all of whom knew better than to smile or even look at anonymous faces.

Carole smiled at a woman walking with a white Pekinese dog on a leash, as people smiled near her home. The woman looked away.

At one end of the lake, the National Carillon's pointed white towers reflected in the sullen waters as grey cloudy skies that morning could not. The small tree-soaked island on which stood the closed Carillon was no place for casual tourists, with unkempt grass and old memorials few people saw. Between the island and shore was a walking bridge, on which stood Andrea Gidley gazing across the water on which the winter rippled, wearing a coat as long and gloves as thick as Carole's coat and gloves. Carole shivered just seeing them, as she approached.

The still air was cold but unobtrusive, a welcome respite from the manufactured air of Parliament House, where they had sat too late the previous night. Unlike Carole, Andrea wasn't wearing a hat.

"When I was first elected," said Andrea as Carole reached her, still gazing across the water, "I often walked around the lake. I wandered across this bridge and around the little island, where I could forget being here. Lakes are peaceful places, as the floor of Parliament and even the party room often aren't, but even lakes conceal struggles for life under the surface."

"Were you responsible for the police harassing my friend Mahmood?" asked Carole.

Andrea turned to her. "Is he your mission, now?"

"The innocent dislike being harassed more than the guilty."

"If police could investigate only the guilty, then they would. A police interview isn't harassment, Carole, but we're MPs. Police like to know who our friends are."

"Is that only our Muslim friends?"

"No, but when one is friends enough to make you intervene to keep his girlfriend in the country without any of the customary reasons, it's your interest as much as anyone to let the police know. Your friend Mahmood refused to tell the policeman his last name and the police didn't push the point as a courtesy to you, but there's no harm in him knowing the police are paying attention."

"There's harm to him," protested Carole. "Your fears aren't mine."

Andrea began walking along the bridge to the island. Carole walked with her. "The police are reviewing this morning's newspaper article about Mahmood," said Andrea.

"Don't you worry I'll tell Mahmood he's being investigated?"

"I expect you to tell him. Leighton Ingles isn't involving himself in the review, but he's asked to be informed. If there's anything to tell you and even if there isn't, Leighton will tell you. He wants to thank you for siding with the Government on our refugee bill yesterday."

The Senate had rejected the refugee bill the previous evening. It would not become law, but Leighton Ingles had already accused the Opposition parties of surrendering Australian sovereignty.

"Will you be embarrassed when Mahmood proves to be everything he says he is?" asked Carole.

"I'll be relieved," answered Andrea, "but we prefer to know anything that might embarrass the Government before others learn of it."

They reached the island and soon the paved space within the three searing towers of the Carillon. "The only people embarrassing this government are the seventeen Rohingya in our high commission in Dhaka," said Carole, "and every other refugee you're not welcoming to this country?"

"How long do conversations with you normally last, Carole, before you mention refugees?" asked Andrea. "You get all starry-eyed and teary-eyed believing tales of the plight of immigrants and asylum seekers. I don't."

Suddenly scores of bells obscured from view above them burst, like the ringing of an absent church in which they'd been confined. Carole pressed her gloved hands under her hat against her ears.

Eventually, the bells stopped. Hesitantly at first, in case they exploded again, Carole pulled her hands from her warm ears. The bells remained silent and still.

"Fifty-five bronze bells ring here every quarter hour," said Andrea. "Didn't you know?"

"You didn't suggest we meet here to watch me squirm, Andrea."

"Be careful, Carole. Sometimes I think you don't realise who your friends are."

"People who meet Mahmood like him, Andrea, so they like Muslims. Is that your fear?"

"Who has met him, Carole, other than you, Xavier Talbot, and I assume Samina Quresh?"

"If you met him, you'd know he's kind; I'm not sure that came through well enough in the newspaper. He couldn't harm anyone; he's a man of peace."

"Everyone is, Carole, until he kills someone, or tries to kill someone."

Andrea stepped away from the Carillon. She pointed across the bridge towards the shore and up the hill.

"Up there is the National Police Memorial," Andrea explained. "Those are the men and women of peace, who died because men, sometimes women, killed them."

"Mahmood drinks margaritas!" cried Carole. "Have you ever met a man who drinks margaritas who did anything bad?"

Andrea laughed, looking back at her. "I've never met a man who drinks margaritas."

Slowly, Andrea started back towards the bridge. Again Carole walked with her.

"Everybody's a bit jumpy," Andrea explained. "The police haven't identified the person in the Canterbury-Bankstown cap. They don't know why he didn't detonate a device, but fear he will."

"Of the tens of millions of people in this country," answered Carole, "is anyone imagining that Mahmood is that man? That's preposterous. Why would a terrorist brazenly come to

Parliament House, presenting himself to all that security? Does he think we're fools?"

Andrea stopped on the bridge and faced her. "Aren't we, Carole?"

"I'm not."

"From here," said Andrea, "I'm going to my department. Leighton Ingles will be at his. He'll call you to meet him, probably at a café or restaurant. Leighton likes cafés and restaurants."

Andrea turned and walked away. Carole's gaze drifted across the rippling waters to the strangely beautiful mountain black on grey. The sounds of the lapping lake rolled through her coat and her, as they would if she weren't there.

Carole checked her watch. The time was after nine thirty.

Old Parliament House had been Australia's parliament house until 1988, when the new Parliament House opened. The three-storey symmetrical white building was no less elegant than it was in retrospect modest, functional and pleasing outside and within.

With its exhibitions and café, the building opened to visitors every day, except Christmas Day. By the time Carole arrived there, the first visitors were already inside. The few arriving outside, slowly climbing the wide steps, did not include Mahmood. Among the cars parked there, she didn't know if any car was his.

Inside, Carole removed her gloves and flexed her finger bones. After removing her hat, she gently loosened without ruffling her hair. After paying the small admission charge and, carrying her coat and hat, with her gloves in her handbag, Carole climbed another flight of stairs.

Mahmood wasn't in the King's Hall, reminding Carole how much smaller but grander was everything about the Old Parliament House than the new. Among the visitors in the carpeted corridors, the green-leather old House of Representatives chamber, and other rooms along that side of the house, she couldn't find Mahmood.

This was not a place to call out. Carole wasn't willing to draw attention to Mahmood or her by asking the ticketing desk to page him. Nor was she impatient.

Carole found Mahmood in the red-leather old Senate chamber. In the chairs in which senators once sat, he sat with a young woman Carole presumed was Samina. Instead of the suit he'd worn when he knew he was seeing her, Mahmood wore a casual striped shirt collared by a fawn cashmere scarf at his neck and long flowing canary white trousers. The woman's long-sleeved, dark-patterned dress covered her arms and legs well, but if Carole had expected to see a silk scarf around her head, she was disappointed. Her shining dark hair flowed sleekly over her shoulders. Her skin was whiter than his.

Slowing her pace when she recognised him, Carole walked towards them. Mahmood stood up and, leaving the woman behind, walked towards Carole.

"An unexpected pleasure," he smiled, as he reached her.

"I've been with Andrea Gidley down by the Carillon," said Carole.

"The Carillon?" asked Mahmood.

"The tower on an island in the lake," explained Carole, "with the bells."

Mahmood nodded. "I heard them," he said. "Bells, church bells, why must there be bells?"

"We try to accommodate all cultures."

"Accommodate mine," Mahmood insisted. "You say this country is multicultural, but it is still so much more Christian than Muslim. Australians prohibit mosques from issuing our calls to prayer beyond their boundaries, denying us our religious observance, but the sounds of church bells ring where Muslims hear them."

"Is that important, now?" asked Carole.

"Only a Christian would ask, Carole."

"I'm as much a Muslim as a Christian," Carole protested. "I'm nice to everyone."

"You're not a Muslim, Carole. Until you feel the pain of people disrespecting Islam..."

"I feel the pain, Mahmood. I do. I wish my Muslim gardener..."

"Your gardener," asked Mahmood, "in the garden?"

"I wish him happiness through the Muslim festivals and never mention Christmas or Easter to him or anyone else," continued Carole. "I never go to church."

"Do you wish him an Eid Saeed, or an Eid Mubarak?"

"Eid Sigh...," Carole struggled to say. "Eid Moo..."

"Do you go to a mosque?"

"There are none near my home."

"That will change," said Mahmood. "Your gardener must have a mosque."

"He lives far away for me; I'm not sure where."

"He comes to your home to garden. Can't you go to his mosque?"

"I'm sorry," said Carole. "I will."

"Will you pray to Allah?"

"Yes, I'm multicultural. I respect all faiths and cultures, but I can't change other people, not at once. When people are more welcoming of Muslims, then we can see what we can do about the bells. More and more churches welcome Muslims, more than they welcome Christians."

"You're English, you're Christian, Carole. Until you renounce the Son of Mary and devote your life to Allah and the Prophet, you're a Christian. You're not multicultural, you only think you are."

"I didn't find you to talk about me," pleaded Carole.

"Please," persisted Mahmood, "tell your friend the journalist that Muslims shouldn't have to hear church bells in a multicultural country. If you want Muslims to integrate with you, then you must integrate with us."

Carole struggled for the words to answer him. He was right, she knew, but that didn't make her answer any easier to find. "I thought you should know the police are still investigating you. I've tried to stop them, but I can't."

"I care less than you care what your police say about me. I've heard it all before, about Samina, about other Muslims, to care what they say about me. You can't stop them. Nobody can stop them, but you don't have to believe them."

"I trust you, Mahmood. I trust what I believe, what we believe, but not everybody does. We need to recognise political reality, the bigotry of others. This is why people need to get to know you, Samina, and other Muslims. They'll trust you when they know you, like I know you."

Mahmood shook his head. "Samina didn't like seeing me mentioned in the newspaper this morning," he told Carole. "She's glad her name wasn't reported, but she worries that it might be. I shouldn't have let you convince me to talk with that journalist."

"We need his help."

"Bureaucratic voyeurs are always looking out for Muslims. They look in mosques, at weddings, and in homes and bedrooms. They're watching our families and friends: most of all, Samina."

Mahmood looked towards Samina. She smiled, acknowledging him, before he turned back to Carole.

"Has anyone followed you home at night or spied upon you in bed, Carole? Has anyone watched you while you pray?"

"I don't pray," she answered, which didn't answer the purpose of his question. "If we're going to improve lives for Muslims, we need journalists' help to change public perceptions. Muslims like you can help us reverse the stereotypes that people have. Andrea Gidley imagined you being the man in the Canterbury-Bankstown football cap. I can't imagine you wearing a football cap."

Mahmood perked up. "I have a football cap," he said.

Carole stepped backwards. She couldn't remember him mentioning it to Xavier Talbot.

Mahmood laughed. "Sydney FC."

Carole also laughed, although she did not know what Sydney FC was. She guessed that it might have been a Sydney football cap.

Mahmood's manner again became earnest. "You talk to your journalist friend about the bells," he told Carole. "Samina and I will enjoy our holiday." He started to walk back to Samina, watching them.

"Where can I contact you?" Carole asked him.

Mahmood turned back to her. "I'll find you," he told her, as he walked, "when I have something to say."

He returned to Samina, again sitting beside her. That wasn't the time for Carole to introduce herself to Samina, if ever there would be a time.

Carole ambled back towards the stairs and entranceway. Again wearing her hat, coat, and gloves, she stepped back into the cool Canberra air. From atop the outdoor steps, she stood in sight of the encampment on the lawns with its banners and smoke from little fires declaring itself the Aboriginal Embassy. That was a visit for her support another day.

From a distance, the Carillon bells rung. Carole must have heard them before that morning, but not noticed them.

Awaiting any word from Leighton Ingles wasn't a reason for Carole remaining in Canberra instead of promptly boarding an aeroplane home to Sydney, except that she wanted to see his face when he had anything to tell her. None of the work she had to do, the reports and correspondence she had to read or answer, were as important as knowing he had nothing to report. None were as important as correcting him if he thought he had.

Much like a tourist on a quiet day, Carole sauntered around the Parliamentary Precinct. If that wasn't the most constructive way to spend a morning, nothing else was more constructive.

The cool air warmed a little, although not very much. Carole's coat remained comfortable. As slow as she walked, she soon slowed even more. Sometime, she started to notice the classic architecture, as she'd not noticed for years.

Inside the National Library, Carole explored the temporary exhibition, forgetting (until she realised she'd forgotten, which reminded her) not just where she was but who she was. The few other people examining the exhibits knew her no more than she remembered being a Member of Parliament.

Soon after eleven o'clock, her mobile telephone rang. Leighton Ingles would meet her at eleven thirty for coffee (for cappuccino) at the café by the exhibition centre on Regatta Point.

Carole walked across the bridge for cars and pedestrians near the Captain Cook Memorial Jet, spouting water high into the air. The water sprayed into a breaking blade against the sky, before finally it splashed back to the shallow wide waters, from which it would rise again.

She reached Regatta Point with time to pause. From there, the distant, solitary Carillion was obvious, above the trees at the far end of the lake. Beside her, the Captain Cook Memorial Globe made the earth no bigger than a person and all the people on it very small. A subtle breeze saved Carole's eyes from becoming damp.

"I noticed you here," a voice interrupted her.

Carole turned to see Leighton Ingles walking towards her. Nobody else was around them.

"A great insecurity has descended over our nation," said Leighton, sounding in private conversation as he did making public speeches. "That fear is now the greatest threat to the multicultural fabric of this nation."

"The Government causes it," protested Carole. "You should alleviate people's fears by not mentioning terrorism."

"We should alleviate people's fears by dealing with it. When did you meet your friend Mahmood, Carole?"

"Two days ago."

"Nothing Mahmood says stacks up," said Leighton. "He's not any of the people named Mahmood who graduated from the University of Sydney with an engineering degree."

"Mahmood warned me that the police don't believe Muslims. Is there any wonder they don't trust us when we don't trust them? You're alienating them with your distrust."

"You're so confident about multiculturalism, you romanticise every immigrant into someone as good as you, even better than you. Is there anything anyone can say to make you consider the possibility that Mahmood is lying to you?"

"Muslims are good and honest people. Saying anything else is a lie. Thinking anything else is prejudice."

"The two terrorists from Tuesday the police have identified were Muslims, Carole."

"How can the police know a person's religion? What databases have they got?"

"Confidential and secure ones."

Never before had anyone mooted a database mentioning

people's religion; being confidential and secure only made it secret. Carole feared secrets more than she feared what everybody knew. "I'm glad I'm not like you, Leighton," she said. "What have we left to defend without our liberties?"

Leighton laughed. "I'd rather live with a little less privacy than not live at all."

"This is not your privacy, Leighton. You might as well ask every Jew to wear a Star of David!"

He turned towards the lake, drawing a weary breath. Carole heard it knowing she was meant to hear it.

"Terrorists aren't real Muslims," she told him.

Leighton looked back at her. "The two we identified in Sydney were real refugees, Carole."

"After all they had suffered, they would have had mental health issues. Would we have been any different if we'd been through their experiences?"

"Yes, Carole, we would. Our soldiers come home from real wars traumatised and don't kill other people. They kill themselves."

"Your wars aren't mine," she told him.

"We don't all choose our wars, Carole."

Carole pulled her arms around her, remembering the cold. "The government and police are always blaming Muslims for crimes and terrorism."

"Carole, we're desperately not blaming them. The public won't hear from me or the police what we've learnt about Mahmood..."

"Good," interrupted Carole. "Then we never need mention it again. Mahmood and I will keep telling the truth and we'll leave the police lies between you and me."

5

THE ELECTORATE OFFICE

Among the flower-spoiled hills in the Upper North Shore of Sydney was Carole's electorate of Seidler. Husbands flew between meetings or accommodated clients or patients through their offices, chambers, or surgeries. Wives prepared their children to lead lives like their parents' lives, attending the same schools, seeing the same people, although to hear her daughter speak sometimes Carole feared she had not done it very well.

Winter's days Carole once called cold affected her much less after so many winter weeks in Canberra. Saturday morning, she dressed into a blouse, skirt and jacket more comfortably casual than she wore during the week: her hybrid of casual wear engaging her constituents on a weekend with the propriety they expected of a parliamentarian. She again affixed to her jacket her silver Amnesty International badge.

The day was one of the weekdays and Saturdays among parliamentary non-sitting days she'd scheduled to be at her electorate office along Tryon Road, Lindfield. Her gold Mercedes-Benz sedan parked in her space in the building basement car park, Carole sat with her constituents presenting her with their complaints about all levels of government: the closure of a government office; the payment of old-age pensions. They were much the same complaints her office received from other constituents by mail.

Carole promised to do all she could. That usually meant talking with or writing a letter to the responsible federal or state government minister or the mayor or responsible councillors of one of the local government areas that her electorate traversed. She and her office repeated those responses back to the constituents.

Sometimes, very rarely, somebody wanted just to thank Carole for what she or the federal government had done. Her electorate office secretary (who had planned to retire with the last member's retirement but remained in the role only because she had known Carole for so long) vetted most appointments and was pleased just to pass those messages along, but still some constituents wanted to see Carole. Along with those who had made appointments, sitting in the vinyl chairs around the waiting area, were those who arrived unheralded for any chance in turn to see Carole.

A glass wall separated the reception area from the building walkway and then footpath of Saturday morning shoppers and children in sports uniforms. Hanging from other waiting area walls were photographs of Carole posed with the Prime Minister and other political figures, along with prominent and less prominent local people. Constituents waiting to see Carole gleaned their eyes across the photographs for any person or place they recognised, and read the captions if they thought they did but were not sure.

They took cold water from the cooler, browsed through newspapers, including the *North Shore Times* in which, as often as not, Carole penned her name to a column promoting government policy. They read copies of her newsletters mailed periodically to every household in the electorate, at the cost of each parliamentarian's allowance. That Saturday, she wanted them to browse through the previous day's edition of the *Sydney Morning Herald* newspaper; Carole had bought extra copies. As well as being delivered to her electorate office, each edition of the newspaper had been delivered to her home every weekday and Saturday morning since she married.

The walls of the windowless meeting room awaited plaques and photographs like those presented to her predecessor by Lions, Rotary, and other clubs, along with local parents and citizens associations. The large long conference table was for formal and large meetings. Carole usually sat with her constituents in a small circle of chairs beside it.

If no one wanted to see her, Carole sat in her private office, relishing the time to catch up with correspondence. Around the walls of her office were several more framed photographs and newspaper pages. Security regulations required her private office to be hidden from public streets and footpaths.

The time Carole had committed to be there ended at eleven o'clock. She remained at her desk in her silent empty offices, reading and writing notes to her office secretary, when she heard the sound of the front door opening. Looking up, she heard it close again. "Hello," she called out, unable to see much of the reception area through her open door.

Nobody answered. A person might have pushed open the door and let it close without entering, but Carole listened. The sound of water coming from the cooler reached her.

"Hello," she said again.

Slowly, Carole stood and walked towards the doorway. Stepping through, she saw Mahmood examining the pictures on the wall, a cup of water in his hand. His suit was dark and close fitting, more staid than other suits Carole had seen him wear, although few constituents dressed so well to see her.

"I thought you were in Canberra," said Carole.

Mahmood turned towards her. "There were no articles in the newspaper today about those awful church bells," he said.

"Church bells, calls to prayer," said Carole. "They're only sounds."

"So are words."

"I'm sorry, Mahmood, I forgot to speak with Xavier Talbot."

"I know. I contacted him through his email address in the *Sydney Morning Herald*. He should be here within the hour."

"I have places to go," Carole told him, "important public events I said I'd attend."

"Aren't Muslims important, Carole? Isn't fighting prejudice

important? If you must go then I can wait for the journalist and talk to him without you."

They were still her offices, although she often allowed meetings in the meeting room without her. "I'll stay," she said.

"I had to promise Xavier Talbot a story, Carole. I shouldn't have to do that."

"What story, Mahmood?"

"Something I didn't mention last Thursday."

His cup of water in his hand, Mahmood walked past Carole into her office, without her invitation, as no other visitor to her offices had. He sat in the only chair other than Carole's there, where Carole's secretary normally sat, facing both Carole and the door. Sipping his water, his legs stretched out, he looked around the room.

Carole sat at her desk, less comfortably than she was sitting with a visitor there than in the meeting room. Her cup of cappuccino she'd bought from a nearby cafeteria was long empty. "After I saw you yesterday, I saw Leighton Ingles," she said. "The police say no person named Mahmood recently graduated from the University of Sydney with an engineering degree."

"Mahmood is a nickname," he explained, again looking around the room. "I enrolled and graduated in my official name: the name on my birth certificate."

"What is that name, Mahmood? Should I call you Mahmood?"

Mahmood continued looking around the room as they conversed. "Actors and actresses use fictitious names. Writers use pseudonyms."

"They give their birth names to anybody asking."

From his chair, Mahmood's eyes dwelt a little on each photograph on the wall. "Who asks them?" he asked, not obviously interested in Carole's reaction. "Everybody calls me Mahmood. If it told you my birth name, then nobody would know who you meant."

"The police could confirm the truth of what you say."

"The police don't confirm the truth of anything that Muslims say."

The papers on Carole's desk remained, her pen part way

through a note. Tending to them seemed rude. Covering them seemed rude. Not covering them seemed rude. She sat wholly unprepared for anyone but her secretary to be in that room with her.

"Can you at least tell me where you live in Thornleigh?" asked Carole. "Can you give me your telephone number?"

"You keep your home address and telephone numbers out of directories. My family's privacy and mine are also precious. We have not been charged with a crime."

"I give my address and telephone numbers to my friends."

"I'm not sure that Muslims have any friends. Wouldn't you give them to the police, or let the police take them from you?"

"No."

"Harry Seidler," said Mahmood, "the architect after whom your electorate was named, was a Jew."

"He lived in Killara," Carole explained. "His old house is unmistakeable, unlike homes built before it."

Mahmood removed something small from his pocket, looked at it, and returned it to his pocket. He placed his cup on the floor, stood up from his chair, and surveyed the carpeted floor around him.

"What is it?" asked Carole.

"Don't disturb me."

Mahmood then raised his hand to his shoulders. "*Allahu Akbar*," he said, before placing his right hand over his left on his chest. He proceeded to speak in what Carole presumed was Arabic.

Carole, in her office, said nothing. She sat uncertain whether to watch him, turn her head away, or even leave the room and close the door after her.

Mahmood bowed, again saying the familiar "*Allahu Akbar*," before more words Carole didn't recognise. He stood, again raised his hand to his shoulders, and again spoke words she didn't know.

Carole leaving the room seemed ruder than remaining. She wished he'd told her what to do.

Mahmood bent down to the floor, reaching it with his hands before kneeling. "*Allahu Akbar*," he said again, resting on the palms of his hands while his forehead, nose, knees, and feet all reached the carpet. He said more unfamiliar words before the familiar "*Allahu Akbar,*" and stood again.

For an instant, Carole presumed he finished, but he continued. Perhaps he repeated what he'd already done. Perhaps it changed. When she was certain he couldn't see her, Carole glanced at a clock. The time was shortly after noon.

Mahmood's prayers continued for many minutes, with Carole in careful silence. She did not so much as move in her chair, less that be disrespectful. She sometimes watched Mahmood and sometimes gazed past him, always trying to be polite. The papers on her desk remained unread, lest Carole looking at them would be disrespectful. Nothing happened in her office while Mahmood prayed, except his prayers.

She checked, relieved, that none of the framed photographs around them pictured clergy. None of the buildings in their backdrops were churches. None of the framed newspaper and magazine pages mentioned Christians, Christianity, or even Christmas. There was nothing potentially offensive among them.

When Mahmood finished, he again sat in his chair. Carole wasn't certain he'd finished until he looked at her.

"What should I have done while you prayed?" she asked him.

"You should have prayed, too," he smiled. "We can get to that later."

Mahmood took his cup from the floor, lifting it high to drink the last of the water, and again stood up. He walked from the room.

Carole followed him. "Have you any beer?" he asked her.

"I think there's wine in the kitchen."

Mahmood dropped his empty cup on the floor, before walking along the corridor. Carole collected the cup and placed it in a wastebasket.

Soon, Mahmood returned, carrying a glass of red wine. He proceeded through the reception area, opened the front door, and went outside, letting the door close behind him.

Carole followed him down the steps to the footpath, where they stood together looking along the quiet street lined with trees, grass, and footpaths. Carole noticed the church on the corner as surely Mahmood had. She thought better than to mention it.

Mahmood held his glass of wine, as Carole hadn't previously seen anybody do on that footpath. "I hope your handbag is safe inside," he said, "without you."

"Which is your car?" asked Carole, checking the various cars parked at the kerbs.

"I came by train." Lindfield railway station was nearby.

"We could have come to your home."

"The journalist can't know my family," answered Mahmood. "I must protect them."

"From what?" asked Carole.

"If the police suspect me of involvement in terrorism, they suspect my family."

"They don't suspect you. They're fearful."

"They suspect all Muslims. We're suspects when there aren't any crimes."

Unusually for Lindfield, an old-model red Holden sedan, with the scrapes and knocks of several years driving that had never troubled anyone enough to warrant repair, parked at the kerb. Soon stepping out of it was Xavier Talbot, not wearing a tie that day, his sloppy pale jacket much like every other jacket Carole had seen him wear. The journalist's belly was more ample in profile every time Carole saw it.

"You drink a lot of alcohol," Xavier told Mahmood as he reached them, "for a Muslim."

"I don't drink alcohol around Muslims unless they also drink it," explained Mahmood. "I don't drink it before cameras." He placed the glass on the ground by a wall. "Where's your photographer?"

"I have my camera," answered Xavier.

Mahmood turned to Carole. "I don't want the only portrait of me on the police files to be whatever pictures the cameras recorded in Parliament House and the policeman secretly took of me in the lobby at the Hotel Canberra," he explained.

"I want this to be quick," said Xavier. "I wouldn't be here at all if my wife wasn't at a health farm or our sons still lived at home."

"You still promise to mention churches and mosques?"

"Yes, yes." Still standing outside, Xavier removed a small dictating machine from a pocket of his jacket, pressed a button to begin recording. He held it close to Mahmood's mouth.

"I'm not particularly religious," said Mahmood, dictating into the machine, "but I can't help but see prejudice when local councils allow church bells to play freely, but ban mosques from broadcasting calls to prayer outside the precincts of a mosque. All we want to do is live peacefully, according to our faith, but church bells deny our faith. Christians would appreciate the sounds of Islamic calls to pray."

Carole waited until she knew Mahmood had finished. "I have some thoughts about your article," she told Xavier.

Xavier stopped his recorder. He withdrew it from Mahmood.

"We need to emphasise the benefits to Australians that Muslims have brought: jobs, culture, cuisine," continued Carole. "Keep up the human angle, stress that Mahmood might not be alive today if we had not accepted his parents as refugees from Lebanon."

Xavier stood studying her. "Are you finished, Carole?" he asked. She nodded, impatient for his response. "What journalism school did you attend?"

Carole shook her head. "None," she said.

"I have some thoughts about your political speeches," said Xavier, becoming professorial. "If you want to connect with our audience, talk to the audience's values. Weave through those values your facts and ideas, not your opinions."

Carole stared at him, trying to comprehend the implications of his advice on the articles he wrote. Those implications eluded her.

"My editor decides my subjects and topics," Xavier explained. "He might decide I write powder pieces, but doesn't lay out the powder, not if he wants my name on the byline."

Xavier reactivated his recorder. Again, he placed it near Mahmood.

"What is this great story you promised me?" Xavier asked Mahmood.

The once brash and confident young man became conspicuously withdrawn, almost afraid, belittled. "My eldest brother," he said, tears collecting in his eyes as he turned to Carole and then away from her. "Hamid was the great hope of our family, who loved us and who we loved very much."

Carole stepped forward, closer to Mahmood. Xavier stood still.

"My parents tried very hard to adopt Australian customs," continued Mahmood. "They encouraged us to play rugby league, took us to parks for picnics, but one Sunday park picnic, late in March four years ago, by the beach at Dee Why, my oldest brother saw a blue-eyed little blonde girl, struggling in the water. The day was sunny, but sunny days can be the most treacherous because we assume they are safe. Hamid was not a good swimmer, but he ventured into the ocean to help her. The water was rough, although none of us knew how rough, but he reached her. She was crying, but his hand held her head above water as he tried to paddle their way to the shore. The current and rips forced them beyond the beach to the rocks, where waves splashed over them, splashed in their mouths and noses, eyes, and ears, but he held her up for me to take her to safety. A man, her father, I suppose, took her from me, without thanking my brother, or me, without even looking at us. He did not wear a shirt, and I saw a crucifix hanging from a chain around his neck."

Xavier raised his free hand close to his lips, holding them tightly. His recorder memorised Mahmood's words. Tears mulled in Carole's eyes.

"I shouldn't have let the Christian distract me," continued Mahmood, "but he did, as he must have distracted my brother. The current quickly dragged Hamid away, back into the waves. I saw him struggling and I began to clamour over the rocks. 'Hamid,' I called, 'Hamid.' I don't know if he heard me, but to my shame I know I should have dived into the water, except that I was scared. He was a better swimmer than I was, he was a better everything than I was, and all I saw was my mortality, my death, not his. 'Help him,' I called out, but the Australians, even the Australians swimming in the water, would not respond. They would not save a Muslim man, a Middle Eastern man. The Christian hugging his blue-eyed blonde daughter stood watching us."

Mahmood's head bowed. Carole reached out her hands to take Mahmood's hand and wrap hers around his, her dry throat almost choking. Her vision blurred.

"Hamid was my parents' eldest child," gasped Mahmood. "Children, especially eldest children, are very important to Muslim families, but he died a hero, even if we were the only people who noticed."

The three stood silently for a time. So did three young boys in matching Lindfield soccer uniforms standing near them on the footpath, one holding a soccer ball.

Mahmood was the first to speak up. "You can take my photograph, now," he told Xavier, his voice subdued.

Xavier switched off his dictating machine and slipped it back into a pocket of his jacket. From another pocket, he removed a camera.

Carole let go of Mahmood's hands. She took the chance to slip back into her electorate office, collect her handbag, switch off the lights, and lock the door.

When she returned, the boys stood as a gallery, watching Mahmood posed on the footpath. He patted down his hair.

"You didn't need to brush your hair," Carole told him.

"I always need to brush my hair," he laughed.

Xavier raised his camera to see the image he was about to photograph. "The setting could be anywhere in Australia," he said, "if we keep the background a little out of focus."

Mahmood threw his chest out before tossing his head to the side and waving his arms through the air, like a baron in a feudal court. The three boys laughed as did Mahmood, until Carole gently nudged him in the side. He stilled, his face becoming comically serious in feigning his submission. Again the boys laughed, as Carole stepped out of the way of the picture.

"They are your audience," Xavier told Mahmood and Carole, taking one photograph and then another.

That audience filled Carole's smile, reaching into an ever-broadening grin across her face. "Politicians need time with people," she said. "They ground us."

"Is our Prime Minister grounded?" asked Mahmood. "I voted for him."

"He tries."

Suddenly, Carole's arm was wrenched out by the force of a man grabbing her handbag. The man ran away from them along the footpath.

"Wait here," said Mahmood, racing after him.

"We should call the police," Carole told Xavier.

Xavier stood beside her. "Do you really want to?" he asked her. "Did you see the colour of his skin?"

"He wore a black, white, and orange football jersey," answered Carole, watching Mahmood chasing the thief along the footpath.

"That's the Western Suburbs rugby league team," said Xavier. "Criminals wear distinctive hats and clothes because witnesses notice them instead of faces, heights, and builds."

The thief and Mahmood disappeared around a corner, out of Carole's view. The three boys remained standing.

"Is there anything in your bag you can't replace?" asked Xavier.

Carole slapped her hand on the left lapel of her jacket, feeling her Amnesty International badge. "Thank God," she said. Sometimes, when she wasn't wearing it, she carried the badge in her handbag. Her credit cards, cash, and make-up were less important. "I've never experienced anything like that before."

"You should spend more time in other parts of Sydney," said Xavier. "Crime isn't news, not anymore, except for readers of the *North Shore Times*. Reporting the theft of your handbag to the police would only contribute to statistics that nobody reads but everyone cites."

Carole again looked along the footpath, seeing Mahmood reappear. He came sprightly towards them, panting a little, carrying her bag.

"The thief dropped it," Mahmood explained as he reached them, returning Carole's unfastened handbag to her.

The contents might have been rummaged through, but only the cash from her purse had gone. Carole couldn't remember how much had been there, but it had been enough so she never ran out.

She turned to Xavier. "Do Muslims rescuing ladies' handbags constitute news," she asked him, "without mentioning my name?"

"Are you worried about you harming his story, or him harming yours?"

"The police interviewed Mahmood in Canberra because I mentioned him to Andrea Gidley."

Xavier slowly nodded, as if thinking more than agreeing. "Did you notice the thief's race?" he asked her. The thief's skin was olive.

"He could have been Jewish," said Mahmood.

"He wasn't Jewish," Carole countered. "He could have been Christian."

"I'm not excusing theft," said Mahmood, turning towards her, "but please understand Carole, rich white people don't notice their losses."

6

THE GARDEN

In Killara, big old trees sheltered homes even older. Leafless liquidambars admitted the sun in winter they had shaded in summer. Streets of simple green would become purple-blue in spring, when the jacaranda trees burst into flower.

Along the front of Carole and Emmet Wynworth's property, the north-facing sunny side, bushes and flat-cropped hedges almost obscured the iron fence of spiked palings. Carole's garden remained important to her, as gardens did in Springdale Road. Too seldom in bloom, the green azalea bushes would in time blossom for three weeks with white and golden flowers, heralding spring. The horticulture-bred camellias would bloom longer. Even if Tessa moved to an apartment closer still to Macquarie University, as she threatened to move, Carole and Emmet wouldn't join the exodus of aged parents retreating into luxurious apartments around the Pacific Highway and railway line.

Carole and Emmet had lived in their secluded century-old home for more than twenty years, since their previous home had become too small for the doctor and his wife carrying their first child. The steep, slate-tiled roof with chimney tops and matching gables enclosed an attic as big as a hall, left closed and dark for years. Below it were two storeys of grey brick, providing more rooms than the family ever needed but always liked to have. Upstairs were the family bedrooms, sitting rooms, and studies, several of which opened to balconies secured with white timber railings. At the side of the house, as happened with old houses, the upward water and downward waste copper pipes to and from the bathrooms were visible outside the walls.

Fastened open for as long as Carole and her family had lived there, white timber shutters decorated many of the white-paned windows upstairs and down. From them and the balconies, Carole looked out onto her garden. Most years, in spring, summer, or autumn, she hosted garden parties, either hers or for the Liberal Party or parents at the Ravenswood School for Girls, who'd vowed to continue seeing each other after their daughters went onto university. Carole's Canberra apartment had no flowers, even if the garden of her Killara home still in winter had too few. Perhaps the jonquils were the reason she always hurried home.

Before dawn the following day, Sunday, much earlier than she normally woke, Carole sat alone in the silent drawing room at the front of her home. Her long satin dressing gown covered her silk nightdress and crossed legs on the flowery upholstered cushion sofa. Among the many complimenting armchairs and sofas, Carole never cared which one she occupied, as Emmet did. A florist's jonquils in a vase were becoming tired and their aroma weak.

Around the house, crystal lights hung freely from the ceilings amidst floral plaster patterns. From the centre of the ceiling in the drawing room, a large chandelier shone upon the fluffy white rug and oak furniture.

A heritage order had not denied the house centrally ducted heating, air conditioning, and vacuum cleaning systems; Carole's home was always slightly warmer than Parliament House. The chimneys were flues to gas-fired heaters that cast flames to replicate old wood fireplaces; none needed to burn anything that morning.

The garden beyond the windows remained in night. Their gardener, Mohammed, came to their home every fortnight to mow the lawns, trim the garden edges, and keep their shrubs and flowers. Since Carole's election took her away from the house most weekdays, he'd come Sunday mornings. He was coming that morning.

Carole's eyes became lost in the comfort of her moment. From the darkness of her mind, unfamiliar faces formed. They taunted her, those seventeen Rohingya still in the Australian High Commission in Dhaka. Those faces she had never seen in photograph or elsewhere, she imagined wailing at barbed wire, pleading for admission and escape. Carole wanted to release them, but didn't think she could. They chided her for having failed to save them, as did all the broken faces she'd been too late to save.

In some little consolation, they were receiving food and other care, whatever that could mean, whatever anything could mean. Should Carole smile for that?

A floorboard upstairs creaked. Somebody or age might make it creak.

Through the window, the sun broke through the trees, slowly brightening the garden greens and greys. Morning filled the room in which Carole sat, as a yellow-crested cockatoo landed on the lawn. Soon another landed and then another, until they were a dozen or more, pecking for food when food was hard to find.

Mahmood had made Carole think of church bells, in the softness of Sunday morning. Only in her garden, with the breeze coming from the direction of a church, could Carole hear them, calling the faithful and faithless. They might also have rung on Christmas mornings, as she recalled. Their tones and intonations echoed among the stone mounts and brass sundials of her garden.

Carole switched off the ceiling light, before sitting down again. The slow, rhythmic creaks of heavy feet in checked cloth slippers came down the stairs. Standing on a shelf, the brass pendulum clock under glass confirmed the time to be soon after seven o'clock. Emmet had woken when he woke every day, including Sunday.

Emmet stood tall in the tall doorway, with his long arms in the pockets of his dark woollen dressing gown with its cord wrapped tight around his waist. The creases of respect and his education stretched like scrolls of honour across his pale secluded skin, as Carole feared her creases were less respectful. They made him seem more than the eight years he was older than she was.

"Am I achieving anything as our elected representative?" she asked him.

"You seem so happy, my dear," answered Emmet, in his customarily measured elocution.

"Happy?" she asked, mocking herself. Her tone again waned.

"You have your home," he said, walking slowly around the sofa in which she sat until he stood behind her, "your friends, people as happy to talk to about the weather as..."

"I am not living my life discussing sunshine and rainy days," she chided him. "I'm not losing my life arbitrating between maids and telling gardeners where to prune, not anymore."

"There are people other than politicians, my dear."

"Like you?"

Emmet rested his large hands on her satin-covered shoulders. "The police are no closer to finding the person in the football cap," he said.

His familiar voice, his recurring presence, let Carole's eyes water, as Canberra rarely let them. "Why do people kill, darling?" she asked.

"People kill for the same reasons that they live, my dear," he said, his unassuming voice carrying the authority of hundreds, perhaps thousands (Carole didn't know), of patients confiding in him more than their physical afflictions. "They kill for love, hate, conviction, doubt. They kill because they believe too much and too little."

Carole dipped her head to one side, resting her cheek against his firm right hand, letting her eyes fall closed. A tear trickled from her face, stumbling through her skin and into his. "Do the killers choose to die?" she asked.

She moved her head, letting Emmet's sturdy hand caress her gentle face. His hand though firm was also soft. It let her face feel soft.

"What might move a person to disregard a life I would have

ached through mine to save?" asked Carole. "If people hurt, we can help them."

She heard Emmet's deep breath behind her, an ambiguous deep breath of disbelief he shared with her or disbelief he cast upon her. He didn't speak.

Resigned to his indifference, Carole's eyes slipped open. "Are principles never more important than in the midst of wilful death, or never less so?" she asked. No tortured faces could plead one case or the other.

Carole raised her head from Emmet's hand. Emmet removed his hands from her shoulders.

He stepped silently around the sofa, until he faced her. "I should prepare some breakfast, my dear," he said, his thin eyebrows rising as he spoke. Breakfast for Emmet was always several rashes of fried bacon and two poached eggs, slightly runny.

She stood up and followed him out of the room and through the high hallway to the kitchen at the rear of the house. While polished oak doors concealed most other modern appliances, Emmet opened the refrigerator door.

Carole stood by the granite-topped bench in the middle of the kitchen. "I want to invite Mohammed, the gardener, to dinner one evening," she told Emmet, so much taller than she was.

Throughout however many years he'd been tending to Carole's garden, since Whiffy Norbluss recommended him to her, Carole had never invited Mohammed inside her home. She had often brought him coffee to drink, sandwiches sometimes to eat, but he had never entered Carole's home. Near the swimming pool was a cubicle if he'd ever needed a washroom.

"Will you invite the Korean woman who cleans the house," asked Emmet, "or your Indian caterers?"

Carole nodded. "I should, but another time. I hope the caterers can serve halal food."

Emmet removed the plastic container for bacon from the refrigerator, along with a carton of free-range chicken eggs. "What is halal food?" he asked.

"The caterers can tell us, or I will find caterers who can."

Rodney Bayne was not there to sanction her if she spoke.

Xavier Talbot could not remind her how unimportant she could be if she did not.

"Our friends are frightfully embarrassed at the way Andrea Gidley treats refugees," said Carole. "I can't see Freddie Lamont or Bambi Pinpare without her mentioning it."

"Is Mohammed a refugee?"

"He's a Muslim."

"I guessed as much, my dear."

From a cupboard, Emmet removed a frying pan. In it, he laid several rashes of bacon.

Carole sat waiting for him at the eating table, although she wouldn't be eating anything, while Emmet cooked. The sounds of bacon sizzling slowly became louder. Louder still were the eggs he dropped into two rings in the pan. They didn't ease until Emmet switched off the stove and served his hot breakfast on a plate. He brought it to the table, where he sat in his dedicated chair. Before eating it, Emmet examined his tender pink bacon, never too cooked.

Their daughter entered the kitchen, dressed in a long pink woollen dressing gown and wearing thick pink cushioned slippers. Nineteen years of age, Tessa was as tall as was her mother but determinedly much thinner, as properly curvaceous as her mother once had been without realising so. Her blonde hair was tied in a ponytail behind her head. Her face without powders was pretty. "You're up early," she said to Carole.

"I'm feeling a little poorly."

Tessa took a muesli bar from a cupboard. She proceeded past her parents at the table into the adjoining entertainment area, in which a large television set stood on a sideboard by a wall. She picked up the remote control from atop a low coffee table, slumped back on the divan, and switched on the television set.

Soon filling the screen were images of the broken wreck of a ferry; Tessa and sometimes Emmet watched commercial television as Carole did not. Sunday morning television reviewed the week.

Carole closed her eyes. "Must you watch horribleness?" she asked.

"Some facts are horrible."

"Can't you watch the ABC?" asked Carole, but the commentary continued. "Please, darling."

After a moment, the commentary stopped. Carole opened her eyes, to see the television set off.

"The only stories on the ABC will be about Islamophobia," Tessa explained.

"The police will catch the third culprit," Carole assured her.

"You don't want to watch more Muslim terrorists."

"You shouldn't even notice their religion," Carole told her. "You'll be humbled if the person in the Canterbury-Bankstown cap isn't Muslim."

"Mother," came Tessa's correcting tone, "you shouldn't even notice his religion."

"There might have been Muslims among the dead and injured," insisted Carole.

"If there were, then the media would have told us," said Tessa, "repeatedly."

"Criminals can be Christians," Carole persisted.

"Christians? Popping out of pews with bombs on their backs?"

Carole looked to Emmet, with his plate clean of his breakfast but for small traces of bacon fat and streaks of yellow yolk. His knife and fork lay neatly together.

"Muslims, Mother," insisted Tessa. "The people killing us across the world in aeroplanes, offices, theatres, schools..."

Carole pressed her hands against her ears. The diatribe continued.

"...nightclubs, railway stations, buses, and ferries are Muslims. Never Christians, nor Buddhists, nor..."

"What have I raised?" asked Carole, pulling her hands from her head.

She again looked at Emmet in his chair. He rose and turned towards the sink.

"The crimes of the few should not cause the many to suffer," Carole continued. "The majority of peace-loving Muslims..."

"Where is this majority?" cried Tessa, her arms open to the air.

"Mohammed," answered Carole confronting her.

"Do you mean the gardener? What's he going to do: decapitate hydrangeas?"

"I'm going to invite him for dinner, whenever is convenient for him."

"Why would he come?"

"He's a very nice man."

"I'll be in my room that night."

"How did you come to be so rude?" asked Carole.

Tessa walked through the kitchen back to the hallway. Carole followed her, to the drawing room at the front of the house.

"According to the radio," said Tessa, standing near the window, "an injured passenger has recovered well enough to report the ferry bomber seemed content. Her lips started to curve, forming a smile, as she opened her coat to reveal a large vest to which several rectangular brown objects were strapped. She pulled a red cord hanging from them to detonate them after uttering, not yelling, the words '*Allahu Akbar*'."

"It's a saying," Carole replied. "It doesn't mean anything."

Tessa shook her head. "They tell us they're killing us for Islam, committing terror in Allah's name."

"They misunderstand what Allah wants."

"Don't you?" asked Tessa. "A war unlike the one your father feared has started, with enemies that don't play by the rules by which he fought."

"There is no war," insisted Carole. "Look about." Carole stretched her arms around her. "We are at peace."

"Within the borders of our home is peace," replied Tessa, "but I want to go outside." Looking out through the windows, she started to laugh, but her laugh wasn't a happy one as much as one resigned to irony. "Mohammed's here now," she said, leaving the room. "Go to him, Mother."

Carole stood at the window. Outside her home, the brown pebble driveway led to tall iron gates, outside which a scratched and dented grey van stood towing a green grid-sealed trailer. An arm reached from the driver's window, pressed the buttons on the security pad, and withdrew.

The gates opened, admitting the van and trailer into the

driveway. The van stopped where it would not obstruct cars that hadn't come or left.

Carole looked down at her long satin dressing gown, suddenly embarrassed of what she wore. She stepped back a little from the window, before looking out again.

Climbing from the van in his usual red flannelette shirt was an aged, thin, and bespectacled man, with sunburnt skin and fine grey hair. Could he know what her daughter thought, so very, very young? Could others think as Tessa thought, in a country Carole often struggled to recognise? Worst still, could vulnerable Mohammed feel her thoughts battering upon him? Did he fear the same in Carole?

Mohammed examined the contents of his trailer: a spindly lawn mower stained with years of spilled drops of oil and fuel; a hedge clipper. Normally Carole spoke to him about his chores, but she did not know how to hold her head when speaking with him that morning, since the ferry bombing. Her questions well intended might upset him.

Carole dressed in a long grey woollen skirt for afternoon tea, not tennis, at the Killara Lawn Tennis Club. Without functions to attend that morning, her light pink cardigan fastened around her blouse was enough to keep her warm.

Emmet dressed for a round of golf at the Killara Golf Club, where he often played of a Sunday morning. He towered above Carole, but to kiss him on his way, she reached her head high and he bowed his until their lips touched.

When next Carole saw Tessa, her blonde hair was clasped clumsily above her head. A wealth of white cream cloaked her face, leaving only round holes in the clouds for her blue eyes and red lips. Tessa returned to her bedroom.

Through the watery old-glass windows of her home, Carole watched Mohammed. The low-lying winter sun rising a short way in the cold, he clipped the hedges before they became unruly. He picked any green blades of grass protruding between the driveway pebbles or from the garden beds. He shaved those along the sides of the winding flagstone pathways. He removed weeds from the smooth soft lawns and dead twigs from the plants before Carole ever noticed them.

Was Mohammed thinking about her as she thought of him, she wondered? Did he fear retribution for nothing he had done? Did he want to ask a question but was feeling too afraid? He was the innocent, for he could do nothing more. Carole and her family with every chance to help were not so innocent.

She should not impose so much upon one journalist when parliamentarians had the platform to write for newspapers and magazines. Carole would pen an article imploring all Australians to invite Muslims they knew into their homes, in a prelude to a subsequent article to invite refugees they didn't. No one person or his late brother could single-handedly sway public opinion about Muslims.

Her gold-enamelled kettle boiled hot steam into the air. Carole had had enough of wondering.

Carrying a mug of tea for warm security, Carole dragged open the heavy front door of her home. Her feet rustling the pebbles, she proceeded along the driveway into the garden, where her feet moved silently, towards Mohammed. He was kneeling on the ground, persevering in his work.

Lying beside Mohammed on the ground was a long gardening fork. A small pile of dirty green bits lay on a green canvas sheet. His head down to where he tended, Mohammed was using a small weeding fork.

"Mohammed," said Carole, holding her mug with both her hands.

He stopped working. Taking the long gardening fork, he used it to push himself upright until he stood before her, balancing himself on his long gardening fork at his side. The back of his dirt-gloved free hand wiped his brow. The summer sun parched his skin each year and winter couldn't heal it.

"Good morning, Mrs Wynworth," he said, his voice thickly accented with Lebanese roots. Patiently he waited for the usual courtesies from Carole or any instructions: the routines of his work or a special task that day.

"Mohammed," she said, preparing her words before she retreated from what she had wanted to say. "Can I pour you some coffee?"

"Thank you, Mrs Wynworth."

She looked at him, began to turn, and then turned back to him. "Mohammed," she said again. "Would you like to come into our home for dinner one evening?"

"No, Mrs Wynworth."

"Are you married, Mohammed? Have you any children? Would your wife and children like to come?" She knew too little of him.

"I garden, Mrs Wynworth."

"Emmet and Tessa also like you ," Carole persisted. "We'd be delighted to host you."

"No, Mrs Wynworth."

"Aren't we friends, Mohammed?"

"We're not friends, Mrs Wynworth," he answered. "I garden. You pay."

"I'm not prejudiced," Carole persevered. "I think Muslims are wonderful people."

"I know, Mrs Wynworth." Mohammed looked back to the ground.

"Do people fear you, Mohammed," she pleaded to know. "Are we so cruel?"

Mohammed continued looking at the soil. "People watch us," he said, "when they see us in the stores or pass us in the streets. They study us, from the corners of their eyes."

"I promise you Mohammed, I shall never succumb to prejudice."

Mohammed stood silently, looking at the ground. Her garden had never before been less important to her.

Carole deliberated over what to say and not to say, in a conversation she needed to have, even if he did not. "I'm sorry, Mohammed," she finally said, holding her cooling mug. "I'll bring you some coffee."

She remained watching him. Without looking at her, Mohammed let his long gardening fork fall over, as he knelt back to the ground. Again taking his small weeding fork, he punctured the ground near an intruding shoot of grass, removing the first sight of a dandelion.

7

TELEVISION

Much as Parliament did little on Fridays to allow members to return home to electorates at the far ends of the country before weekends, it normally did little on Mondays to allow them to come back again afterwards. Formally, the House of Representatives sat, but most of the business was the presentation of committee reports, private members' business, and the presentation of petitions; few parliamentarians not directly involved in each matter sat in the chamber, if they were in Canberra at all. Coming from Sydney, Carole didn't need to board an aeroplane flight to Canberra until the evening.

At nine o'clock, Monday morning, Carole, Xavier, and Mahmood sat in a small café near her electorate offices in Lindfield, as they'd arranged to do on Saturday. On their table was the *Sydney Morning Herald* newspaper Carole had already read at home, publishing the stories of Mahmood's brother and of Mahmood retrieving a woman's handbag in Lindfield. A single sentence at the end quoted Mahmood's complaint that allowing churches to sound bells but not mosques to call to prayer was discriminatory.

"ABC Television called me," said Xavier. "Current affairs and news programmes are always looking for stories of good Muslims to tell, weaning the public away from crime and terrorism. Newspapers put into print what television stations then broadcast."

Mahmood leant back in his chair, stretching his arms wide. "All Australia will see me," he smiled, looking down at the long flowing pale jacket in a suit he wore as if to check it was suitable for television. "It is my chance to demand that mosques be free to call the faithful to pray."

Carole shook her head. "I'm not certain most Australians are ready..."

Mahmood turned towards her. "Aren't Muslims Australian, Carole? Do you believe in fairness, in freedom? Muslims should be free to experience our cultures: our beautiful religion."

"Let people learn more about Muslims first, and choose to give you everything you want."

His fists gripped the armrests of the chair in which he sat, his body beginning to quiver. The veins rose from the back of his hands. "I feel we must demand what we want for people to notice."

"If you demand anything, we'll lose everything. We don't want people to fear you."

"Without risks Carole, we achieve nothing. Newspaper articles touch you but do nothing for Muslims. What do we gain if people like me, before my media images disappear into libraries that nobody enters? Muslims will remain lesser citizens every time a church bell rings."

"Please, Mahmood, I am in Canberra tomorrow. Don't say anything today that we'll regret."

"Do you want multiculturalism, Carole, or compliance?"

"Give me one day to help."

"I'll think about it," said Mahmood, before turning back to Xavier. His mood slowly settling, the veins vanished from his hands. "Do you want Samina with me on the television?" he asked Xavier. "She is very pretty."

"I thought she didn't want publicity," interjected Carole.

"We're past that now," replied Mahmood. "I'll bring her with me to the studio."

Xavier looked at Carole. "You don't need me there."

Before they could stand, a man appeared at the table,

towering over them. His muscular body blended into his muscular face, with little neck in between. His short-cropped brown hair was similar in shade to his clumsy and oafish suit, much less fashionable than the threads flowing from Mahmood but crisper than Xavier kept his suits. "Mrs Wynworth?" he asked. "Your office told me I'd find you here."

"And you're?"

"Samuel Dempsey, Superintendent, New South Wales Police Force Counter Terrorism Unit."

Carole had met the senior policemen and women from the police stations responsible for her electorate, but never anyone from the counterterrorism unit. She had been unaware there was such a unit.

The Superintendent turned to Mahmood. "You would be Mister Mahmood?" he asked. "May I sit with you?"

Sitting upright, her back away from the back of the chair, Carole wished they'd sat at a table with only three chairs, instead of four. "We should ask Emmet's lawyer to join us," she told Mahmood. "You have the right to a lawyer to represent you."

"We have no need for lawyers," replied Mahmood, his hand fobbing her away. "No one has need for lawyers."

"The innocent need lawyers more than the guilty," added Xavier, checking his scratched round old watch. "The guilty are more careful."

"What is your name?" the Superintendent asked him.

"Xavier Talbot, *Sydney Morning Herald*."

"You don't have to stay, Mister Talbot."

"None of us have to stay, Superintendent, but I'm not missing this."

"I was hoping you wouldn't," smiled the Superintendent, sitting down. He faced Mahmood, with Carole and Xavier to each side of him.

"Police inquiries only exacerbate the prejudice Muslims feel," said Carole. "Everything you need to know about Mahmood you can learn from the newspaper."

"I have read Mister Talbot's articles."

"You should understand, Superintendent, the politics behind

your inquiry," said Carole. "Would you be here if Mahmood were not Muslim?"

Dempsey turned to her. "Would you, Mrs Wynworth? Would Mister Talbot be?"

"I do worry about the way our security forces watch Muslims," said Carole. "It's very unfair."

The Superintendent turned back to Mahmood. "What is your full name, Mister Mahmood?"

"I don't want police persecuting my family."

"We're chatting."

Mahmood turned to Carole. "Would you think my family were paranoid for fearing our home could be wired with hidden microphones?"

"No," she smiled, resting back in her chair. "Rational, well-founded fears are not paranoia."

"I could insist you disclose your name and age," the Superintendent told Mahmood.

"Not of my friends, you won't," Carole told him.

The Superintendent looked at her, rubbing his hand around his jaw, too obviously thinking, before looking back at Mahmood. "There is no record of anyone drowning at the beach at Dee Why or anyone named Hamid drowning anywhere in this country four years ago."

"He was my brother," Mahmood insisted, "he drowned as I said. What more can I say to people who don't believe us?"

"Where were you during the ferry bombing last Tuesday?"

"I was at home, in my bedroom."

"Did anyone see you?"

Mahmood shook his head. "I hadn't realised I needed an alibi."

"You don't," Carole interrupted, before looking at the Superintendent. "Trust me, Superintendent. Muslims are the most honest people. Record that in your file, and close it."

The Superintendent sat studying her for several moments, never quite looking as if he was about to speak, before looking back at Mahmood. "Can I telephone you, Mahmood?"

Carole answered. "Any messages you have for Mahmood,

Superintendent, you can leave with my office. If Mahmood wants them, he can get them there."

The Superintendent again looked at her, more briefly this time, before standing. "This is my card," he said, removing from his pocket a small wad of business cards and leaving one each in front of Carole, Xavier, and Mahmood. "Good day."

He left the table. Carole watched him leave the café.

"Thank you, Carole," said Mahmood. "Most Muslims don't have someone like you at their side."

Carole smiled, before turning to Xavier. "Is there a newspaper record of Hamid drowning?" she asked.

"I couldn't find one."

"Everything I have ever said to you is true," said Mahmood, "all of it."

"What is your real name?" asked Xavier.

Carole turned to Xavier. She was as angry with him for having asked that question as she was desperate to hear Mahmood's answer.

"Does you trusting me depend on that, Xavier?" asked Mahmood.

Xavier turned to Carole. "The Superintendent expects me to report what he said."

"You don't have to report it," replied Carole.

Mahmood interjected. "Let people see the police persecuting Muslims."

Xavier continued looking at Carole. "I don't have to mention you," he told her. "Mahmood and Samina don't have to mention you on television."

Carole continued looking at him, before nodding. "The story should be about Mahmood, Hamid, and Samina."

Early that afternoon, Carole paced about the footpath outside the television studios in Ultimo. Harris Street was busy with cars and the footpath busy with pedestrians. Looking at her watch every few minutes did not quicken the time, between studying every taxi that might be slowing and pedestrian appearing for Mahmood and Samina.

Finally, they came around a corner on the footpath. Slightly shorter than Mahmood, Samina dressed as fashionably as modestly, in a long-sleeved, dark long dress a little more formal perhaps than the dress she'd worn when Carole saw her in Canberra. They walked close together but apart, conspicuously not touching each other. They didn't hold hands, as Australians did.

Seeing Carole, Mahmood seemed to smile, striding with expectation towards her. Samina didn't try to keep up with him.

"Carole!" he exclaimed as he approached her, his arms stretched out. Reaching her, he placed his hands on her arms and kissed her cheek.

She grinned, a little embarrassed, as the younger woman reached them. "You must be Samina," said Carole.

Her red lips gleamed from her skin. Her brown eyes were gentle.

"You may kiss her, Carole," said Mahmood.

Samina blushed as Carole kissed her cheek. The two women stepped apart.

"Thank you for helping me stay," said Samina, her voice thickly accented with Jordanian roots.

"I want to support you both," said Carole, "quietly."

"Quietly?"

Carole shook her head, grasping for anything more useful to say. "I'm sorry," she said.

Samina's smile slipped into just a hint of what it had been. Behind her, two young women stood looking at Mahmood. Carole's attention upon them soon drew Samina, turning around to face them.

"You were in the newspaper," said one young woman.

Samina stepped beside Mahmood and put her arm through his, again facing the other young women. They laughed and walked away.

Carole looked around, to see two small boys standing with their bicycles along the footpath near the kerb, watching her. They were Middle Eastern: more reason to feel good about immigrants, although Carole could not know the boys' religion. She smiled.

They did not respond. Slowly, Carole realised they were

looking at Mahmood, watching them. He smiled. He winked, flashing his eyes.

A loud horn blasted the air, jarring Carole. Mahmood pushed her aside, surging along the footpath. Tyres screeched as Carole turned to see a truck coming along the kerbside lane. The boys were on the footpath, but their bicycles had fallen on the road. Mahmood bundled the boys back from the kerb, as the truck crashed through and over the bicycles. The truck passed, before Mahmood hurriedly pulled the two twisted bicycles back from the road.

Carole turned back to the truck, its rear and sides unmarked sheets of steel. A sack caught in a rear panel door covered the registration plates.

"Thank you," said one boy to Mahmood, before the boys collected their bicycles. One boy and then the other tried to mount his bicycle, but couldn't. They rolled them away.

Mahmood remained there, watching them leave. When they had turned around a corner, he wandered back to Carole and Samina.

"You might have saved their lives," said Carole.

"I didn't save their bicycles," replied Mahmood, leading Carole and Samina into the studios building.

Standing beside a long white desk were two black-dressed security guards. "We need to check your bags," said one.

"You're targeting us," said Mahmood.

"Everyone is subject to security checks," the guard insisted, "even the Queen of England." He looked at Carole. "Sorry, Ma'am."

The guards' prying eyes examined Carole's handbag. They delved into Samina's smaller bag.

Mahmood looked back at Carole. "I forgot," he said. "I don't look Muslim. If I did, I wouldn't be on television and you wouldn't think I could change public opinion." Carole was too embarrassed to reply.

A reception desk summoned an officious programme producer, for whom any smile was lost in the intensity of her expression. Held close to her chest was a dark clipboard, while her free hand firmly shook Mahmood's and Samina's hands. "Who are you?" she asked Carole.

"I'm a friend of Mahmood."

The woman turned to Mahmood and Samina. "I'll take you to the Green Room: a private lounge where the drinks try valiantly to still the nerves of guests and sometimes hosts."

"Mahmood," Carole said quickly. "Will you allow me to help you? Will you give me a day before demanding that churches cease playing their bells or that mosques be allowed their calls to prayer?"

"You'll know you have your one day, Carole, if I look at you from the set and wink." The producer whisked Mahmood and Samina away.

Carole waited, looking up at the floors of offices, some people noticing Carole standing idly. In the long banners promoting the network's television and radio personalities, Carole recognised the older ones, photographed in serious and solitary close portraiture amidst their black garbs and backgrounds, but not the younger ones photographed full length in colour. Carole had never appeared on television, not even among a group of political figures or crowd of faces to background someone else's story, so far as she was aware.

The programme producer eventually returned, when she led Carole into a studio and the darkness behind the cameras. "Keep out of the way," she told Carole, "keep quiet during recording, and do everything the staff tell you to do and not do."

Carole stood alone, in sight of a small set of chairs behind an oval desk. Behind them were the coloured wall and logo of the show. Near Carole, several huge black cameras stood idle across the shining floor, facing the set.

Samina and Mahmood wandered into the studio, their pale faces powdered paler. His hair was tinged a subtle turn of brown.

Behind them, appeared the programme hostess, Eileen, her jaw lines square and smile serious. "Mahmood, Samina," her voice beamed. "I'm sorry I missed you."

Eileen shook their hands. Her red dress wrapped around her exposed her broad authoritative shoulders, without a need for shoulder pads that other women wore. Below them were her formidable cleavage, allowing her the beauty of gender and credibility of experience, to the extent any public figure still had credibility.

"You should not dress like that in the presence of Muslims," Mahmood told her.

Eileen glanced down into the dip of her freckled bare cleavage, before glancing at Samina's concealed chest. "I will see you both shortly," she smiled, before leaving.

Mahmood turned to Samina. "Not married," he told her, drawing up his right arm and with the palm of his hand gently touching her cheek.

"I'm sorry that happened," said Carole.

"Please, tell me Carole," inquired Mahmood. "Who do all your apologies help, but you?"

If he had been rude then Carole could deal with him more readily than she could answer so straightforward an inquiry. She looked at Samina, hoping the answer to Mahmood's question was so self-evident that Samina could respond, but Samina said nothing. Like Mahmood, her gaze remained inquiring.

The producer returned. "This way, please," she said, before qualifying her instruction, "Mahmood and Samina."

Leaving Carole behind, she led them to the oval desk and chairs in which they sat. A man popped in to leave glasses of water on the table. Other men, dressed in black shirts and trousers and wearing thin headsets and small microphones near their mouths, came to the cameras. Technicians checked the lights and sound. Teleprompter script reflected in the camera glass. A man ushered Carole further out of the way.

Eileen returned, wearing a red jacket covering her shoulders and chest. She laid several sheets of paper on the oval desk at which she sat.

After a final touch of powders to the three dollied faces, Eileen faced the camera poised before her. People fell quiet. Cameras focussed upon Mahmood and Samina's concentrating faces, preparing for the coming exposition. Bright lights became brighter, blazing from all sides upon the television desk. The red light atop the camera facing Eileen shone.

Behind the cameramen watching, stood Carole in the

shadows. Mahmood adjusted himself in his chair, looked at her, and winked.

Her smile balanced with the seriousness of the story, Eileen faced the camera underway. "Australians have taken Mahmood and his girlfriend Samina Quresh into their hearts," she read. Her television voice was forcefully feminine: personable but businesslike. "Their story has elicited unprecedented support and sympathy from people around the country." She turned to face her guests, as a red light on a camera pointed towards them shone. "Mahmood," she said, "if I may call you that. What *is* your name?"

"Eileen, my family and my friends call me Mahmood," he answered, and so told every Australian watching the interview that night or in subsequent replay.

"Mahmood then," said Eileen, "tell me your life."

Mahmood repeated in more flourishing detail the tales and traumas that Carole already knew: his sorrows and joys, failures and success. Carole listened proudly as if she had allowed his life to happen.

"Samina and I have not committed any crime," said Mahmood, "but still the police took time away from real policing, from hunting the third Sydney bomber they have still not identified, to investigate me. Eileen, we wanted you to see not just police harassment of Muslims in this country, but also their sheer incompetence." Carole basked in every phrase that Leighton Ingles would soon be forced to hear, while Mahmood leant forward and pressed his hands against his chest. "I exist, don't I, but the police would have you think I don't."

"Why have the police been unable to corroborate anything about you?" asked Eileen, in a tone Carole feared to be a little doubting.

"My brother didn't die on television," Mahmood melancholically replied. "He didn't die among policemen or journalists to document his death. If there is a certificate of his death, then I don't know what it says, but our traditions don't demand affidavits from witnesses to prove the worst calamity my family could incur. We wouldn't need them now if Hamid had not been a Muslim."

Eileen turned to Samina. "Samina, you're Mahmood's girlfriend, how did you two meet?"

"We met at the Islamic Community Centre in Greenacre," she said, her soft brown eyes beginning to glow. "Mahmood was the most handsome man in the room."

"Do you trust Mahmood, Samina?"

"I do," she beamed.

"Are you a loving girlfriend?"

Carole stepped forward, but a man in black with a headset on his ears held out his hand to stop her. He ushered her back.

"Please Eileen," said Mahmood. Carole saw his hand down low reach across and gently hold Samina's hands, rested on her lap. "We have a friend, an important friend, who believes us." Carole slumped a little back. "We don't blame her for not wanting to say anything." Carole might have felt less ashamed if Mahmood were angry with her. "Defending multiculturalism has become a very difficult task to take."

Carole had never thought of herself as brave; women were not brave doing what they did, as some men thought they were. Nor had she thought of herself as being cowardly, until she stood there watching a young woman on holiday from another country trying to help a beleaguered friend Carole was less willing to help. Carole turned her face to the floor, feeling Mahmood's fantasy and fear, his dream and sombre dread.

"Mahmood," said Eileen. "What do you tell people who feel uneasy that you conceal your real name?"

Carole looked up. Mahmood's smile was conspicuously reserved. "I wish I could tell you the name to which I was born," he lamented. A whisper of a tear collected in his eye nearest the camera. "I wish I could use that name as freely as you use yours, but Muslims need to take precautions."

Eileen allowed the moment to resolve, before turning to Samina. "Do you know his real name?"

Carole edged forward. The man in black again moved his arm across Carole's way and glared at her.

"He's always been Mahmood," Samina answered. "I'm happy with that."

"Eileen," interjected Mahmood, "my family don't want to

suffer because people don't want good Muslim stories in the newspapers or television."

Carole thought of calling out indignantly, while the man in black turned back to face the set. Her red face seethed.

"No one is more Australian than I am," said Mahmood, "but this country only intrudes upon the privacy of Muslims."

Carole bounded past the man in black and his arms lunging out to catch her, hurrying up the step into the brightly burning lights. "Mahmood is not the issue," protested Carole from the television stage.

Two men with headsets on their ears began to rush and apprehend the snap intruder. Eileen shook her head, keeping those men away.

"I don't need to know his name to know him," declared Carole.

A camera with a shining light turned upwards and trained upon her. In the light and dark small studio, she steeled her eyes upon it, bearing down upon small homes watching their television sets and scribes who would repeat her words nationwide in countless news reports.

"Every Australian who has foregone our multicultural ideal because of a few criminals should dip his head against the floor in disgrace," Carole continued. "The real victims of terrorism are the Muslim men and women who suffer their exclusion from this country that has so cruelly turned upon them." Her voice rose, becoming more voracious with every syllable she spoke. "The rest of us would not so graciously accept the scrutiny drilled upon this admirable young man. I should tell you about the two boys' lives he saved today."

"Who are you?" asked Eileen.

"Carole Wynworth," she answered, rising in her high-heeled shoes, "the Member for Seidler."

8

MEETINGS

Winter had returned to Canberra by Tuesday morning, although it had never really been away. Few people were outside who didn't need to be.

Far from the shopping centres Canberrans entered with free arms and left with full hands, was the Australian War Memorial. In its grounds was the modern Poppy's Café, where outdoors tables filled in better weather stood empty, the chairs inside. Far enough from Parliament House for nobody to recognise her, in a city through which politicians fleeted like showers of frosty sleet, Carole sat with Xavier Talbot.

Xavier drank from a large glass of sparkling mineral water, the green bottle near him on the table. His pale coat lay over a chair beside him. On another chair, lay Carole's black leather handbag, over which she'd draped her coat and hat. Shining from her blue padded jacket was her silver Amnesty International badge.

Eating his hot Diggers Breakfast didn't deter Xavier from speaking. "I'm more accustomed to interviewing than being interviewed," he told Carole. "Last night, the federal police visited me."

"I'm surprised you haven't reported it."

"I wanted to speak with you and give Leighton Ingles a chance to explain."

"Police harassment," said Carole, "police incompetence, I thought you'd like it."

"They wanted to hear everything I knew about Mahmood and about you."

"What did you tell them?"

"Everything I know. I gave them my notes and the electronic mail between us. He's not exactly a confidential source, and you're so pure of heart the truth can only help you, but this story is no longer about the friendly Muslim boy who's a reason we should admit however many Rohingya and other refugees wanting to come here. The story is becoming one about the Government. It's about the backbencher and her relationship with a Muslim man who lies..."

"He doesn't lie."

"...whose stories nobody can corroborate."

A waitress stood beside them. "May I get you something, Madam?" she asked.

Their audience, however ignorant and anonymous, silenced Carole. Suddenly unable to think, she looked up at the waitress. "Not just now, thank you."

The waitress left. Carole looked again at Xavier.

"I had to order my breakfast from the counter," remarked Xavier.

"We've talked about trust," resumed Carole. "Please don't let Mahmood down."

Xavier took another portion of bacon. "Mahmood attracts news like flypaper collects flies," he said, as he chewed. "We had a thief taking your handbag on Saturday, a speeding truck yesterday."

"Why don't you ask those two Middle Eastern boys with their bicycles to come forward?"

"You might have found two Middle Eastern boys in the North Shore, where you'd all be clamouring to hug them, apologise to them, and give them presents, even while they're picking your pockets, but they'd be two among the packs in most parts of Sydney."

Carole pulled back in her chair. "You shouldn't be like that, Xavier."

Xavier's eyes left her as he put another cut of sausage in his mouth. He again sat back, studying her and chewing.

"If you want my reaction to the police visiting you," said Carole, "then print my total confidence this country is better for all the more Mahmoods."

Xavier finished chewing. His glass of mineral water continued sparkling.

"I'll also speak to Leighton Ingles," said Carole, "after I've placated Mahmood."

With Andrea Gidley's busy schedule that morning, the only time she might be able to see Carole was briefly before she addressed a conference at the Rex Hotel (not quite as nice since the renovations) at eleven o'clock. Carole found Andrea with her aide and other people near the Grand Ballroom, by the tables of hot urns and open boxes displaying varieties of tea. Andrea's aide led Carole to a small meeting room nearby. "You'll have two minutes," said the aide, "be quick." The aide closed the door.

Carole had no time to sit among the chairs before the door again opened and Andrea entered. "I saw your performance on television, Carole," said Andrea, as the aide closed the door again. "Were those colours you nailed to your mast those of your friend Mahmood or those of all Islam?"

"Aren't local councils breaking our international obligations," asked Carole, more as a statement than a question, "when they ban mosques from broadcasting calls to prayer while churches can play bells?"

"Don't you like the sounds of bells, Carole, prancing through the air?"

"The issue is discrimination, not what we like," insisted Carole. "We can't let Muslims feel their religion is less Australian than the religion of bells. What do we allow them if we don't allow them to live according to their faith?"

"What is your faith, Carole?"

Tears graced the small corners of her eyes. "Humanity," Carole answered.

"Local councils decide whether their residents have to hear wailing calls to prayer," said Andrea, "five times a day."

Carole straightened up. "What if curtailing the rights of Muslims to enjoy their religion is a surreptitious means of excluding them from the neighbourhood?"

"Leave the councils to decide," Andrea told you. "I'm not trampling on neighbourhood daffodils."

"I could embarrass you," said Carole, watching Andrea's every expression for an excuse to pause. "I could tell the press of every threat that Rodney Bayne made against me to vote for your changes to refugee law last week."

"People expect political party discipline."

"People don't expect parties to bully women."

"Would you forgo the last of your career, Carole, for calls to other people's prayer?"

"This is my prayer, Andrea."

The two women stood pointedly studying each other. "Don't neglect people who vote for you in favour of people who don't," said Andrea.

"The people voting for me in my electorate aren't the same people voting for you in yours."

A rapid little knock came through the door. "You refer your complaint to the Human Rights and Equal Opportunity Commission to decide," Andrea told Carole. "It wouldn't be the first time the majority suffered because a minority demanded what it called its human rights."

"You could disregard the Commission's decision."

"So could you."

A long smile filled Carole's face, more profoundly than had been her small smiles for many days. She began to beam.

"Be careful," said Andrea, edging towards the door. "If the Commission insists upon equality, councils will ban church bells."

Sounds of medieval bells ringing from sandstone churches mumbled in Carole's mind. "Religion," she said, "it's not as if any of it's true."

"You mightn't want to say that to your Muslim friend."

"I wouldn't be so rude," said Carole, before laughing,

"although I remember the look on the poor reverend's face from St Martin's Church when I said the same thing to him."

Andrea departed, leaving the door open behind her. Carole started to believe she could precipitate a change.

Returning to Parliament House, Carole should have thought more about the reason she'd found meeting Leighton Ingles that morning even harder to arrange than she'd found meeting Andrea Gidley, in spite of him apparently being there. At the end of another wide corridor in the Ministerial Wing were Leighton's offices.

The first person she saw there was a young woman, sitting at the round desk beneath the window. "Where is Leighton Ingles?" Carole asked her.

"I told your office that the Attorney General can't see you."

Carole looked around. Adjoining the waiting area was a room, in which a young man stood holding a bundle of reports. Beside that room was a short hallway towards a half-open office door, in which were several empty chairs and beyond them a tall window.

"I might be able to secure you an appointment on Friday," the young woman told Carole.

Carole looked back at her. "I want to know to what Leighton Ingles objects in my friend Mahmood," said Carole. Whatever the reply, Carole would refute it.

"I will pass your request to the Attorney."

Carole continued staring at her. Her older woman's heart throbbed through her jacket.

The younger woman didn't move. "He cannot see you today."

A sound, like that of a book being set on a wooden desk, broke from the far end of the corridor. As if it had been a starter's pistol, Carole turned and strode towards it.

"Please…," said the young woman behind her. Carole strode faster than she normally moved to the half-open office door and thrust it open.

Sitting at a file and paper-littered desk was Leighton, with his half-spectacles resting on his nose. He looked up from his chair, as the door Carole had thrust open crashed into a block of shelves. Standing next to Leighton, his arms leaning on the desk, another suited young man looked across at her. Leighton slowly removed the spectacles from his nose.

The thump on Carole's back was the young woman she'd left behind too slow to stop, bundling into her. "I'm sorry, Leighton," said the young woman. "I told her…"

Carole turned to the young woman. "My name is Carole," she said, "or Mrs Wynworth." Carole faced down at her, although they were roughly the same height.

The young woman looked back at Leighton. "I told *Carole* she needed an appointment."

Carole also looked at Leighton, as she stepped towards his desk. "You invade *my* privacy," she told him.

Calmly, Leighton sat up in his chair, placing his spectacles on his desk. He turned to the young woman. "Thank you, Brenda. Carole has her appointment."

Without looking again at Carole, the young woman left. The suited young man slowly stood upright.

"Why, Leighton, please tell me why?" Carole asked him.

Leighton looked at the young man standing beside him. "The report on Carole Wynworth?" he asked.

The young man walked from the room. From his desk, Leighton took a brown mug in his hands. Carole's mouth was dry.

Leighton leant back in his chair, grasping the mug with both hands. "Ours is the time of terrorism, Carole," said Leighton, his voice calm and measured.

Carole sat in the chair nearest to him. "You once had optimism, Leighton," she told him, "before you found fear."

Leighton laughed. "With every week," he told her, "the likelihood of terrorist assaults grows." He sipped from his mug. "Some days we learn something, interrupt a plan, even arrest some people, but for every small win we score, another ten plots unfold. There are more and more people willing to kill us and willing to shelter them. The next victim might be you."

"I might fall down the stairs in my home, Leighton, or choke on a fishbone."

"The police are no closer to identifying the third Sydney bomber a week since fifteen people died."

"There are other unsolved murders, Leighton," said Carole leaning forward, "other murderers walking free."

"Our co-operation from Muslims is patchy..."

"That's an outrageous statement, Leighton," snapped Carole, before slowly resting back in her chair. "What do you expect from calling the bombers Muslim? You were once more sympathetic."

The young suited man returned to the office, carrying a cream-coloured cardboard file. The file was unmarked: no more than a cover to carry the paper or papers Carole was not meant to see.

"Thank you, Douglas," said Leighton, coming forward in his chair close to his desk to which he returned his brown mug. "You better close the door."

The young man retrieved a second brown mug from a corner of the desk. He walked from the room, closing the door after him.

Leighton returned his spectacles to his nose and opened the file, far from Carole's short reach. From her side of the desk and from that angle, Carole could not decipher the upside-down paragraphs.

Too few moments after opening the file, enough time only to have refreshed a memory than read a page, Leighton turned the page, then another, and another. He closed the file.

"Samina Quresh's brother Zaki Quresh appears to be what he says he is," said Leighton, again removing his spectacles so his blue eyes focused upon Carole. "He is a moderately successful importer of shirts, not really to my taste, too flowery, and I would have thought not really to yours. He lives in a fibro cottage according to his means, except for a car he drives that is a little more costly than he should spend. We're not worried about some discrepancies in his income tax returns. He likes martial arts movies, rarely reads books, and would like his sons to play squash when they're older. He travels as his business would suggest he should travel, and his banking transactions and religious, cultural, and social activities don't raise any red flags."

The breadth and detail of the report overwhelmed her. "Do you take such an interest in all Muslims?" asked Carole.

"The police look around whenever somebody influences Members of Parliament," Leighton answered. "They look around most thoroughly when members declare their devotion to somebody on national television."

Carole concealed her reaction. She admitted no blink of her eyes or change to her breath, from which Leighton studying her could draw any inference.

"Jordanian and other intelligence agencies have no evidence of militant activities or associations by Samina Quresh or her family," Leighton continued. "We won't fault everyone whose friends and family think they fared better in their studies than they fared in fact." His voice became coy. "To the extent there are more salacious stories, I leave others to decide what to reveal."

Carole sat unsure whether the exoneration, thus far, should console her. "Don't you worry I'll tell them what you've told me," she asked, before realising she already knew his reply, "or do you expect me to do so?"

"Xavier Talbot will be seeing me later today, after his police visit last night. Whatever I end up telling you, I'll tell him, except for the detail about Zaki Quresh he would not report anyway."

"Records can be erroneous," Carole insisted, "databases incomplete." Her tone was more than mere gall. "With prejudice against Muslims, is it any wonder if nobody reported Hamid's death?"

"Not to the police, nor to the coroner, nor to the New South Wales or any other state Registry of Births, Deaths, and Marriages?"

"Some people live and die unrecorded, but their families know they lived and died," Carole told him. "You shouldn't dismiss oral histories because of government files."

"Don't believe folklore above evidence," snapped Leighton, leaning forward in his chair, bearing his deepening blue eyes down upon her. "No man we can pinpoint who might have been

Mahmood's brother drowned, Carole, not even having a bath. No small girl was saved."

The telephone beside him rang. Leighton lifted the handset. "Ingles," he said. Silently, he listened, his eyes turned down.

Wearily, Carole's gaze drifted around the room, examining for the first time the den she had entered. Along the shelves were black leather-bound volumes of parliamentary rules and laws Carole hadn't read. By them were photographs of Leighton smiling with his casually dressed wife and more casually dressed teenage children, so alien to the man sitting before her.

His smiles were no less natural, and yet were a little less effusive, in the photographs of him with well-suited men and women. One face among the several not drawn from European stock drew Carole's gaze. She leant forward, checking what she thought she could see. Like Leighton's face beside it, like so many faces among the photographs, this face grinned warmly. Atop it was the white cap and below it the white cassock of an imam.

"Carole's with me now," said Leighton.

Carole turned back towards him. Leighton's eyes flicked up at Carole.

"Yes," said Leighton, "thank you." Leighton hung up the telephone, before again directing his eyes upon Carole. "When will you next see Mahmood?"

She thought of hiding her reply, until doing so seemed pointless. "He contacts me," she told him. "I'll see him when he arranges it. Do you want to come, too?"

"Police and security agencies have images of the man you call Mahmood entering and leaving mosques and Muslim community centres but can't identify him."

"Spies should spend more time watching television and reading newspapers," Carole retorted, "instead of peeking out van windows and through curtains."

"The police want your help watching him, letting them know if he says anything that might identify him or anyone he knows. The plate from which he eats or the glass from which he drinks might identify his DNA."

"I'm nobody's spy," insisted Carole, shaking her head.

"If Mahmood is what you think he is," Leighton told her, "then you can prove it. If he's not, then the best thing for you is to be the one to expose him."

"He's my friend."

Leighton studied her face, the face Carole kept taut with her resolve, before his eyes dropped back to his great timber desk. His right hand fidgeted over the file, before opening it. Keeping the words hidden from Carole, Leighton removed every sheet of paper bar one and placed it in a short pile face down on his desk. He again closed the file, took it in his hand, and rose slowly from his chair.

The tall man stood towering over his files unseen and unknowable to Carole, staring down towards her. Slowly he stepped around his desk until he reached her, when he handed her the file of one page.

Cautiously, as if it were a trap that might spring shut and catch her, Carole took the file in her fingers. Her eyes quickly trained back upon him, walking towards the window. The sun had become bright and Carole's eyes flinched as Leighton stood before the glass and sunlight. "Carole," he said, turning back towards her, "*my* friend."

If that greeting was meant to comfort her, it failed. Carole's shoulders began to seize, deep within the padded shoulders of her jacket, although she would not allow Leighton to see her trepidation.

The Attorney-General again sighed, before proceeding. "None of the Lebanese Muslims living in Thornleigh or who studied engineering at the University of Sydney are your friend Mahmood, whatever his name," said Leighton. "There is no evidence that your friend does or has done anything he says he does or has done, except meet Samina Quresh and now you."

"He doesn't need evidence."

"Why do you think he won't tell you his name? All these problems might vanish and I mightn't have to worry so much about one of my parliamentary colleagues befriending him if he would just tell people his name: the name he enrolled at university; the family name of his late brother."

Carole pulled a little back in her chair, before humbly

venturing a thought. "People change their names for many good reasons. They might hide their names because of these crude intrusions upon them."

Leighton again studied her. If he was thinking what more he could tell Carole, then he was thinking what more he could tell Xavier Talbot. "Linguists have proven adept at catching asylum seekers lying about their places of origin," he told her.

"Your linguists are obviously wrong," Carole insisted, as she had each time they'd been cited to her.

"Hear me out, Carole," said Leighton, walking back towards his desk. "Samina Quresh is twenty-two years old, but they suspect your friend is much older than you might think he is: well into his thirties, if not forty or more. They believe he was probably born in Sydney, or has lived there since he was young. He was probably raised among Lebanese, but we know he is none of their refugee sons named Mahmood."

"You cannot possibly know so much about so many people," Carole said. "Security agencies make mistakes; they have in the past."

"When will you start questioning suspects instead of police?" snapped Leighton, before sitting back down in his chair. "Our police and security agencies are completely committed to stamping out Islamophobia, but they can't help it if criminals and terrorists are Muslim."

"Criminals and terrorists are not Muslim," insisted Carole. "Police should spend more time worrying about Christians."

"Might the police be wrong about exonerating Zaki and Samina Quresh?"

Carole smiled. "Everybody gets something right sometimes."

"However much you might hate me for it, Carole," Leighton told her, "I am trying to protect you. Please, be careful."

Slowly, holding the cardboard file tight in her fingers, Carole rose from her chair. Preparing to leave, she looked down at Leighton in his chair.

"Why would anybody want not to exist, Carole?" asked Leighton, looking up at her. "The man you call Mahmood, your perfect Muslim to promote to a stubbornly sceptical populace, does not exist."

9

THE ULTIMATUM

Underground car parks in Parliament House allowed parliamentarians to arrive and depart unseen. When they wanted journalists to see them, they arrived at the securely guarded Ministerial, Senate, or House of Representatives entrances, forming three points of a huge compass with the paved public forecourt at the front of Capital Hill. The mornings of parliamentary sitting days, when news required it, journalists gathered for the door-stop interviews of the arriving prime minister or relevant minister, parliamentary secretary, or shadow minister from the Opposition, while irrelevant backbenchers hoped to be asked to comment.

The Wednesday morning air was cold, but not as cold as other Canberra days had been. For the first time, the pack of journalists converged upon Carole in her hat and coat, following publication of Xavier Talbot's article reporting the police investigations of Mahmood and inquiry of Xavier.

Carole slowed and let the journalists surround her, marshalling them around her, as the bulky black cameras pointed at her and microphones thrust towards her. A litany of questions barrelled towards her. "What is your relationship with Mahmood?" asked one.

"He is a friend," Carole confidently answered, slowly noticing that Xavier was not among the group.

"Have you any concerns about a friend that the federal police consider a security risk?" asked another.

"The federal police are the security risk," answered Carole, basking in her forum. Some journalists laughed. "We should be far more worried about prejudice than about Muslims."

"What about Islamic terrorism?" asked a third journalist.

"There is no Islamic terrorism," Carole told them, finally able to broadcast across the country what she had said among small audiences for so long. "Terrorism has no religion."

"Could Mahmood be the third Sydney ferry bomber?"

Carole laughed. "No more than I could," she said. "Criminals come from every faith."

"The Prime Minister will shortly be making a statement about you and Mahmood," said a fourth journalist. The Prime Minister had returned to Canberra the previous weekend. "Do you know what he will say?"

Carole studied the journalist's searching face, as cameras continued recording and microphones continued jostling. "I remain totally confident this country is better for all the more Muslims," she said, before pushing through the throng towards privacy.

The warm air and relative silence of Parliament House wasn't really respite; journalists would want to talk to her all day. When journalists finished taking comments from politicians desperate to be heard, they'd come inside too.

Walking along the corridors, Carole saw a familiar face. "Kieran," she said.

He kept walking. Parliamentarians normally greeted each other, however little they liked each other.

"Gretchen," Carole said to another.

"Carole," replied Gretchen without greeting, hurrying her pace. Perhaps Carole had only greeted her to hear a reply.

Approaching Carole was a parliamentarian from the Labor Party. Francis saw her and smiled, grinning excitedly from ear to ear. Carole prepared to say something, but his grin was at her and the Government's expense. Carole kept walking.

In her offices, Heidi was on a telephone call. Seeing Carole, she rapidly waved her hands, without confessing the distraction in her voice. "Thank you," said Heidi, quickly ending the call. She stood up to face Carole. "The telephones," she told her, panting as she spoke, "the email, they're burning with people relying upon you and with people worried about you."

Political staffers normally discarded correspondence from voters in other electorates, never to be read, but when the messages were an opinion poll about the member, staffers became pollsters. Heidi picked up a notepad of paper from her desk.

"Forty-one support you," read Heidi, "forty-four don't." The telephone again began ringing, but Heidi ignored it. "Why didn't you tell me what you were planning?"

"I have no plan," said Carole, "but I have principles." The telephone continued ringing. "I'm otherwise engaged," she said, starting towards her office as Heidi reached for the telephone, before Carole corrected herself, "unless Mahmood calls."

Carole pushed open her private office door to see Rodney Bayne sitting comfortably in a chair, his legs crossed and arms on the rests. He looked up at her, without his usual crafted smile. "You could have arrived through the members' private car park to avoid the media," he told her, as she had already known. "While you were conducting your first door-stop press conference, the rest of us have been up to our vocal chords in talkback radio, talking about you."

"You've been in here, Rodney," Carole corrected him, as she closed her office door behind her. Carole walked slowly towards her hat and coat stand, on which she quietly hung her outdoor clothes. She paused at the silver mirror, checking that her hair and face were still as they were when last she checked them. In the reflection she saw Rodney, looking up at her.

Rodney stood up, stepped across her office, and switched on the television set. Carole turned to watch it with him.

Soon, the television set showed the Parliament House Blue Room, with its pale timber lectern before the sharp lights of cameras and array of jostling microphones. The Prime Minister stepped up to the lectern; a few more camera lights seemed to brighten as he did.

He was taller than his detractors described him, with hair darker than the hair of most men more than sixty years of age. The powders on his face were for television: to make it seem he didn't need them. Around his purposeful deep eyes were his studious spectacles, thinly rimmed in recent years as they followed the fashions for his age, until he removed them. "Ladies and Gentlemen," he said, "thank you for coming." He began every formal press conference the same way.

"You know what he's about to say, don't you Rodney?" said Carole.

"This government places the safety of people above any one person," continued the Prime Minister. "I will ensure that there are no security risks from any association between the Member for Seidler and the man known as Mahmood, whatever that takes."

The most powerful political figure in the land had set the national defence against her. Only her hands rested on her desk kept Carole standing.

"I invite Mahmood," the Prime Minister continued, "to present himself to any police officer before noon tomorrow to enable our security agencies to confirm his bona fides, failing which I shall report to the Australian people tomorrow afternoon the measures we will take."

Carole's office door burst open and Heidi's face appeared, before seeming to realise what she should do. She pulled her head away and closed the door.

The television set broadcast the sounds of journalists jousting to be heard, until Rodney stepped across and switched it off. He stood before Carole, much taller than she.

"The Labor Party won't upset its Muslim supporters by saying much more today," explained Rodney. "Giving your friend a day to bail you out demonstrates the Prime Minister's reasonableness. It also makes your friend a cad if he doesn't."

"Why should Mahmood submit to bullying?"

"If Mahmood contacts you," said Rodney, his voice restrained, "then you insist he contact the police and the police clear him before you see him, for the sake of public confidence in the Government."

"What about public confidence in Mahmood?" Carole protested. "Why isn't the Prime Minister telling people they have nothing to fear, instead of catering to their fear?"

"The police..."

"The police worry so much about criminals they forget the people who aren't," interrupted Carole, leaning forward and bearing the full force of her conviction upon him. "This party used to be about individuals like Mahmood, people with legitimate concerns we should accommodate, not the ignorant masses."

"This government governs for everyone, Carole," answered Rodney, as Government members did and Opposition members denied. "The Prime Minister wants this issue resolved before we go home on Friday."

After sitting for two weeks, the Parliament would again adjourn, this time for three weeks. Ministers would fan out around the country for meetings and speeches, while backbenchers generally remained in or near their electorates.

"I have spoken with your conference president," Rodney resumed, intruding upon her electorate as Carole thought wasn't his concern, except that Rodney Bayne thought everything was his concern. "She expects several party members to challenge you for endorsement at the next election."

Party members had the right to challenge any parliamentarian for endorsement before each election. Very few did, least of all in Seidler.

"The Government's majority is big enough not to need you," continued Rodney, "but your conference president doesn't want the people of Seidler punished, unless the security of the Australian people requires it."

"I have friends," said Carole.

"There are no friends in Parliament, only allies and the enemies you've not realised. I've been here long enough to make a gutful of enemies. You're only new enough to have made a few, but that can change quickly."

"Is that the reason there's no paranoia in politics?" asked

Carole. "There's only knowledge of the people who'll hurt you and ignorance of everyone else."

Rodney smiled. "You are learning, aren't you Carole?"

Without facing her, Rodney walked towards the door. His hand rested on the handle, he turned back to face her.

"If this situation is unresolved before Question Time tomorrow," resumed Rodney, "then the Prime Minister expects you to refuse all further contact with Mahmood, until the security agencies are no longer concerned. If you do not, then the Prime Minister will tell the Parliament that you are excluded from the governing party room. Who will you help then?"

Exclusion from the party room could become a precursor to the Liberal Party expelling Carole from its parliamentary team altogether, in spite of her having been a party member for so long. She would remain an independent Member of Parliament, but however little Carole had achieved in Parliament, she could achieve nothing then. She could scream and shout and the only people who would listen were people who already agreed with her: people whose opinions would not sway a single ministerial discretion. At the next election, the voters of her electorate would probably elect whomever the Liberal Party endorsed.

"Whatever you decide," concluded Rodney, "the Prime Minister wants to see you in his office after Question Time tomorrow." Rodney Bayne closed the door after he left.

Carole blew a long breath into the air of her parliamentary space, too warm to feel. She checked the time on the wall clock, as if every extra hour that day as well as those until two o'clock the next afternoon mattered. The time was not yet nine o'clock.

She slumped into a chair, not hers behind the desk. Carole's bent elbows fell onto her chest and her hands grasped her hair and throbbing head. Whirls of raged frustration blurred her vision of the floor, her mind grappled with her two options: to comply, and still try to save the world; or not comply, trying to save the world. She would, in either case, be alone within the Parliament, but she did not mind being alone within the Parliament as she would at home.

Returning to her chair behind the desk, Carole took a letter from the pile to read. A constituent complained. She put the letter to the side.

She picked up a report and tried to concentrate. Soon her mind wandered into the space between thought and nothingness.

Carole stood before her window without a view. The trees, private gardens, and paths were not as nice as those around her home.

She lay in the tardy sofa. It was not comfortable to rest.

She flexed her shoulder muscles, rolling them forward through circles trying to loosen them. She washed her hands and face at the small washbasin in her private office washroom, before reapplying her most subtle powders and colours to her face.

Outside her closed office door, her staff compiled more messages: the polling of the people concerned enough to vote where no election had been called. Their votes mattered more to the Prime Minister and Rodney Bayne than it meant to Carole. If she was deciding to do anything, it was not to dignify Rodney Bayne with a reply, not yet.

A gentle double-knock, Heidi's knock, breached the door. "Come in," answered Carole.

The door opened. "Do you want to see Xavier Talbot?" asked Heidi.

"Xavier," asked Carole, surprised as much that he had come to her office at all as that he had come to it then, "why not?"

The big man entered her office, looking around. He had surely seen many parliamentary offices, although the only time he had seen Carole's office was the morning of the ferry bombing, when their attention was on the television set. Heidi closed the door.

"I know about your ultimatum, Carole," said Xavier, stopping by the chairs without sitting down.

"How do you know?"

"I know because the Prime Minister wanted me to know."

"Did he want you to see me, too?"

"He wants people to know that he's a strong leader, but that he's giving you a chance."

"In which event, he expects you to report his ultimatum."

"I'm not here taking notes," Xavier assured her. "I switched off my memory at the door." Political lore insisted that no conversation with a journalist was ever really off the record. "Is the Prime Minister in control?"

"He thinks he is."

"Have you decided your response?"

"I won't surrender to prejudice, Xavier. I won't let Muslim people think I'd put my career ahead of them."

"As a journalist," Xavier continued, "I should sit back and report the downfall of the Member for Seidler." He smiled, as Carole didn't think she had previously seen him smile. "As your friend, I suggest you say nothing, not to me, not to anyone, until you're certain what you're doing."

"I am certain, Xavier. Promises alone won't bring people to our side. Not everyone equates words with deeds, as if we're good because of what we say, whatever we do or don't."

"If you were ending your relationship with Mahmood, then I would report it, but I want to allow you time to reconsider."

"I won't..."

"I know you won't, but let me hope you will. The ultimatum I'll report today. I'll draft a report to file tomorrow afternoon, if the Prime Minister slaps his chains on you and throws you out of the castle, and hope against hope I'll delete it unpublished. I keep thinking you can do more good as a little lamb inside this farmyard than another sheep sent to slaughter."

If Xavier offered Carole a reason to end her association with Mahmood, then she didn't want it, without being certain she didn't need it. If she should appreciate his words, then they might be reason to wonder whether perhaps she ought to trust him, just a little, but that was falling too far down a hole from which she might never escape. "Life was easier just holding principles, Xavier," said Carole, "instead of having to act upon them."

He smiled. "Sometimes, Carole, the saints inside their heads bring hell upon themselves, and others."

Xavier stepped back towards her office door and placed his hand on the handle. Before he opened the door, he turned to speak to her, as it seemed everybody visiting Carole in her office of late did.

"If you want a deaf ear not to hear you speak," he said, "or someone with whom to drink cappuccino or walk the gardens, then let me know."

He then departed. Everyone eventually did.

Heidi brought Carole a cup of cappuccino coffee. Holding an undemanding paper cup was as much a distraction as drinking; Carole had little mood to taste anything.

If the Prime Minister was going to ostracise her then let the blood be his; Carole was not so crude as to save herself. She would sacrifice herself the hostage to save the people she tried desperately to save: Mahmood, the Rohingya, and all the refugees in leaky boats and immigrants under tin shelters.

The only person her sacrifice might save was the Prime Minister. He did not need her saving.

Carole's office door left open, as she normally left it, Heidi came back and forth throughout the morning. The telephone on Carole's desk often rang.

"Answer that, please Heidi," said Carole each time.

Heidi picked up the telephone. "Carole Wynworth's office," she said.

Most calls were those of any day, until one shortly before lunchtime. Carole was sitting at her desk.

"I'll let her know," said Heidi, before hanging up the telephone. "Zaki Quresh telephoned," she told Carole. "He said he is Samina Quresh's brother and he's coming to the Ministerial entrance."

"I don't know what he expects me to do," sighed Carole.

"Shall I meet him?" asked Heidi.

"I need a break away from here," answered Carole, drawing her energy into her legs to stand up.

Wearing her coat, Carole set off. A colleague she passed in the corridors did not acknowledge her. Rodney Bayne might have glared a little more than normal when he saw her.

The Ministerial entrance was the furthest entrance from the public forecourt and facade of Parliament House, almost a kilometre away. Without decorations or motifs, it was the entrance for people coming to work or meetings. It was also an entrance for the family and friends of parliamentarians, although Carole's family had not visited since her swearing in.

Carole stood inside by the security guards and gate, looking out through the glass doors. The journalists were elsewhere, preparing their hurried articles and analyses or garnering more comment.

Between the ornamental rows of trees, the long narrow pond was still. The blue sky of a cool day reflected in the water. To the sides of the trees, a handful of cars were parked at the bays. Driving close to the entranceway was a white taxi, from which alighted a businessman in a grey suit carrying a black briefcase. He did not acknowledge Carole as he passed her, and stood by the desk at which a security guard telephoned the office of the person he was appointed to meet.

A long yellow sports car glided towards the parking bays. The sky reflected in the windscreen obscured Carole's view of the driver. The car stopped before a sign reserving the bay for disabled people, reversed, and parked in another space.

Stepping from the car was a Middle Eastern man, as Carole had taken to noticing. He wore an ordinary brown suit, indistinguishable from any other, with a diagonally striped tie. The wind that had not stirred the pond stirred his black hair. There was nothing impressive about him, beyond his car, but Carole felt relieved to see someone of whom she should have no expectations.

He paused to look around, before walking towards the entranceway. Carole pushed open the door to step outside.

"I recognise you, Mrs Wynworth," he said, his voice accented much as his sister's was. He studied her for several moments, their faces at one height, until his scrutinising eyes forced her gaze away. "I should introduce myself."

He removed a gold cardholder from his pocket and offered his business card to her. The thick printed ink of his name, Zaki Quresh, in scrolled lettering rose from the board, caressing the soft skin of her thumb. His address was in Sydney. "You have driven a long way," said Carole.

"I would drive to Tel Aviv to protect my sister," he told her, "but please don't tell Samina or Mahmood I have come. Don't tell anybody."

Security cameras were already recording both of them, knew Carole. They recorded the registration plates of his motor vehicle.

"I know why you like Mahmood," he told her. "He dresses as you dress and speaks as you speak Mrs Wynworth, very beautifully." She cringed, but smiled. "My priority is my sister. Every doubt that your security services have about Mahmood, I must also have. If he is up to something bad, I want my sister safe."

"I want everyone safe, Mister Quresh."

"If Mahmood is a man the police should arrest, then I want him arrested, before he gets my sister hurt. I don't want you protecting him so she gets killed."

"Who would hurt Samina?" asked Carole.

"All I know is what I read in the newspaper," said Zaki, "which is nothing. Samina can't ever contact him. I don't know whether Mahmood likes my sister, loves her, possesses her, or whatever else an Arab man does with his women, but none of those might keep him from hurting her or getting her killed. You should know that I will do anything to protect my sister and anything to avenge her. Mahmood knows."

Carole felt certain that he didn't mean to sound as menacing as he did. That feeling didn't alleviate her.

"With all the support I know you have given Muslims," Zaki continued, "I know that if you believe Mahmood is what he appears to be, that you and the other Australians are safe with him near you, then you believe my sister is safe. My sister trusts Mahmood and I trust my sister, but if you believe that you must walk away from him, then you believe my sister must."

10

QUESTION TIME

Whenever Parliament was in session, parliamentarians trickled in and out of their respective chambers: the Senate and the House of Representatives. The major parties only required one member to represent them in a chamber at a time, except when a member called a spill on a vote and during the daily spectacle of Question Time, in the House of Representatives.

Question Time allowed Opposition members to ask prepared questions of ministers intended to embarrass the Government. Government members read aloud set questions provided to them by ministers beforehand, enabling ministers to speak in self-congratulation and denigration of the Opposition. (Any real questions within the Government were reserved for private broaching or the closed-door party room.) A small group in each party privately prepared questions and tactics beforehand. From far above the chambers, the public sat in silent galleries watching the theatre, their cameras and telephones barred.

Thursday afternoon, shortly before two o'clock, members in their parliamentary offices combed and brushed their crafted hair. They checked their skin for blemishes. They dressed into their television jackets in preparation for the show.

Carole stood at the small mirror in her office. Her eyes centred on the reflection of her deep-blue jacket lapel, and upon her barbed wire and lighted candle badge. She had somehow failed to notice it since affixing it to her jacket that morning, as much a part of her formal wear as the two rings on her ring finger and watch on her wrist. Mahmood had not contacted her since Monday or the police.

Five minutes before two o'clock, the infernal bells began ringing, audible in every room and cupboard, corner, and corral of Parliament House. The green lights on every synchronised clock began flashing, denoting the House of Representatives, summoning her.

Among the members bustling towards the House, Carole continued along the corridors and most of the way through the members' lounge. She braced herself, patting down her jacket and sleek skirt. Amidst the ringing bells and flashing lights, she entered the chamber.

Throughout the long broken horseshoe of backbench wooden desks and front benches, almost a hundred and fifty members on green leather cast their eyes at Carole. She looked upwards, where the ceiling and its bright fluorescent lights rose so high they could have been the sky. Near them was the gallery for journalists, from which Xavier Talbot sat watching her. He nodded, in his distant, silent greeting.

Segregated from the press were the public galleries, from which visitors gazed down to the political square pit. Parliamentarians normally only looked up at them when their electoral assistants had informed them that their constituents were there, so that the Speaker in his remarks to the House acknowledged them. One man in the public gallery pointed towards Carole, for the benefit presumably of people sitting around him. Near him, pointed another.

Beyond that audience was anyone watching parliamentary proceedings through their computers or government television. Carole hurried up the steps towards her seat and desk, among the rows of them.

Ministers and shadow ministers spoke from their sides of the centre table, on which stood the wooden dispatch box. Behind their place for speaking were the seats visible to television cameras when they spoke, but they were dedicated to women members of marginal electorates. Carole's place among the Government majority was invisible, far from each debate. Only in her maiden speech and when given a question to read had her face and voice been broadcast, with the caption on the screen informing viewers she was the Member for Seidler.

The Prime Minister sat at the table with the dispatch box. Ministers sat along the front bench ahead of Carole. The bells ceased ringing and lights ceased flashing; the time was two o'clock.

Rodney Bayne stood looking towards Carole. She shook her head.

A calming deep relief settled inside her, choices and righteousness seemed hers. Rodney leant close to the Prime Minister, before hurrying to his seat like Carole's.

Presiding from his grey-timber boxed podium and marquetry was the Speaker of the House. "Questions without notice," he introduced Question Time. "Are there any questions?" he by tradition asked, although the answer was well known. Tradition afforded the first question to the Leader of the Opposition, whenever he rose to ask it.

"My question is to the Prime Minister," began the Opposition Leader, standing earnestly. "How does the Prime Minister respond to the Member for Seidler's shame to be part of this Government?"

Government members shouted their disdain. Opposition members retorted with their calls for a reply. Members behaved much as they always did, while Carole remained still and the Opposition Leader sat back down.

The Prime Minister rose from his chair. There he surveyed the rabble, with the smile of long experience. "Does the Opposition Leader worry more about one member's shame to be part of Government," he asked, swirling his tall self around to face all members in the House, "than he worries about his parliamentary colleagues satisfied to be in Opposition?"

Government members laughed. Opposition members protested. The Prime Minister sat down. The Opposition Leader could have persevered, but remained silent in his seat.

Continuing the tradition, the Speaker accepted the next

question from a member of the Government, who rose from behind her desk close to Carole. "My question is to the Prime Minister," she began. "How will the Prime Minister ensure there are no risks to national security flowing from any association between the Member for Seidler and the man known as Mahmood?"

Opposition members booed. Trying to drown away their noise, Government members cheered. Carole stared aghast at the question from a colleague, not the Opposition, supplied to her by Rodney Bayne or someone like him.

The Prime Minister rose again. "I thank the honourable member for her question," he said, without a short speech about his last visit to her electorate or the good job she was doing, as he ordinarily began his answers from Government members. "The Member for Seidler has many friends who don't threaten national security." Some Opposition members laughed. "I can inform the House that until such time as the police exonerate Mahmood of any interest in terrorism or the Member for Seidler ends her association with him, she will not attend any Liberal Party room meetings."

"Here, here," cried her colleagues in the Government, chastising Carole in the crowd, as the Prime Minister sat down. Opposition members stared at Carole alone in her seat, while she looked up to the press gallery from which Xavier Talbot watched her.

An Opposition member asked a question of the Minister for Health and Aged Care. Carole's head lifted. The House had moved beyond the story of Mahmood to another: an unimportant little gripe, thought Carole, about a hospital somewhere. The journalists watched the member speaking, as did the public gallery. Some members across the chamber still studied Carole, for any political implication, but they became fewer with every question.

Carole sat indifferently, while each side lobbed its predetermined questions and responses back and forth. They could be short snippets of fine eloquence for evening news bulletins or detailed exposition for the commentators preparing analyses they would claim as their own. None of them mentioned the Rohingya, still the subject of consultation and inquiry. The Opposition passed another chance to aid them.

The members who had scoffed at their adversaries' humour snapped into laughter with their colleagues' humour, as they would in turn throughout every hour-long Question Time. Members whispered words to those beside them, who nodded their affirmation.

Carole looked up again at Xavier Talbot, at his desk in the high gallery of journalists. If he was searching for a story, she was searching no less for one to give him. Her head turned up too long was cricking at her neck.

Her neck relaxed. Her head slipped down, until she gazed down towards the jacket she wore. Carole raised her ringed left hand and lifted her lapel. The bright fluorescent ceiling lights reflected in her silver badge: that infernal barbed wire encircling a lighted candle.

What might Xavier write if she dared ask a question there, inside the people's House, she thought, where all the people heard? She had said enough in confidence and almost enough in public without eliciting response. If Carole were to breach the hidden protocol and ask a question of her own, it needed to be more potent and personal than anything she had already said. It needed to rile the people still unstirred, seizing public attention too soon abating.

From all the words that charged the air and all the facts of recent weeks, one question slowly formed inside her mind. It grew from words through phrases until it blazed in bold black lettering in space that only Carole saw. Her belly began to seize, as her rush before the cameras that past Monday had not given her chance to feel. Her breath became pronounced, bubbling and struggling to bubble, against her tightening lungs. She looked again around the members not seeing her; surely none of them could sense what she imagined. She looked back up towards the gallery; the only story left to tell would be set from her parliamentary seat.

The Speaker turned to the Government benches for the next question, when Carole and another member began to stand. "I call the Member for Tablelands," said the Speaker. Carole sat back down.

He asked his question, members cheered and jeered, while Carole's question resounded in her mind. Her stilted breath released a trace of doubt she should proceed to ask it, while an Opposition member asked a question through the usual repartee.

When next the Speaker turned to the Government benches, Carole and another member stood. "I call the Member for Bradfield," said the Speaker. Carole sat back down.

The dance continued back and forth, the silent screams in Carole's mind, while the nominally independent Speaker elected from the governing majority accepted questions from anyone but Carole. Each time, she sat back down more slowly, her face becoming stern, to the increasing attention of members from all sides and journalists, if not from the public unaware of what was happening. The same tradition that expected the Speaker to alternate questions between each side of the House expected him to share the questions among the members standing each time he turned to face their side. Her jaw remained locked fast, for everybody watching her to see.

The time on the clock so conspicuous in the chamber neared three o'clock. Soon the Prime Minister would move that further questions be put on notice ending Question Time that day. Carole's spoken words had already cast her as a rebel from which she daren't retreat, and she took a sheet of paper and pen from her desk. "*What must a Government member do to ask a question in the House?*" she wrote. Carole folded the note twice, scrawled "*The PM*" across the face, and passed it to the member sitting beside her.

Her message passed from member to member, each reading only the covering inscription before passing it along. Carole watched it move, as did each person who had passed it and every person who had watched her rise and sit. More members and journalists saw the ripple through the chamber, their mumblings and mutterings increasing. An Opposition member asked a question of the Treasurer, to less effect than other questions, as members watching the trail of Carole's message saw it reach the Prime Minister.

Beside him, Leighton Ingles turned to Carole, inquiring but confessing no judgement on her. The two men looked towards the clock so close to ending time.

The Treasurer returned to his seat on the front bench. The Speaker turned again to the members of the Government. Carole and another member rose up from their places, when the Prime Minister raised his left hand and index finger, catching the Speaker's attention. He tipped his finger back towards Carole and nodded.

"I call the Member for Seidler," said the Speaker.

Carole rose, without a piece of paper from which to read. The mumblings and mutterings ceased. All eyes among the seats and front benches, bar those of the Prime Minister, scrutinised her as they did not scrutinise the usual tacit questions of Government backbenchers. Her fellow party members might have thought their glares could diminish or destroy her question, as much as the expectant gaze from Opposition members across the chamber might have yearned to encourage her to further what she had already said. She looked up towards the gallery, where Xavier Talbot leant forward and downward for the few extra inches it brought her closer to him, so far away.

The question once so clear in bold black lettering across her mind wavered in the space, but Carole recalled enough to grapple for it. Her lungs that once had struggled rose with fulsome breasted air, as she turned back to face the Speaker. "My question is to the Prime Minister," she said, her heartbeat racing from her chest. The mutterings from across the House resumed. "When the Prime Minister speaks of my friends who do not threaten national security, is he talking about my Christian friends?"

The House erupted. Her colleagues roared their rancour. The Opposition hollers encouraged her to battle. Members waved their hands and rolls of paper they had brought into the House for the most virulent confrontations.

"Order," bellowed the Speaker, in his deepest commander voice.

"I rise on a point of order," yelled another Government member. He stood, eliciting great laughs from the Opposition benches.

Carole ought to have sat back down until the Speaker adjudicated the point, but she remained standing. Her heartbeat threatened to explode, but her calves and legs were iron stays to keep her body still.

"The Member for Cooper will resume his seat," instructed the Speaker, through the cacophony of catcalls and the cheers. "Order, order!" he commanded. The Prime Minister might have motioned something to the Speaker. "The Member for Seidler will be heard!"

Opposition members hushed each other, preparing the spectacle ahead. Government members eased their jeers to mutter their contempt.

Bracing herself more for fire within than fire without, Carole drew upon her most forthright voice and drove her voice above all other noise. "Are the security agencies spying upon my Christian friends or just my Muslim friends?"

Again the House erupted with shouts and heckles. Rolls of paper waved like army batons from the arms of members stretching forward from their seats and shouting epithets across the floor towards each other.

"Order, order, order!" the Speaker demanded, as Carole sat back down in her Parliamentary pew. Palpitations raging through her lungs and heart and brain, she gazed around the waving arms and shouting faces.

Members throughout the House, observers in the galleries, and the parliamentary clerks below the Speaker in his seat watched the Prime Minister slowly rise. Braving the storms of words against him, he stood before the timber box aloof from the entire ruckus. The Speaker could have beckoned him to sit until order was resumed, but members quickly stilled to turn to him and hear his answer. Carole again disappeared among the crowd.

The Prime Minister surveyed the chamber, compelling it to wait. He glanced toward the clock stumbling past the hour, when Question Time could end. "This country, Mister Speaker," he said, "does not discriminate between religions."

The Opposition resumed hollering. Government members, bar Carole, cheered.

"Mister Speaker," said the Prime Minister, closing Question Time. "I ask that further questions be placed on the Notice Paper."

The Opposition members persisted hollering, waving their reams of paper and hurling abuse across the floor. The Prime Minister and most other Government members strode quickly from the House. Opposition members soon did the same.

Carole remained in her seat, becoming more alone. The few other members who remained had been rostered to attend by their parties to ensure a quorum, or were interested in the matters pending to be heard. Routine presentations of government documents and ministerial statements would soon follow, along with matters of importance (or that the Opposition called important) on the notice paper.

Slowly, Carole rose and trudged away. Pushing open the door into the members' lounge, where parliamentarians conversed in comfortable leather armchairs, she faced Rodney Bayne.

Carole proceeded towards the nearest door into the rest of Parliament House, as Rodney moved towards her. Without a word, they walked together along the corridors towards the Prime Minister's office.

The waiting area to the Prime Minister's office was larger than that to any other parliamentary office Carole had seen, but they were otherwise much alike as everything was much alike. Public property pictures of Australia with captions and catalogue numbers hung from the walls, behind pale Australian timber furniture with clothed upholstery.

The two open doors were clearly not to the Prime Minister's private office. A third door was closed. "He's asked you both to wait," an oldish woman behind the desk told Rodney.

Rodney sat in the middle of one sofa, implicitly directing Carole to sit in the other. There she sat quietly, overhearing a television set playing the sounds of Parliament proceeding, looking around the room. If she was the errant schoolgirl called to the headmaster's private office, then she should be glad for the chance to see it. If the Prime Minister's private office wasn't interesting, then at least she would know.

Sometimes Carole followed the time passing on the synchronised clock on the wall, or the less synchronised watch on her wrist, but time didn't matter much to her. Staffers took telephone calls, speaking in voices Carole heard but could not understand from one short side.

Finally, a staffer approached Rodney. "I can take you both through now," she told him.

Rodney rose, as Carole did, while the staffer stepped towards the closed door, knocked, and opened it. Rodney stepped back to allow Carole the courtesy of entering ahead of him.

Inside the office, sitting in the high black leather chair beside the red, white, and blue Australian flag and behind the double-barrelled desk, was the Prime Minister. Standing to one side before the timber-panelled wall was Leighton Ingles, watching Carole. Sitting in a chair on the other side, under the glass window, was Andrea Gidley, also watching Carole. Rodney closed the door behind him, walked across the smooth carpet, and sat quietly by Andrea.

"I'm sorry, Carole," said the Prime Minister. "I have been too busy to spend more time with you."

She sat down in the last chair, facing his desk, in which the four surrounded her. "My husband says I'm too busy," Carole smiled.

The Prime Minister also smiled. "Emmet is well, and Tessa?"

"Yes, thank you."

The Prime Minister rose from his chair. "You know, Carole," he said, walking slowly around his desk without looking at Carole. Her head turned with him. "Multiculturalism requires tolerance," he said, "not just of immigrants but also of police and security forces."

The Prime Minister continued walking around his office. Leighton stepped back to let him pass. He proceeded behind Carole, encircling her, when she stopped trying to watch him. She turned her head the other way and waited until he returned to sight again, near Rodney and Andrea. He stopped by the bright window; windows, however small they seemed, were holes through which a person could escape. He turned to Carole. His silence was her invitation to speak.

"I'm sorry about my question in the House," said Carole, "but I can't walk away from what I've always believed to be right, even if everybody else has."

"Nobody else has Carole, but we're learning what being right means." The Prime Minster studied her for several moments, as she studied him. "What do you think we should do, Carole, assuming you still refuse to dissociate yourself from this man Mahmood?"

"He is not a criminal," she insisted. "He hasn't lied. He simply hasn't told us everything he could. I'd stake my life on it."

"You've staked this government on it, but would you stake your seat in Parliament on it?"

Again she studied him, trying to understand. "Haven't I already staked my seat on it?"

"You have only staked it after the next election." The Prime Minister stepped back to his chair behind his desk and sat down. "That could be years away."

Carole looked around the office: Andrea, Rodney, and Leighton all scrutinised her. Slowly their expectation became clear. She turned again to the Prime Minister and leant forward in her chair. "Would you resign if the third Sydney bomber proves not to be a Muslim, proving religious profiling to be the abomination I know it to be?"

"Nobody thinks the party should expel me," the Prime Minister answered, although Carole knew otherwise. "I think the third bomber is probably a Muslim because the police think it, but I have never suggested that he certainly is."

Carole looked into her lap, thinking carefully about what she was prepared to say. She raised her face again. "If Mahmood is in any way concerned with the Sydney ferry bombing or other terrorism," she told him, conscious of the three witnesses around the room, "I will resign from Parliament."

The Prime Minister slowly opened a desk drawer, removed a blank sheet of paper, and passed it to her. He picked up a pen and laid it on the paper.

Carole picked up the pen. "Will you show my letter of undertaking to the Speaker?" she asked, as she began to write.

"No," the Prime Minister replied, "Xavier Talbot."

11

MOUNT AINSLIE

From the Mount Ainslie lookout, Canberra lay along valleys, cradled among low mountains, resting around her lake. The city could seem very big or very little, according to whether Carole dwelt upon the sprawling suburbs or her gaze reached the mountains beyond them. With only countryside beyond them, aircraft landing and taking off from the airport could seem rather small and slow. The artificial lake, part of the artificial city (as perhaps all cities are artificial), would have been still, but for the Captain Cook fountain quietly at work.

Around the lake was a plethora of landmarks and monuments most of which Carole had not visited for a while, although she worked in one. Parliament House and every other building was a model ornament for adults, set neatly to view. They were a toy set for children, expecting to push around the tiny cars along the little roads and lift those little aeroplanes into the air. Friday morning, there were no threats or conflicts, no talk of terror and its recriminatory aftermath. From above, even cities were serene.

Without anybody speaking, the scene was silent. Whatever once affected people, their lives righted again.

A breeze chilled the winter air already cold. Carole shivered, drawing her arms close to her side. Her widest woollen hat concealed her face from cold and recognition, her heaviest dark woollen coat embroiled her, and her fine black leather gloves sealed her hands. The sun had not warmed the day enough to keep her from needing so much clothing; it probably never would, not in Canberra. Hidden beneath her coat was a dress for her flight home to Sydney that afternoon. Sitting in one of the benches would have prolonged her time there.

Down the steps from the road and parking spaces came the wide girth of Xavier Talbot. The pale trench coat he filled was remarkably creased, so early on a cold day.

"I thought this was better than meeting by the lake," said Xavier, as he neared her. "Anything might wash up from the water."

"I'm glad to see you somewhere you're not eating," said Carole, as he reached her.

"In all the years I've been meeting people here," said Xavier, "I've never encountered a politician, staffer, or journalist I'd not expected to see."

Carole looked around. Few woollen huddled tourists had yet come to the lookout, standing by the boards telling them what they saw. At the top of the steps from the road, partly concealed by a bush, a young man stood. His hair was thick and blond, brushed arrogantly across his head. His face was athletic, as was his build. His arms were close to his sides and his hands seemed comfortably rested in the pockets of a long navy blue coat. Those hands could have held anything. He wasn't looking at someone with him or at the view, as other people did.

"Is that man watching us?" asked Carole.

Xavier turned towards him. "You worry too much about white people," said Xavier.

"You don't worry enough," answered Carole.

"I didn't want to report your resignation letter before speaking with you," Xavier told her.

Carole looked back at Xavier. "I wrote that letter because I knew it would never be called upon," she explained. "Why does Leighton Ingles have such influence?"

"He has influence because people think he has influence." Xavier stepped to the front of the lookout, facing across

Canberra to Parliament House. "If you want to end your association with Mahmood this morning, the Prime Minister will return your letter to you."

"I don't want it returned," insisted Carole. "Leighton Ingles will be humbled if the third Sydney bomber isn't even a Muslim."

"Leighton Ingles will be stronger than ever if he is, especially if he's a refugee..."

"He's not," snapped Carole.

Xavier faced her, leaning against the low wall around the lookout. "Please play with people, Carole. You have too little left to lose."

"I can't play," said Carole, laughing almost frivolously. "I have everything to lose."

Xavier stared at her. "I think Mahmood staged the theft of your handbag last Saturday," he told her. "A woman standing with two men outside a small office building in Lindfield is a strange setting for stealing a handbag, unless you know the person running after you won't catch you. I think the thief waited for Mahmood around the corner, took your cash as his fee, and gave Mahmood your handbag to give to you. The hero's brother became a hero, too."

"You wrote the article reporting it, Xavier," answered Carole.

"What could Mahmood have learnt from the contents of your handbag, especially your purse? Check the entries on your banking and credit cards, although Mahmood doesn't appear to need money. Do you keep your driver licence in your purse? That would tell him where you live."

"Did you want to meet me here so I could hear your prejudice, Xavier?"

"I wasn't with you on Monday afternoon," Xavier continued, "but I think Mahmood also staged saving those two boys from a truck. The boys weren't on the road, but from what you said their bicycles were left where a truck would hit them. The truck driver might have been part of the cast or might not, but the boys were never in danger and all Mahmood needed to do was pick up their wrecked bicycles. They knew to leave immediately, away from you."

"Sounding thoughtful and intelligent doesn't make someone any less Islamophobic," Carole told him.

"Thought and reason aren't phobias, Carole."

"Why, Xavier? Why would Mahmood go to the trouble to concoct such a show? Why would he lie?"

"We encouraged him. We made him famous and he gave us something for which to be famous. He fabricated the hero we wanted him to be. We need heroes so much."

Carole's eyes remained trained upon him, choosing her words carefully to be truthful. "We weren't looking for heroes, Xavier," she said. "We were looking for normal men and women when people in this country think Muslims and refugees aren't. Muddling through my mind every minute are the Rohingya in our high commission in Dhaka. I'd do anything for them to be here with us now, sharing the view."

Xavier threw his hands in the air. "Maybe everything about Mahmood is a coincidence," he said. "Maybe he thought he could slip into Canberra and get a friendly Member of Parliament to extend his girlfriend's visa and then slip out of sight again, until that policeman stopped him at the Hotel Canberra, or maybe he wanted a witness that he was away from Sydney, on a holiday, a day after the ferry bombing. You might want to be careful. I am."

"I am careful when I need to be," said Carole, "but we have no need to be careful with Muslims."

Xavier began walking, past her, forcing her to walk with him. "Mahmood would not be the first immigrant paraded as a reason to admit refugees proving to be no hero or victim," he said, "but we quickly pick a fresh one to promote. When the immigrants we trust without question are found to be liars, or worse, we move on effortlessly to the next impeccable objects of our affections, as if we'd never been misled and never been wrong. We don't need them all to be perfect. We only need the ones we're presently talking about to seem perfect."

"We have Zaki and Samina Quresh," said Carole. "Leighton Ingles told you they're clear of allegation."

"I'll let the cadet journalists know, but if Mahmood starts killing people, all we're going to write about his girlfriend and her brother is that they had no idea what he was capable of doing, and that they're victims too."

"You've lost your fire, Xavier. What happens if Zaki and Samina's stories falter? Do we move along to Zaki's wife, her friends, the people they sit with in a hall? I've not heard anything to make me doubt the truth of everything Mahmood has said and done, although I've heard a lot of prejudice and suspicion against him."

"You understand principles better than facts," Xavier told her. "Facts can be prejudicial."

"People want to see multiculturalism succeed, not fail as Leighton Ingles imputes each time he says that immigrants enrich us but then flies his spectre of terror."

Xavier stood across her path. "Do you want to win the argument or make arguments we lose?"

Carole stopped. "Does not Mahmood's pain also pain us?"

"Why is Mahmood's pain worse than anyone else's?"

"He is our guest."

Xavier turned to walk onwards. "Welcoming immigrants had more merit before the bombs began."

"Are you now a xenophobe, Xavier?" asked Carole. "People dying makes preventing prejudice even more imperative, not less."

Again Xavier stopped, facing her again. "What if you were a person dying, Carole?" he asked her.

Carole again stopped. "Then I will die for something, Xavier."

Xavier shook his head. "My life's worth more than that, Carole. Did you know I have a family: a wife, two sons, who sometimes catch ferries?"

Carole stepped forward, resting her hand on his arm. "For them," she softly reassured him, "we need multiculturalism, whatever the cost. Multiculturalism matters, not me, or Mahmood."

"Mahmood *is* multiculturalism. Principle and the people it promotes are inseparable. You knew that when you thought Mahmood and his friends would move public opinion enough to bring the Rohingya here."

Carole pulled back her hand. "Millions, billions, of people

all over the world need us to help them," she said. "When you malign Mahmood because you can't verify his bravery or nobility, I don't mind that you malign me, but you affect the opinions of the people with whom we can't sit down to explain. You make it all much harder for me to affect my government, and you punish every immigrant or refugee denied shelter in this land."

Having reached the place the view was no longer of the city but was becoming countryside, they stopped. Xavier removed from his pocket a chocolate bar he offered to Carole.

She shook her head, turned, and began walking more quickly back. Xavier hurried to keep up with her.

"For many people," said Carole, "Mahmood is still a hero."

"The Prime Minister doesn't worry about Members of Parliament associating with heroes."

"I don't abandon anyone," said Carole, "but if we abandon Mahmood, we abandon ourselves. We condemn him and us to his genocide."

"Please," laughed Xavier, between mouthfuls of chocolate.

Xavier stopped suddenly. A man in a long grey tracksuit almost crashed into him. "Hey," the man called out, stepping around Xavier as he ran onward.

Carole also stopped. She and Xavier looked back along the path, saw no one else running, and again faced each other. The sun had become a little warmer on her face since last she noticed it. A soft wind through the trees had become audible. "Did that man run all the way up this mountain?" asked Carole.

If Xavier was preparing more words to cast Mahmood aside then she would quickly jump upon them. He ate the last of his chocolate.

"Xavier," said Carole, "before you begged me to wait until you'd seen me..."

"I didn't beg, Carole."

"I thought my resignation letter was something you could use to prove Mahmood's goodness."

"Our trust in people doesn't mean it's warranted."

A heavily French-accented voice interrupted them. "Not everything real appears in newspapers."

Carole and Xavier turned to see an old man with a beard not certain if a beard was what it wanted to be, sitting on a bench with his legs crossed. Wearing a black hat and duffel coat, his hands grasped a dulled wooden cane close to him. His shoes were polished black, shining incongruously with the rest of his attire.

"*Pardon*," he said. "*Madame* Wynworth?"

"Have we met, Monsieur?"

He looked at Xavier Talbot. "*Monsieur* Talbot," he said.

Carole looked at Xavier expecting him to introduce her. Xavier shook his head.

"I have seen your pictures in the newspaper and seen you on television," the old man explained.

Gratified by the recognition, Carole stepped towards him. "Do you read newspapers, watch television, often?"

"I am old," he said, pulling his hands apart without letting slip his wooden stick. "What else do I do, between conversations?"

Carole retreated a little. Xavier again stood beside her.

"Can we get on with it?" asked Xavier.

"You mean to be kind, I think, Madame Wynworth," smiled the Frenchman. "Making war with the Islamists is not the French way."

"What is the French way, Monsieur?" asked Carole, again stepping towards him.

"Not just the French way, but the German way, now, the European way," he explained. "Our way is not to be afraid but to listen to the Islamists, accommodate them, collaborate."

Carole sat beside him; the bench chilled her layers of coat and other clothes. "Will that be enough?" she asked.

The Frenchman placed his hand on hers. "You reap," he said, "what you deserve."

Carole gradually imagined herself gasping for breath, as might the passengers in a death car bustling along a train track to a death camp. "What did we fight for in the last great war if not for Mahmood?"

"We fought for us," answered Xavier, looking down at them.

She looked back up at him. "We fought for principle."

"No, Carole. We fought for us."

"You weren't there."

"Were you?"

Carole withdrew into the bench, before her voice slowed from vehemence to sorrow. "I've seen the serial number branded in blue on a Jewish arm," she said. "I fought the war every time Mister Schimmelmann unbuttoned his cuff and dragged up his woollen sleeve."

Xavier fell silent. His pose pulled back.

"I did not recognise you when I began watching you, *Madame* Wynworth," the Frenchman continued, drawing Carole's attention back to him. "I sit here to watch, and I watched a man who walked when you walked, stopped when you stopped." His age-withered eyes turned towards the path from which they had come. "Do you know that man?"

Her coat hindered her movements, but Carole pulled herself around on the bench to look back along the path. Some distance away from them, a couple passed a young man dressed in a long navy blue coat, standing still and watching them: the same man, Carole felt sure, she'd earlier sensed watching her and Xavier.

"Who is he?" asked Carole.

"I haven't seen him before today," answered the Frenchman.

An old man with a cane and a fat man slow to move seemed inadequate protection against the young man watching them. He could surely ran faster than Carole could, was surely stronger than she was. Carole pulled her handbag close to her side, grasping it.

"We can ask him," said Xavier, starting towards the man.

"Please excuse me, Monsieur," said Carole, rising from the bench. She followed Xavier, walking in pace behind him in his wake and with her hand clutching her bag close to her side. She expected the young man to turn and run, or at least to turn and look behind him for a reason they were coming, but he remained unmoved, watching them. His hands in his coat pockets remained still.

Their pace quickened with each step, more quickly than Carole had known Xavier to move. Perhaps her thoughts of doubt about Xavier had offended him.

Approaching the young unfamiliar face, a face more tanned

than most faces in Canberra, Carole could more readily discern its sharp features. Xavier reached close enough to him to stop. Carole stopped behind and beside Xavier.

"Mrs Wynworth," said the young man, nodding his head in greeting towards her. He turned towards Xavier, revealing to Carole a small flesh-coloured object in his right ear: a signal receiver and speaker only the man wearing it could hear. "Mister Talbot."

"Who are you, man?" demanded Xavier.

"That man with whom you were speaking. Do you know his name?"

Carole looked back at the Frenchman. Struggling to bear the weight of his age upon his crippling cane, he was slowly standing up. He was old enough to have been alive during the Second World War, or to have had parents who were. "Was he encouraging us to collaborate with our enemy," asked Carole, as much of herself as of Xavier, "or accusing me of already doing so?"

"Why are you watching us?" Xavier asked the young man.

"I'm watching Mrs Wynworth."

Again looking at the young man, Carole stepped further behind Xavier. "Why?" asked Xavier.

"I'm Luke Parmeter, with the Australian Federal Police."

"What!" exclaimed Xavier, stepping back towards Carole.

Carole quickly stepped out of Xavier's way. "Am I under surveillance?" she asked.

"Would you like to be?"

"Am I under investigation?"

"I'm protecting you."

"I don't need protection from an old man with a cane," said Carole.

Luke laughed. "You might from the man you call Mahmood," he told her.

"Mahmood!" laughed Carole. She stepped to the side to face Xavier and Luke. "Are both of you xenophobes?"

"Leighton Ingles said I should tell you that he's looking after you," continued Luke.

"I don't need looking after," roared Carole. "Muslims do, from the likes of Leighton Ingles."

"Oh dear," said Luke. "The people most difficult to protect are those refusing protection."

"Go away!" snapped Carole, rushing towards Luke. "Shoo, shoo!" Crouched forward, she flicked her hands at him as she might frighten away birds from a picnic. "Scram!"

Luke stepped backwards and backwards, as fast as he needed to step to keep away from her, but she followed him. Turning, he climbed up the steps towards the road and parking spaces, glancing back at her as he did.

Carole stopped at the foot of the steps. He stopped when she did, close to the top of the steps. "Go find a damsel," she told him. "This lady doesn't want you!"

Luke remained on the steps. He continued watching Carole and Xavier.

Carole turned to Xavier. "I can manage the police," she told him. "I can't manage the public, not without your help."

"Journalists aren't supposed to obey politicians; we do so too often."

"All I need is your time to type, whenever I tell you something good to report."

"You don't need me, Carole. The government and police run their programmes promoting the reputations of Muslims, while there are plenty of other media players salivating over a story that racist Australia let a Muslim martyr drown four years ago. They'll believe a Muslim recovering a woman's stolen handbag and saving two boys from being killed by a truck, rather than the police or a conservative government. They'll produce newspaper articles and television programmes profiling the famous and nearly famous, generous in their treatment of Mahmood and scornful of critics."

"They should," said Carole, pulling away from him. The smile swelling in her face threatened to lift her whole body from the ground.

"I'll keep writing about you and report your resignation letter," continued Xavier, "along with your certainty it will never be invoked, but soon enough, journalists move onto the next news. The ferry bombing is already ancient history, and people don't remember ancient history. They're already onto their next television game show or the problem with the hinge on a cupboard.

"Mahmood will soon become another name people have forgotten, until someone with that name pops up on a cricket team somewhere or something like it and someone associates it with him, before forgetting both of them. Don't summon me to see your friend Mahmood again, even if you see him walking across the water."

12

REFUGE

Saturday morning, Emmet dressed for a medical conference much as he dressed for his medical practice: in a tweed woollen suit. His brown-leather spectacles pouch protruded from his top pocket. Carole's jacket and skirt were more formal and businesslike as constituents expected of their elected representatives, which aged patients did not expect of aging doctors. Tessa's clothes were the clothes of university age: her woollen blouse beneath a woollen jumper and tight blue denim jeans hugging her hips and legs. She was meeting some friends later that morning to study.

Carole, Emmet, and Tessa sat at the kitchen table of their home. Carole held her mug of warm coffee with both hands. The smells of fried eggs and bacon, which Emmet had cooked for breakfast, still wafted through the air.

Spread beside the *Sydney Morning Herald* newspaper were the morning editions of the *Australian* and *Daily Telegraph* newspapers, which Carole had rushed out to buy that morning as she had bought them the previous day. "I never thought I'd see any newspapers but the *Sydney Morning Herald* and *North Shore Times* in this house," remarked Tessa. "Who told you where to find them?"

Editions from both mornings lay open to their pictures and

stories about Carole's suspension from the Liberal Party room but not the party. The three weeks through which Parliament had adjourned was time for the police and security agencies to become relaxed about Mahmood, thought Carole, before the suspension had any practical implications. She, Emmet, and Tessa read Xavier Talbot's and every other journalist's report.

"Conviction is hardly conviction unless a person risks everything on it," said Carole.

"You sound like a politician," said Tessa, her head over a newspaper. "I never thought you would." She returned to another newspaper, before looking up. "Will Mahmood be pleased with what you've done?"

"I haven't heard from him."

"If he hasn't contacted you when you go back to Canberra," asked Tessa, "will the Prime Minister presume he won't anymore and let you back into the team?"

"I think so."

With Emmet about to leave for the day, the electronic buzzer sounded from the security control panels on walls in the kitchen and hallway. A person outside the security gates to the driveway had pressed the communication button, wanting attention.

Carole went to the panel on a kitchen wall. "Yes," she answered, speaking into the small microphone, pressing the button broadcasting her voice to the person outside.

"I have a Mister Mahmood in the car," answered a very proper voice, from the small speaker on the panel.

Carole looked at Emmet. Tessa slowly rose from her chair.

From the kitchen along the hallway, Carole led them to a window by the front door, through which she looked along the driveway. A long white limousine stood outside the closed iron gates, ready to enter.

"Hello?" said the proper voice, from the speaker on the panel along the hallway wall.

Carole looked at Emmet, wanting his reaction. "He's your friend, my dear," answered Emmet.

She looked at Tessa. "He has nothing to do with me," answered Tessa.

"May we please enter?" the proper voice asked.

Carole turned back to the panel on the wall. She pressed the button to open the gates. She then opened the front door.

From the sheltered landing outside the door, Carole, Emmet, and Tessa watched the gates finish opening. The white limousine drove slowly along the driveway to where they stood, finally stopping close to them.

Dark-tinted side windows obscured Carole's vision into the car. From the driver's seat stepped the driver in his black uniform and cap. He walked around the front of the car and opened a passenger door in front of Carole, Emmet, and Tessa.

Out of the car stepped Mahmood, dressed in a pale suit without a tie, flowing as fashionably as always. In his hand was a margarita glass, from which he took a final mouthful. He then handed his empty glass to the driver.

"Carole!" cried out Mahmood. Confidently as always, he fleeted up the steps, his arms out wide to greet her. She offered him her hand, but he kissed her powdered clean cheek. Her arms did not hug him as his hugged her.

Mahmood turned to Emmet, becoming even later for his conference. "Are you Emmet?" he asked, energetically shaking Emmet's hand.

He turned to Tessa. "Are you Tessa?"

Winter was fortuitous in dictating that Tessa was well covered, in spite of the figure her clothing suggested. Mahmood started towards her as if about to kiss her, but she stepped back and offered him her hand to shake. "How do know our names?" she asked.

"I read Carole's maiden speech to Parliament," Mahmood explained, "but you're white, Anglo." Mahmood turned to Carole. "All the children pictured with you on your website and in your electorate office are black."

"Poor Mummy," lamented Tessa, although she did not normally refer to her mother as such. "There weren't any black doctors she could marry."

"How did you know where we live, Mahmood?" asked Carole.

"Aren't I welcome here, Carole? You told the newspaper you welcomed everyone."

Carole looked around, trying to remember what she'd said to

Xavier Talbot the day of the ferry bombing, before looking back at Mahmood. "I was thinking about the Rohingya," she said.

"You don't want those savages."

"They're Muslims."

"I pray for their safety, but we can't have them here. Send them to Melbourne."

"What about your home, with your family, in Thornleigh?" asked Carole.

"My parents are worried about the police harassing me and know I can come here. They asked me to live here."

Her meeting with Leighton Ingles that past Tuesday came back to Carole's mind. "How old are you?" Carole asked him.

"Do you tell everyone your age?" retorted Mahmood.

"Linguists suspect you're thirty or forty years old."

"Linguists aren't as clever as they think they are," said Mahmood. "The government pays them to lie."

"Can't you live with Samina?"

"I couldn't impose upon her brother."

Carole shook her head. "I'm sorry, Mahmood, but I don't think of you being a refugee."

"You do. Ever since I mentioned my parents coming as refugees from Lebanon, you've liked us being refugees. Refugees don't stop being refugees."

Carole again looked around her, grappling for an answer she couldn't find, slowly becoming embarrassed she had. "How long will you be here?"

"Is that a question to ask a refugee?"

Mahmood looked back at the driver and nodded. From the car, the driver removed a white suitcase. He placed it on the ground near them.

Carole turned back to Mahmood. "Where is your car?" she asked him.

"I left it with my family for my brother to drive."

"Your brother drowned?"

"Hamid drowned. I have four other brothers. My sisters can't drive."

The driver removed another suitcase from the car, and another. Finally, six matching white suitcases stood by the car.

"Couldn't you pretend to be persecuted, poor, and needy?" Tessa asked Mahmood. "Other refugees do. It would help my mother think she's saving you."

Mahmood stepped back into the driveway, where his wide eyes surveyed the home Carole had long stopped studying. "Christians have beautiful homes," he said. "You have beautiful gardens."

"I'll find you a room," said Carole, beckoning Mahmood back to her and up the steps. The limousine driver remained on the driveway, beside the suitcases.

"Can I see your room, Carole?" asked Mahmood.

"No," answered Emmet. "There is a spare room downstairs."

Carole led Mahmood into the house, where Mahmood suddenly stopped. He gazed at the long, tall hallway. "It's like a museum," he said, his head slowly turning.

The chandeliers hanging by long chains from the ceiling weren't alight. Mahmood stepped to the wall and flicked a switch, as if to check the chandeliers glowed. They did.

Along the walls were rows of pictures in gilded frames, hanging by hooks and wires from wooden rails above them. "It's like an art gallery," said Mahmood.

Inside an oval frame and glass was a portrait of Carole's father, while paintings were of farmyards and lakes. Mahmood dwelt upon an engraving.

"That is Hobart," Emmet explained, "in Tasmania."

Suddenly obvious among the many buildings from 1874, along a sloping street, was a church. "I'm sorry, Mahmood," said Carole, quickly stepping forward. She removed the picture from its hook and wire, placing it on the floor, facing the wall. "I'll hide it somewhere."

"Haven't you a garbage bin?" asked Mahmood.

Carole resumed leading Mahmood along the hallway towards the rear of the house. Carole opened a closed door, seeing again a spare bed set with pillows, sheets, and blankets, unused for years. Near the bed was a wardrobe. A tall free-standing light stood on shining brass with a golden yellow shade. Through the window lay the gardens. The room was clean because Carole instructed her maids to wipe all the glass, polish all the furniture, and vacuum every floor throughout the house, without exception.

Her current maid, Nari, normally came to the house on Mondays. Carole would ask her to come that day, two days early, to clean everything. She would remove the sheets, pillows, and blankets from Mahmood's bed, before setting clean ones there.

Mahmood inspected the room, before looking at Carole. "May I see another room?" he asked.

"No," said Emmet from the door, beyond the point of rudeness as Carole had never before seen in him.

"I'm feeling unwelcome," said Mahmood.

"The bed in our other spare room isn't made up," Carole explained.

"I can wait," said Mahmood.

"No," again said Emmet.

"Please, darling," Carole told her husband, before looking back at Mahmood. "That room is the same as this one, but upstairs."

"I'd like to be upstairs," said Mahmood.

"No, Mahmood," Emmet repeated. "We do not allow visitors upstairs."

"I'm not a visitor," said Mahmood. "I've been invited."

"My wife invited you," Emmet told him. "I did not invite you, and I do not allow visitors upstairs."

Mahmood looked back to Carole. "I am not welcome in your home unless I am welcome in every room," he told her. "What will happen when a second refugee comes?"

"Are you expecting another refugee to come?" asked Carole.

"Someone will when I tell my friends how good everything here is."

"Then," Emmet interjected, "we should ensure that everything is not good."

"Please, Emmet," Carole told him. "I want everything to be good."

Mahmood responded, still facing Carole. "You might want to make up that bed in the other room."

The limousine driver carried Mahmood's six white suitcases in turn from the driveway into what quickly became Mahmood's room. After words between them that Carole couldn't hear, the driver and his limousine then departed. Pressing the button in the control panel on the wall in the hallway, Carole closed the front gates.

"Shouldn't we leave the gates open?" Tessa asked her. "We might need to run away."

"Please, Tessa," countered Carole.

Mahmood was already in the drawing room at the front of the house, Emmet having followed him, when Carole and Tessa joined them. Mahmood removed his jacket, which he hung over Emmet's favourite armchair. Emmet removed the jacket and draped it over a spare chair by a wall. Before Emmet could sit there, Mahmood sat in Emmet's armchair, his arms along the rests.

Carole felt the thoughts in Emmet's head, relegated to another armchair, quietly facing Mahmood. Carole and Tessa sat together on a sofa. The four faced each other.

"The Ku-ring-gai Municipality is a Refugee Welcome Zone," smiled Carole.

Emmet responded. "Do you genuinely consider yourself a refugee, Mahmood?"

Carole interjected. "Definitions are less important than being inclusive," she said. "Definitions are for people wanting excuses."

"We don't simply allow refugees to come, do we?" said Emmet. "We invite them, but the local council resolution was not to admit refugees into our homes. It was to admit refugees into other people's homes."

"We welcome," Carole insisted.

"I never supported council's resolution," resumed the doctor's discord. "I don't welcome people because they claim to be refugees. I don't welcome refugees."

"Emmet!" said Carole, "darling."

"Won't you need to go to a mosque for your prayers, Mahmood?" asked Emmet, more forcefully than he needed to ask.

"I can pray here. 'The whole earth is a mosque,' said the Prophet."

"That will be lovely," smiled Carole. "We haven't had prayers in this house for a long time." There mightn't have been any prayers in the house since Carole and Emmet bought it.

Tessa, almost under her breath, remarked, "I'm ready to start praying."

"I can teach you," said Mahmood. He winked at her, smiling as he did.

"That wasn't what I meant."

Again, Mahmood winked at Tessa. Looking back at Carole beside her, he must have blinked.

"Are you blinking," Emmet asked him, "or are both your eyes winking simultaneously?"

"Emmet," said Carole, "please."

"Do you have a job, Mahmood?" asked Emmet.

"I've applied for many jobs, but most employers refuse to employ Muslims, without admitting it."

"For which jobs have you applied?" Emmet persisted.

"Why must businesses be so prejudiced against Muslims?" asked Mahmood.

Emmet scoffed. "Most businesses nowadays would employ Satan himself in the name of religious diversity."

Carole interjected. "Isn't it time you set off to your conference, darling?" she asked her husband. "You're already late."

Emmet sat silently, conspicuously studying Mahmood as one lion might study another. If he had spoken then Carole would have answered. Instead, he slowly stood up. Walking to his wife and bending forward, he briefly kissed her cheek. "I'm never too far away, my dear," he told her, for Mahmood to hear. "Will you tell Xavier Talbot or the Prime Minister that Mahmood is here?"

"They don't have to know."

Tessa stood for her father to kiss her cheek, before he departed. She then sat down again. "The police wanted Mother to spy on you," Tessa told Mahmood, "in case you know something about the third Sydney bomber."

"I refused," Carole assured him.

"My mother looks after you," smiled Tessa.

"Muslims don't spy on each other," Mahmood responded. "We don't betray each other as Christians do."

"That's true," sighed Tessa.

"Today," Carole told Mahmood, "I have some appointments."

Tessa responded. "We shouldn't both leave the house."

Mahmood interjected. "I can watch everything," he said.

"Who watches you?" Tessa asked him.

"What about your studies?" Carole asked her. "I can defer my appointments."

"For how long, Mother? How long will he be here?"

"Tessa!" said Carole, looking back at Mahmood sitting calmly, before turning back to her daughter. "Mahmood will be here for as long as he wants to be here."

"I'll need a lock on my bedroom door."

"We need to build trust, darling."

Tessa suddenly stood up, staring down at her. "You're more interested in him having a home here than me!" She stormed out of the room.

Only Carole and Mahmood remained. "I'm sorry, Mahmood," said Carole, turning towards him. "She can be very selfish."

Mahmood stood and walked around the room. Carole watched him inspect the pictures on the wall, leaning close to some of them. The paintings there were oils.

Above the fireplace was a mirror, in which Mahmood paused before his reflection. With his hand, he brushed down his hair.

Standing on the mantelpiece was a Royal Doulton porcelain figurine from the fine ladies in delicate dresses collection, which Nari carefully kept clean. Mahmood took the figurine in his hand, examining it, before it slipped from his fingers.

Carole sat up, as the figurine fell to the floor and broke; the head and hat coming apart from the rest of it. Carole rushed around to pick it up from the floor, as Mahmood stood silently, watching her.

Holding a piece of broken figurine in each of her hands, she looked at him, uncertain whether she expected him to react. Carole walked from the room into the hallway and then the kitchen.

The kitchen might have been Carole's place for wondering

what to do, as she placed the broken figurine on the kitchen table. The break was clean, and Carole gently placed the broken head and hat against the broken neck. Whether the figurine was reparable with glue, what glue, and whether she should repair it, weren't obvious; Nari might know. She laid the pieces out again.

Stepping towards her from the entertainment area was Tessa. "You loved that lady," Tessa told her.

"It was only an ornament," said Carole. "We all have to make sacrifices."

Tessa looked up and past her, as Mahmood's voice came from behind her. "This is the biggest kitchen I've ever seen," he said. Carole turned to see him looking around, although there was probably nothing more impressive about the kitchen than its size.

Mahmood proceeded past Carole and Tessa into the entertainment area. The television didn't seem to attract his attention as did the framed posters around the walls; the artwork made the room feel more contemporary than other rooms in the house.

He stopped before a poster picturing an Afghan cameleer in the Australian Outback. "Have you Afghan blood?" he asked.

"God, no," replied Tessa.

"Tessa, please," Carole scolded her. "A little respect from you wouldn't be too much to ask."

Carole and Tessa watched Mahmood inspecting everything. He pulled open a drawer, leaving it open until Carole followed him and closed it. He paused at windows to look out into the garden and swimming pool.

The doors to the formal dining room Carole kept closed, so that opening them for a dinner party was something special. Mahmood opened the door from the hallway and entered.

Carole and Tessa followed. In the centre of the long, shining black dining table, below a small chandelier, stood three unlit candles in a sterling silver candelabrum. Mahmood examined the etched images of Australian landscapes high on the wall.

From the hallway was a closed door. Mahmood turned the old knob, like every other doorknob in the house, and pushed the door open. Carole normally only entered the library to stow unread any books she was given, after politely perusing them, or bought as frivolities. Most of the books, she and Emmet had inherited, or accumulated when they were young.

Mahmood flicked the light switch by the door, although the room didn't need it; a solitary closed window looked out upon the garden. Hanging from the centre of the ceiling, a single round light shone from the end of a metal chain.

The pictures on the library walls were those Emmet had chosen: castles from throughout the British Isles. They could be so dreary, thought Carole, and she didn't want them elsewhere in the house, but they complemented the old tomes on the bookcase shelves.

From the open doorway, Carole and Tessa watched Mahmood look through the glass-panelled bookcase doors, shielding shelves of books. The spines of all of them were plain to see.

Brass hinges squeaked and the oak frame creaked as Mahmood opened a bookcase door. Reaching in his hand, he slowly removed a book, leaving behind a conspicuous dark space between the books left standing. He carried the leather-bound book to Carole. The dry book was a Bible.

"I didn't know we had that," said Carole, intuitively opening it to see its creaming dulled pages without reading them, before closing it again. "We have a bin for recycling paper."

Mahmood returned to the bookcase, where he resumed examining the books. Eventually, he opened another glass-panelled door and removed another book. He examined the book, before sitting in one of the two red-leather armchairs in the room and reading. There, he seemed to settle. Two glass-panelled doors remained open in the bookcases.

Carole looked at Tessa, who quietly stepped back into the hallway. Carole also quietly stepped back, leaving Mahmood alone in the room. Carole pulled closed the door.

13

MEALTIMES

Sunday morning, Carole dressed a little more formally than she'd dressed the previous Sunday. She felt a little less at home with Mahmood living there.

Tessa dressed in different clothes to those she'd worn the previous day, but looking much the same. When Carole entered the kitchen, she found Tessa watching the television set in the adjoining entertainment area. With the police still searching for the man wearing the Canterbury-Bankstown cap photographed with the two Sydney bombers, the morning news repeated images from the attack twelve days earlier.

Carole strode across the rug and picked up the remote control device. After taking a moment to recall which button to press, as she always took, Carole switched off the set.

"Mother!" complained Tessa.

"We don't need to be reminded of that horrible morning," Carole told her.

Mahmood soon entered the kitchen. He wore an ivory suit and a golden scarf, with every sense of an occasion when Carole hadn't realised there was one.

Emmet dressed much as he'd dressed the previous Sunday, pausing briefly to see Mahmood dressed as he was. Ready to prepare his breakfast, Emmet opened the refrigerator door. "Where is the bacon, my dear?" he asked Carole.

Mahmood replied for her. "I told the maid to remove it and clean everything," he said. "Muslims can't eat food from kitchens in which unclean animals have been."

Emmet looked at Carole. "We all have to make allowances," she told him, "if we're going to get along."

Her husband continued looking at her. His consternation didn't need another voice.

Carole turned to Mahmood. "This house will be bacon-free, pork-free, and ham-free," she assured him, "for as long as you're our guest."

"I'll get my breakfast from a café," said Emmet, moving towards Carole.

"I wish I could eat with you," said Mahmood, "but how can Muslims integrate with others when restaurants and cafes serve pigs without regard for us?"

"Let me arrange a dinner tonight that I know we'll all enjoy," said Carole. "Would you like to invite Samina?"

"Will she be living here, too?" asked Emmet. "She won't be taking any room upstairs."

"We can't share a room," answered Mahmood.

"Then if she does stay here," retorted Emmet, "claiming refugee status, you will have to leave."

"Please, darling," said Carole. "If it must come to that, then I'm sure we can work something out."

Emmet stared long at Carole, before stepping towards her and kissing her cheek. He left the house.

Tessa took a mandarin orange from the bowl on a bench. She left the kitchen, without speaking.

Carole turned back to Mahmood, watching Tessa parting from view. "I'll prepare us all some coffee," said Carole.

Mahmood followed Tessa from the kitchen. Carole followed him, along a hallway, and outside. Ahead of them, amidst a tidy flagstone patio kept warm with the sun, was a deep blue swimming pool. Beside it were two long reclining lounges, on one of which sat Tessa.

Mahmood proceeded towards her. "You have a beautiful home," he told Tessa.

"It doesn't feel like *my* home," said Tessa, peeling her mandarin. "Nowhere feels like *my* home."

"Tess...," started Carole.

"That's how I feel!" exclaimed Mahmood, raising his arms and hands and pressing his fingers into his chest as he again faced her.

"I'm trying," Carole begged of him.

Tessa looked up. "When *you* feel without a home," she told Mahmood, "my mother tells *me* to make you feel more welcome. When *I* feel without a home, she tells *me* to accept it."

"Tessa, please," Carole scolded her. "Our guest..."

"Huh!" mocked Tessa, standing up and walking away. She threw her mandarin skin in the garden.

"I'm so sorry, Mahmood," said Carole. "I'll talk to her."

Mahmood stepped towards the edge of the swimming pool. His face turned down to the water beneath him, as if looking for something.

Carole stood beside him, looking down. All she saw was the small vacuum cleaner plying the deep blue bottom, collecting leaves before she noticed them.

Mahmood crouched down and dipped his fingers in the water. "It's heated," he said.

Carole continued watching him. "Are you remembering your brother?" she asked him.

"I never forget him."

"Are you any less heroic?" asked Carole, throwing her hand and arm into the air over the swimming pool. "You could save *me*," she said, as she unbalanced. "Aah!" she cried, trying desperately to pull herself back. Losing all control, she crashed down into the water.

The warm water flooded Carole's clothes, her thick woollen dress rising around her, as her body and head slipped under the surface. Gasping for breath, the weight of water in everything she wore dragged her down. Her legs twisted to the side meant her feet in awkward shoes couldn't feel the pool bottom. Carole struggled to get upright and her head above the water. Her hair held down covered much of her face, but between the fallen hair and falling water she saw Mahmood crouched by the poolside, reaching his hand towards her.

"I can't swim," he told her.

Struggling with each breath, Carole's right hand dragged the hair from her eyes, as she paddled towards him. Her clothes dragged her back and down, but she reached her hand out not to Mahmood's hand but to the side of the pool and took hold if it.

Her grip kept her there, her head above the pool edge from which she saw her home, water pouring from her hair over her face. A door from the house rushed open and Tessa stepped out. Tessa paused, before slipping back inside.

Carole's body straightened in the water, her shoes still on her feet resting where the pool wall began to turn to the pool bottom. Hopelessly embarrassed for her clumsiness, she clawed along the side of the pool. The warm water quickly cooled in the wide-open cold air and her teeth and jaw shivered, as she waded into the shallow end of the pool.

She reached the steps heading out, as Tessa came again from the house carrying a long white towel. Carole grasped the cold handrail, wearily pulling herself up the steps with one hand and her other hand again pushing her wet hair from her face, as her daughter wrapped the towel around her.

Out of the swimming pool, Carole removed her shoes. Standing in her tender freezing feet, her stockings scratching on the ground, she was shorter than Mahmood. Perhaps he pitied her.

"I'll dress into dry clothes," said Carole, water still falling from her drenched clothes. "We can all have tea."

"What is the security code for the driveway gate?" asked Mahmood.

"Why do you want to know that?" asked Carole.

"I'll visit Samina. You wanted me to invite her to dinner."

"I'll be here when you return."

"Don't you trust me?" asked Mahmood. "You're not really welcoming me if I can't come and go as I please, and I don't want to trouble you when I get back."

Carole continued staring at him. He was living there. "One,

nine, five, one," she told him. "It was the year of the refugee convention."

Mahmood turned and left, while Tessa walked with Carole towards the laundry. "He pops up all over the house," complained Tessa, "our house with many rooms."

"Has he been upstairs?" asked Carole.

"He said he hasn't."

"I'd have preferred to escort him," said Carole, "but what can I do?"

"You can insist upon it, but you don't insist upon anything. You're so busy welcoming him, you let him ramble all over us."

Carole left her wet clothes drying in the laundry. Wearing another brown dress, she undertook a day much like the day she would have undertaken without Mahmood there, apart from organising dinner that night.

Early in the evening, with the warm lights of their home overwhelming the winter night outside, Carole and Emmet relaxed in their drawing room. They sat with their red wine glasses resting with their hands on the armrests of their chairs. There, they sat, until only a few flecks of red residue remained in Carole's glass.

Appearing at the door from the hallway was Mahmood, having entered through a door at the rear of the house. "I should get a key," Mahmood told them.

"Where is Samina?" asked Carole, sitting up.

"Samina and I have split," answered Mahmood, looking down and away. "The media pressure became too much for her."

"I am sorry," said Carole.

"Will that affect her visa?" asked Emmet.

"I won't let it," insisted Carole.

Tessa appeared at the door from the hallway. "Mother," she said.

"Please, Tessa," said Carole. "Mahmood and I were talking about something important." Tessa turned and left.

"I had hoped for a margarita," said Mahmood, "but I couldn't find any margarita glasses in your cupboards."

"We have other cocktail glasses," answered Carole.

"I do like my margaritas in margarita glasses. Can you collect some tomorrow?"

"I am busy tomorrow, Mahmood."

"Can Emmet or Tessa collect them?"

"We are busy too, Mahmood," answered Emmet.

"Please," said Mahmood, "I am trying to adjust here, to fit in with you all, but I need some support from you."

"Let me see what I can do," said Carole, as the front doorbell rang. "That would be Ariel." She had entrusted her occasional waiter with the code for the driveway gates but not a key to the front door. "I've asked him to prepare us dinner."

"Where is Kunal?" asked Emmet.

"Kunal can't prepare halal meals," Carole answered, leaving her empty wine glass left behind on the coffee table. "Ariel said he can. He wants to."

Mahmood followed Carole into the hallway. Among the pictures hanging from the walls, a native Australian landscape hung where the engraving of old Hobart had. Carole opened the front door, admitting a thinly built, young waiter in a black bow tie and dinner suit; Carole hadn't thought to tell him he didn't need to wear them that evening. His black hair was cut finer than Mahmood's slightly longer, waving black hair. His black eyebrows had been trimmed thinner than Mahmood's.

"You're Mahmood," enthused Ariel, his voice demure. He offered Mahmood his right hand in greeting.

Mahmood looked at Ariel's hand close to him. He didn't offer his.

"I love what Carole and Emmet are doing," smiled Ariel, leaning forward and shaking Mahmood's hand. "Folks of your faith, folks of mine, we should be friends."

Ariel's wrist was loose, his grip was weak. Mahmood pulled his hand away.

"Ariel's studying at university," Carole told Mahmood, assuming that would create affinity between them. "His parents have been friends of ours for years."

"I know you'll love the meal I'm preparing," gushed Ariel. "In matters of meals, quality depends more on the cook than the cuisine, along with the ingredients." In his hand was a white paper-wrapped parcel, he lifted up. "Fresh barramundi," he said, licking his lips, "with a soft curry sauce." He sauntered along the hallway towards the kitchen, as Emmet came to stand with them.

"You should never introduce Muslims to people like that," Mahmood told Carole, when Ariel was probably out of earshot.

Emmet laughed, not too loudly. His tall frame rarely laughed.

Carole looked up the hallway towards Ariel, her mind drawn to Ariel's features she had never before considered. She again looked at Mahmood. "He amuses," she whispered, "but I'll ask that he stay in the kitchen."

"I like Ariel's parents, my dear," said Emmet, "but I never much liked Ariel either."

Much as he'd set it for dinner parties, Ariel covered the dining room table with a large tablecloth. He set four cork place mats, picturing pretty country scenes. Around them were four sterling silver napkin rings clasping four white cloth napkins and four sets of sterling silver fish knives and forks, along with four wine glasses. In the centre of the table was a bottle of chilled white wine on a round silver coaster, although Ariel prepared a margarita cocktail that Carole took Mahmood.

Mahmood held the cocktail glass in his hand, examining it more than the cocktail. "You do need to get proper margarita glasses," he said.

Appearing at the door from the hallway was Tessa. The young woman was dressed in a long black woollen dress that accentuated her gleaming blonde hair. Her make-up, blue shadow around her eyes and red gloss on her lips, might have been more explicit than she normally wore, but should not cause offence. Black sashes bound her shoes to her feet. "May I sit down?" she asked.

The question, in her home, was impertinent. "Of course, darling," answered Carole.

From the four sides of the table, Carole, Emmet, Tessa, and Mahmood sat silently. Emmet and Mahmood sat on opposite sides, facing each other. It was all more formal than Carole had imagined, but the dining room was well separated from the kitchen where Ariel prepared the food. Carole brought two fine china plates of baked fish from the kitchen, which she set before Mahmood and Emmet. She then brought Tessa's and her meals, before sitting down.

His cocktail finished before the food had arrived, Mahmood picked up the bottle of wine from the coaster. He poured some into the glass in front of him, before returning the wine to the tablecloth. He held his glass close to his nose, visibly savouring the bouquet.

Emmet remarked, "I might never become accustomed to you drinking as much alcohol as you do."

"I drink alcohol among Christians."

Taking the bottle, Emmet poured wine into Carole's glass and then filled Tessa's and his glasses, before returning it to the coaster. They drank without moment.

Mahmood surveyed the food in front of him. Emmet waited for Carole to begin eating before he would begin. Carole waited for Mahmood to begin.

"Dear God," said Tessa.

All attention in the room turned to Tessa, with her hands placed together in prayer and eyes closed. Mahmood picked up his knife and fork.

"For the good food you have brought us," continued Tessa, "for your Lord Jesus Christ..."

Emmet's eyebrows rose with surprise. Carole's eyes widened with shock.

"...We are truly thankful, Amen." Tessa opened her eyes. She smiled at her mother, father, and Mahmood in turn, before picking up her knife and fork.

Emmet looked at Carole. Carole turned to Mahmood, already chewing on a mouthful of food. "She doesn't normally do that," Carole assured him. "She didn't learn it from us."

"I found an old card inside our Bible I recovered from the recycling bin and began reading in my bedroom," explained Tessa, cutting some fish for her fork. "I've hung our picture of old Hobart near my bed."

"How do you think that makes Mahmood feel?" Carole asked her.

Tessa swallowed her first piece of fish before responding.

"People assuming my religion from my heritage made me think about my heritage," she continued. "People attacking me for my religion made me wonder what my religion was."

"Do you attend church, Tessa?" asked Mahmood, again pressing his fork into his fish.

Carole replied on her family's behalf. "We taught our daughter to embrace all religions," she told Mahmood. Emmet picked up his knife and fork and began eating.

Mahmood glanced at Carole, before again looking at Tessa. "Do you embrace all religions, Tessa?"

"Muslims have taught me some things," answered Tessa, her tone pleasant and friendly. "Truly embracing your religion makes it impossible for you to believe any other." Tessa glanced at her mother across the table, before again looking at Mahmood. "I've realised the same of my religion."

"She's very young," Carole told Mahmood.

"The atheists reject both of us," said Tessa. "Pretending they don't insults us."

"There are no atheists here," smiled Carole.

"I like the sounds of church bells," said Tessa. "Calling us Christians because we used to be is a compliment."

"Now, please Tessa," said Carole. "Talk to Mahmood about university."

"The laws of this country are Christian laws," lamented Mahmood, as he ate.

Tessa looked at her mother, grinning. "Christian laws without Christmas," muttered Tessa.

"Muslim laws would be good for you," said Mahmood.

"Where do we go then?" asked Tessa.

"Tessa, please darling," again interrupted Carole, her knife and fork still untouched on the table. "We have no need to go anywhere."

"You have Lebanon," Tessa told Mahmood. "We only have here, and we don't have here anymore."

"Tessa!" said Carole, her face reddening. "Mahmood was born in Australia."

"Have you not England?" Mahmood asked Tessa.

"Not anymore."

Mahmood and Tessa fell silent, eating their meal as Emmet did. Finally, Carole picked up her knife and fork to begin eating hers. The curry was a little spicier than Carole was accustomed to eating. She took a quick glass of wine to ease the heat in her tongue.

"You should think about how Muslims feel, Tessa," said Mahmood.

"Do you think about how Christians feel, Mahmood?" asked Tessa.

"Please, Tessa," interrupted Carole.

"Christians invaded Muslim countries," Mahmood replied.

Tessa laughed. "Muslims invaded Christian countries."

"Tessa!" retorted Carole.

"Please let her speak, my dear," said Emmet. Carole turned to her husband.

Mahmood pulled back in his chair. "Arab cultures were at their peak," he declared.

"Where are the science, invention, art, and knowledge now?" inquired Tessa.

"Tessa!" Carole snapped across the table. "Where are your manners?"

"Today," lamented Mahmood, "Muslims live in poverty, alienated from the riches of the earth."

"Plenty don't," responded Tessa. "Consider all the money we're giving you. You say you studied engineering, but oil lets you produce a pittance of the world's patents and technologies but buy other people's work and cleverness."

"We would do the same," Carole sniped.

"Oil is a gift from Allah," Mahmood told her.

Tessa turned her head away and muttered under her breath. "God knows, intelligence isn't."

"Tessa, Tessa, Tessa," insisted Carole. "Don't you think you should apologise to Mahmood?"

Tessa fell silent, but for the sound of her knife and fork returning to the plate. She cut another small portion of fish, her fork spilling a little before it arrived at her lips. She kept the food in her mouth, chewing, while her eyes gazed into the space over the table.

Emmet observed his daughter. Mahmood watched him.

Finally, Tessa swallowed her mouthful. "No, Mother," she said. "I do not think I should apologise to Mahmood." Tessa straightened her knife and fork on the unfinished plate. She sat up in her chair and looked at Mahmood. "Please excuse me, Mahmood," she said.

Mahmood nodded. Carole looked back at her daughter.

Tessa rose from her chair, pausing only to look at her father. "I'll be in the kitchen, Daddy," she told him, before picking up her plate and leaving the dining room.

"I don't know what's come over her," said Carole. "Please excuse me, Mahmood."

Carole left the dining room, closing the door behind her. She entered the kitchen, also closing that door behind her. There, she found Tessa standing with Ariel. "What is wrong with you?" Carole demanded to know.

Tessa's eyes began watering, as Emmet appeared. "May we please have a few minutes alone, Ariel?" he asked.

Ariel turned to Carole, slowly concentrating her breath. Shyly, he nodded and left the kitchen. He closed the door after him.

Emmet faced his wife. "I have always supported you in your confrontations with Tessa, my dear," he told her, placing his arm around Tessa, "but when the confrontation is between our daughter and your politics, principle, career, or whatever else you wish us to call it, then the time has come to honour my blood."

"*My* principle!" scoffed Carole, "my career!" She drew Tessa's attention to her. "When did you defer tending to your patients to tend to your daughter?"

"*She* never needed me..."

"*I* needed you!*"

Her confession held the air between them, Emmet and Carole staring at each other, Tessa staring at her mother. Carole's stare was hard, committed and driven, determined that Emmet understand what she had said, although she was uncertain.

Emmet stepped a short way from his daughter. She let him go, his arms falling by his side.

The telephone rang without breaking the moment. Part way

through the second pair of rings, it stopped, replaced by a voice from the hallway subdued by the closed walls.

"I'm sorry, my dear," said Emmet, dipping his tall head.

Carole turned away. Tessa stepped forward, her feet uncommonly loud on the floor, before stopping.

The door from the hallway pushed open, revealing Mahmood. Carole quickly checked her eyes were dry; they were.

"I am tired," said Emmet. He lent forward and tensely kissed Carole's cheek, before stepping past Mahmood and out of the kitchen. Tessa looked at her mother and Mahmood, before hurrying after her father.

Only Carole and Mahmood remained. "Where's Ariel?" she asked Mahmood.

"I sent him home. He won't be back."

14

WITNESSES

Carole's duties, if anyone called them that, for Monday morning included meeting the Roseville College headmistress. Later, she would join a morning tea with patients and staff at the Dalcross Private Hospital. In the evening she and Emmet would attend an Ethnic Communities Council dinner; she'd enjoyed those she'd attended since her election to Parliament and her support for refugees qualified her and Emmet for an invitation.

Dressed in another set of smart casual clothes, a pale shirt and loose fitting trousers, the breadth of Mahmood's wardrobe was remarkable. She restrained herself from remarking upon it, but Carole couldn't recall him wearing the same clothes twice. Even his pale leather shoes were unlike those she'd previously seen him wear.

Preparing to leave her home, Carole sat in her gold Mercedes Benz at her side of the garage. Opening the mirror behind the sun visor, she checked her face and hair.

Taking the small handset she kept in her car, Carole pressed the button opening the garage. The timber-slatted door rolled upwards and she ignited the engine, heading her car out onto the brown pebble driveway. Facing the iron gates keeping her car from the road, her long fingers again reached down to the button preparing to open the gates, when an unfamiliar bronze-coloured car approached. It stopped outside the gates. The arm that should have reached from the driver-side window to the control panel by the gates did not.

Carole left the gates closed, driving her car slowly towards them. The unfamiliar car door opened, and stepping out was a tall stocky man slowly becoming familiar, wearing sunglasses and a dark brown suit. He approached the iron palings as Carole's car slowed still further, finally stopping. The day did not seem bright enough to warrant sunglasses.

She stepped out of her car; her first time that morning in the cool open air. Carole walked towards him until she stood before him, separated from him by the tall iron bars of the closed gates.

"Superintendent Samuel Dempsey," he reminded her, "New South Wales Police Force Counter Terrorism Unit."

"These bars make you look like a prisoner," she told him.

"Cages are consequences of perspective, Mrs Wynworth. From where I'm standing, the cage surrounds you."

Carole placed her hand on a gate, but the iron bar was cold and she pulled it away. "Some cages protect the people in them, Superintendent. They protect deep sea divers from sharks."

"You *should* be careful whom you let into your home, Mrs Wynworth."

She looked more closely into his deep blue eyes than she previously had, longing for anything clever to say. "Will you let me leave, Superintendent?"

"You're free to leave, Mrs Wynworth. I'll move my car out of your way." He looked towards the house. "I want to speak with your ward, Mahmood."

"My ward?" asked Carole, before she thought better than to investigate the Superintendent's mockery. "Why would you expect to find Mahmood here?"

"The limousine driver that brought Mahmood here two days ago says he collected him and his luggage from Oakleigh Park, Thornleigh," the Superintendent told her, without really answering her question. "We can't prove otherwise, and the cameras that observed his limousine headed and leaving there couldn't see through the tinted windows, but we can't find anyone around Oakleigh Park who might be Mahmood's family. Unsurprisingly, Mahmood paid him in cash."

Carole continued looking at him. His knowledge of her home intruded upon her as no person ever could.

"A word of advice, Mrs Wynworth," said the Superintendent. "Always tell the police, like the media, what we will soon learn anyway. We'll trust you because of it, and you can shape our understanding before others do."

Silently and slowly, Carole returned to her car. Sitting there again, she opened the front gates.

The Superintendent returned to his car, as Carole reversed far enough towards her garage to allow the Superintendent plenty of space to drive onto her driveway and park. Carole left the front gates open.

Leading the Superintendent into her home, his footsteps following her along the hallway, Carole found Mahmood resting in front of the television set in the entertainment area adjoining the kitchen. "Superintendent Samuel Dempsey would like to speak with you," she told him.

Mahmood looked up from his sofa. "I was about to go out," he said.

The Superintendent stepped past her towards Mahmood. He stood tall over him, glaring down.

"I can wait," Mahmood added.

Another heavy footstep came from the hallway. Carole turned to see Emmet.

"Darling," said Carole. "We weren't expecting you."

"This seemed a day I should drink my morning tea at home," said Emmet, continuing towards her, "my dear." He leant down and kissed Carole's cheek.

The small sitting room at the front of the house, across the hallway from the larger drawing room, was where Carole hosted people she did not want in her home. The furnishings were the most antique in the house; Carole still liked to make a good impression. She offered her guests coffee or tea when etiquette required it, but only if they shouldn't know she didn't want them there.

Samuel sat in the armchair by a window, adjusting to the old springs. His suit was brighter than the one he had worn when last Carole saw him, if no more fashionable. Mahmood sat in another armchair and Carole in the third armchair, from which she could see the time on the grandfather clock by the door. Emmet stood at the open door. The coffee table lay empty.

"Mister Mahmood," said the Superintendent. The inquisitor took a small notebook and silver pen from his pocket.

"I didn't think policemen really had notebooks," said Mahmood.

"Did you know Ojala Kassab?"

"Ojala Kassab?"

"She was one of the Sydney suicide bombers."

Early news reports after the ferry bombing named Ojala Kassab among the victims, when she had been intuitively, in Carole's eyes, an ordinary young woman aboard a ferry. When the police called her the bomber, the victim became a murderess: transformed into a horrid exaggeration of other people's fears. Worse than the traditional maladjusted criminals who could be taught to understand their crimes and atone, after just and open courts of law brought them to account, Ojala had become something more Carole needed to comprehend.

Mahmood shook his head. "Why, Samuel?" Carole couldn't imagine addressing a police officer conducting an investigation by his Christian name.

The Superintendent took a photograph from his pocket and gave it to Mahmood. "This might help."

Mahmood examined the photograph. "I don't think so, Samuel, although I meet so many people." He offered the photograph back to the Superintendent.

"Keep it," said the Superintendent. "I have others."

"The media reported the ferry bombers carrying Myer shopping bags," said Mahmood.

"What do you know about that?" asked the Superintendent.

"Myer is a Jewish name," Mahmood explained.

"Sidney Myer was a refugee," Carole interjected, as she liked to mention, "from tsarist Russia."

"Refugees aren't all alike," said Mahmood, before turning back to the Superintendent. "Shouldn't you worry about Jews?"

"My wife shops at Myer," said the Superintendent. "She isn't Jewish."

"Myer is almost as fashionable as David Jones," added Carole, trying to keep pace with the conversation.

Mahmood looked at Carole and then back at the Superintendent. "Do either one of you know Ojala Kassab?" Mahmood asked them.

"Mahmood," the Superintendent raised his voice a little, "a witness recognised your face in the newspaper and on television as a person with Ojala Kassab. She believes you might have been her boyfriend."

"How credible is the witness?" asked Carole.

The Superintendent paused, thinking as he seemed suddenly so often to think. "The witness is as credible and not as most witnesses, Mrs Wynworth."

"Is your witness a Muslim?" asked Mahmood. "You can't believe the evidence of a non-Muslim against a Muslim."

The Superintendent continued staring at Mahmood. If Carole realised that he wasn't about to answer Mahmood's question, then so did Mahmood.

"No Muslim would say such a thing about Ojala Kassab or me," said Mahmood. "Your witness isn't Muslim, but memories mix, they muddle. Your witness is confused, or do you think the memory muddled might be mine?"

The Superintendent sat silently studying Mahmood, his suspicious eyes and ears snooping. He'd not written in his notebook.

"May I leave now?" asked Mahmood.

The Superintendent began flexing his mouth and lips as if preparing to gnaw on something in his mouth. Slowly he rose.

Carole also rose. "I always open the front door to guests leaving my home," she explained to Mahmood, before following the Superintendent out of the room, never getting too close. "Thank you, Superintendent," she said, although she did not know why she did.

From her open door, she watched the Superintendent start his car engine and drive away, through the open gates to the road. Emmet stood beside her.

"How did he know Mahmood was here?" asked Emmet.

"I have an idea," said Carole.

They walked together along their driveway through the open gates, where Carole looked up and down the quiet street for parked cars. Few were there, as few normally were unless somebody was entertaining.

The closest car to them was a blue sedan across the street, facing her. It became incongruous, in a street where most cars parked were luxury cars or closer to being luxury than was that blue sedan. Daylight reflected from the windscreen, through which driver headrests could appear like drivers, from a distance.

With Emmet following, Carole walked towards the car. The closer she came to it, the more there could have been a person sitting in the driver's seat. She became certain a man sat there, watching her approach.

She went to the driver's side window, but the tinted windows made looking through it difficult. She heard the door unlock and stepped backwards. Emmet stood beside her.

The door opened. A man in a blue suit stepped out: another policeman without uniform.

"Luke Parmeter," said Carole. "May I introduce you to my husband, Emmet?"

"Mister Wynworth," said Luke.

"Luke says he's a protective officer protecting me," Carole explained to Emmet, continuing to look at Luke. "Didn't I free myself from you in Canberra?"

"We don't cease protecting people because they don't want to be protected."

"Is your responsibility protecting me or watching Mahmood?" asked Carole.

"Protecting you means watching Mahmood."

"Don't you live in Canberra?"

"I live in Sydney. I went to Canberra to keep you safe coming home."

Carole looked around them; no people walked the footpaths. She looked back at Luke. "Have you been watching me all the time, everywhere I've been?"

"I have my shifts. Other officers have theirs."

"I won't live in fear."

"Caution isn't fear," Luke assured her.

A car came along Springdale Road. Carole didn't recognise it, as it passed. She watched it head away. Another car approached from that end of Springdale Road, suddenly busy of a Monday morning when people should have long gone to work and the school runs should have been completed.

Carole turned back to Luke. "Is there anything I can say to make you leave?" she asked him.

"Don't you think I'd prefer doing something more constructive?" Luke asked her. "I'd have preferred to spend my Saturday watching my sons play football or daughters play netball than watch a limousine roll up to your home, from which Mahmood steps out."

"Doesn't your family miss you, spending so much time watching this house?"

"They understand, Mrs Wynworth, better than I do. If you want me not to sit in a crammed car seat, you could invite me into your home?"

Carole laughed, before starting back to her home. Emmet walked with her.

"I like him being here," said Emmet, a few paces onward. "I feel better about getting back to work."

Carole stopped. She looked up at Emmet; the cold air around her slowly seemed a little less cool. She looked back to Luke. "Let me know if you want any tea," she told him.

They returned to their driveway, through the open front gates. Emmet returned to his car and drove away.

Standing beside Carole's car was Mahmood, dressed for the open air in a jacket to complement everything else he wore. "You doubt me," he told Carole. "You think I've lied."

Carole reached him, looking into his eyes lower than hers. "If you could just tell them your real name, your age..."

"Is that what our friendship depends upon, Carole?" asked Mahmood, his hands open before her. "Is that what your commitment to multiculturalism depends?"

She stepped backwards, not knowing whether to shake her

head or nod. She was pleading, but she was pleading for him. She might shout her answer "No!" or beg her answer "Yes!"

Mahmood spoke again before she needed to decide. "If I died too, would you believe me?"

Carole gazed down to the brown pebbles on the driveway, her mind reworking her thoughts and convictions. "I believe you, Mahmood."

"I better go," he said.

"You better stay," replied Carole, looking up at him. "The police are watching the house."

"I need to talk to people," he told her. "I need to understand why anyone would think a terrorist was my girlfriend."

Carole deliberated upon anything more she wanted to say, before releasing him. "Go out through the laundry," she told him, "leaving the door unlocked. Take the path by the birdbath to the gate in our rear fence." Without fear from their neighbours, the boundary fences between homes and gardens, often hidden behind shrubbery, were wooden. "The gate is unlocked. The Haughtons are in Europe and their house is alarmed but not the grounds. Please keep to the paths and don't step on any plants. You won't need a key to unlock the small gate in their front fence by their letter box. Head right, not left; don't walk anywhere near the front of our house."

"What will you tell the police if they come looking for me?"

"A little white lie can save people from getting the wrong idea."

"Be quiet," said Mahmood, gazing nowhere, standing silently before speaking again. "Did you hear that?"

"What did you hear?"

He looked around. "Do any of your neighbours own dogs?"

Carole took a moment to think about it; she'd not heard a dog barking. "Yvette Uppley has a Samoyed," she told Mahmood, "a pedigree says Yvette, named Phineas."

"Does she know you have a Muslim living here now? She should send it away."

"I'll have a word to her."

"Thank you, Carole," said Mahmood, smiling specially for her.

He placed his hands on her shoulders and kissed her cheek, before returning to the house.

Carole proceeded to her duties for the day, meeting people who didn't want to talk about the news reports they'd seen of Carole that past week: Mahmood and her letter of resignation if he should prove to be associated with terrorism. They weren't even people wanting to talk about the seventeen Rohingya refugees, still in the Australian High Commission in Dhaka, demanding to come to Australia. None of her more relaxed conversations or more formal discussions kept Carole from remembering them, or remembering Mahmood.

He'd not returned to the house when Carole returned home. He'd not returned by sunset, when Carole dressed into a long evening dress. With the aid of her shoehorn, she slipped her feet into her highest-heeled black leather shoes. She picked out her neat black-beaded handbag. A pair of pearl rings was affixed through her ears.

Being among their less formal evenings out, Emmet dressed into one of his many lounge suits, dark blue not quite black, with a conventional club tie. "Will our sentry policeman keep watch over our home or us, my dear," Emmet postulated, as he fastened Carole's simplest pearl necklace around her neck. "If he remains watching our home then by being out tonight, will we miss the changing of the guard?"

"I have told him where we are going," said Carole. "I wanted him to dress appropriately."

Carole left lights in the house shining. The lights by their driveway also shone, as did lights illuminating features of their house frontage. Emmet drove him and Carole away from their garage through the open driveway gates to the street, where Emmet pressed his button to close and lock the gates behind them. Emmet stopped their car near where Luke Parmeter sat in his car.

Luke stepped out of his car. He remained dressed in the suit he'd worn earlier that day.

Carole stepped from her car to speak with him. "Aren't you coming with us to the dinner?" Carole asked him.

"I don't like Indian food," he smiled. "With Mahmood in your home, I'll keep watching him."

At an Indian restaurant function room, Carole and Emmet attended their Ethnic Communities Council dinner. In the company of strangers, a hundred or more immigrant men and women, Australian-born and not, crammed into a dozen round tables between the orange walls and lights. With them was a smattering of Anglo-Saxons and Celts, paying and invited guests. Political aspirants, local councillors and the like, sat together at one table, away from Carole and Emmet.

The dinner honoured the retirement from an ethnic radio station (to which Carole had never listened) of a Vietnamese presenter, whose few words in halting English Carole could not discern; the only language most people in the room understood other than their own (if they understood any) was English. White-suited waiters and waitresses served plates of food on the Lazy Susans, swivelling on each table.

A past chairman jovially heckled the speakers, but adjourned to allow their parliamentary guest to speak. Politicians did not normally speak at Ethnic Communities Council dinners, but Carole had asked for the chance to do so.

"Multiculturalism is under threat," Carole solemnly told them, "but not from the actions of a few misguided criminals such as those we recently suffered."

Some guests nodded. Most continued eating.

"Multiculturalism is under threat," she continued, "I must confess, not from bombing but from bigotry, from the ignorance of white Australians, from religious prejudice, which you can be assured this government bitterly opposes."

Her audience politely clapped; Emmet's long upright hands clapped deferentially as they always clapped. Carole smiled and sat down.

An old Indian man at another table rose to thank their guests. When he finished, the tables resumed their interrupted conversations.

Emmet looked down at the plate of somethings a waiter had set before him, before leaning closer to Carole. "When would you like us to leave, my dear?"

"Shush," said Carole, hurriedly looking towards the only person watching them: a man at another table. She smiled.

Emmet reimmersed in a conversation to the other side of him. The man who watched her came towards Carole.

He was a short man, no more than thirty-five years old, with trim black hair, smooth brown skin, and a rounded unassuming face. The pride with which he filled his black jacket made the jacket seem too small, convincing Carole that his black suit must be his best attire. "Mrs Wynworth," inquired his South Asian voice, with a hint of London education.

She smiled, back to his black-brown eyes; near his left eye was a black mole she would not acknowledge. She glanced at the name card before him. "Hello, Mister Iqbal," said Carole. Assuming he was a Muslim, although she was not so rude as to ask, Carole returned her glass of wine to the table.

"Courage is a difficult burden," said Mister Iqbal. "Thank you for supporting Mahmood."

"You know him?" said Carole. "What can you tell me about him?"

Mister Iqbal stepped back. "I met him at the Islamic Community Centre. All I know is that he is very friendly."

Carole smiled. "Thank you, Mister Iqbal."

"You can't expect anyone here to trust the police," he told her, looking around the room. "We trust our own, and we trust you."

The man in the seat beside Carole moved away to another table, as people often did after finishing their desserts at Ethnic Communities Council dinners and even beforehand. Mister Iqbal took that seat.

"Did you also know Ojala Kassab?" asked Carole.

Mister Iqbal looked back at her. "Why should you ask, Mrs Wynworth?"

"I enjoy learning about people."

"I can see that," he smiled. "She was not devout, not that I saw, not a good Muslim. She liked boys, more than she should, but I never thought she'd hurt anyone; nobody did."

A waitress removed the finished plate before him. Mister Iqbal leant back in his new chair, stretched his chest, and scratched a small itch at his waistline.

"Do you know whether Mahmood knew Ojala Kassab?" asked Carole.

Mister Iqbal again looked at her. Sitting back up in his chair, he moved a little closer to her. "You know we can't assume anything from their friendship."

15

ALIBIS

Without the need for more formal clothes on Tuesday morning, Carole dressed in woollen slacks. Emmet remained at home longer than he normally did. Tessa remained long in her room, having not returned home until sometime after Carole and Emmet finally got to bed the previous night. Mahmood remained somewhere in the house, awaiting the arrival of Superintendent Dempsey.

The grass around Carole's home was damp, from the last of the dew not dried. Winding through the lawns and gardens were stone paths, along which she and Emmet walked, in spite of the threat of rain. Emmet used his rackety black umbrella as if it were a walking stick, its taps pacing them as his and Carole's slow steps slipped into unison. Her tidy tartan umbrella remained folded in her hand.

"Do you think Mahmood might flee before the police arrive?" asked Carole.

"I wish he would flee, my dear, but when we think about it, why would he?"

White picket fences separated the more private rear garden from the front garden more for exhibition. Small, unlockable gates admitted Carole, her family, and her closest friends through them.

"For the first since I met Mahmood," said Carole, "I know where he is. Am I a saint for granting him refuge, or the secret police for keeping him where I can watch him?"

"Saints can be secret police, my dear."

"Can spies and the spied upon be friends?" asked Carole.

"I'm sure they can, but not at the same time."

Carole paused beside a tarnished brass sundial atop a mildewy stone pedestal. "I think I felt proud that Mahmood wanted to make our home his," she admitted.

"You don't need people wanting to live here to be proud of the home you've made."

Carole resumed walking. "I never spent much time with Tessa, except at school hockey games or violin concerts," she said. "Perhaps, in the same house, Tessa and Mahmood can moderate what they think of each other, and what Mahmood thinks of..." The sounds of birds and Emmet's umbrella tapping on the garden path became the only sounds outside Carole's head, reverberating with the word she was unwilling to say.

"Were you about to say 'Jews'?" asked Emmet.

"No," snapped Carole, stopping.

Emmet stopped and faced her. He smiled with her, not at her expense, as the birds continued to sound.

"Yes," sighed Carole, as she resumed walking, letting Emmet walk with her again. She laughed, at herself.

The sunshine broke through the clouds above them. It lit, if only briefly, the ground around them.

Superintendent Samuel Dempsey arrived when he said he would. This time, Carole led him to the drawing room.

Mahmood sat again in Emmet's usual armchair, relegating Emmet to the sofa with Carole. The Superintendent sat in the armchair of his choosing. Again, Carole declined to offer anyone coffee or tea, although Mahmood continued drinking the coffee he was drinking when the Superintendent arrived.

Leaning forward from his armchair, the Superintendent placed a disc recorder on the coffee table in the centre of the room. He set it recording, stating his name and the date, time, and venue. "Mrs Wynworth secured several concessions for you,

Mahmood," he said, his deep voice becoming familiar. "One concession is your right not to give your true name or your age."

At the Superintendent's invitation, without moving from his chair, Mahmood identified himself and affirmed his consent to the interview being recorded. Leaning towards the recorder in turn, Carole and then Emmet stated their names and affirmed their consents, before sitting back.

"I will ask you again, Mahmood," said the Superintendent, still leaning forward. "Did you know Ojala Kassab?"

"I did," said Mahmood, drawing his arms closer to himself and clasping his hands. He described meeting Ojala Kassab at the same Islamic Cultural Centre at which he later met Samina. "Ojala and her family did not attend mosques," he explained. "Her father told them that being in Australia now his wife and daughters should be like Aussies, as she said he called them, as he would have called you, and he would have called me. She said he was proud of his new Citroen motor car and bought an Audi coupe for Ojala, although he tried to confiscate her car when she withdrew from college because studies interfered with her personal life."

Concealing her curiosity, Carole listened attentively. With every phrase from Mahmood's lips, the killer again became the victim in Carole's first impression, indistinguishable in profile from any other person. Her courtship with Mahmood was of picnics in parks and walks along beaches without entering the water, as Carole imagined it being with Samina.

Mahmood laughed. "Ojala even owned a bikini, she told me, although I never saw her wear it."

After any pause long enough to know Mahmood had nothing more to say, the Superintendent proceeded into the coming question. "Who did you see with Ojala Kassab?" he asked Mahmood. "Who did she talk about?"

"No one," he said. "Our time was too short before I met Samina Quresh. I liked Ojala, but I knew I could never love Ojala and yet I could love Samina; not loving is no less irrational than loving. Being with Ojala became pointless."

Carole thought of leaving the sofa to rest her hand on him. She kept her distance.

"Did you meet her family?" asked the Superintendent. "Did she meet yours?"

"Meeting families is for marriage," answered Mahmood. "Women who wear bikinis can be fun to date, but they're not for marrying."

The recorder continued plying. "Why do you believe Ojala Kassab became involved in terrorism?" asked the Superintendent.

Mahmood shook his head. He opened the palms of his hands. "She never spoke of politics," he said. "She rarely spoke of religion except for other people. She didn't object to religion, I couldn't have spent time with her if she did, but she had no interest in it. She liked being alive; I would have said she could never harm anyone, least of all herself."

"When did you last see her?"

Mahmood took longer to answer to that question than any other. "Three months ago," he said.

For all she'd heard, Carole was none the wiser as to the reason Ojala Kassab killed herself and other passengers on a ferry. She had suffered no poverty to corrupt her, nor fervour to inspire her.

"Why didn't you tell us yesterday that you knew Ojala Kassab?" asked the Superintendent. If the question seemed confrontational to Carole, then it was because the rest of the interview had seemed not so.

"Gentlemen don't speak of past relationships," explained Mahmood. "In this anti-Muslim atmosphere, and with the government legitimising prejudice, I didn't want Carole looking at me as she's looking at me now."

Carole immediately became conscious of the expression on her face. She changed it, to nothing at all.

"Yesterday," the Superintendent continued, "I mentioned a witness who recognised you with Ojala Kassab. She knew her quite well, and recalled seeing her by chance in a park several months ago, talking intensely with a handsome young man. The witness later enquired of Ojala Kassab whether the young man might be her boyfriend, but she became agitated and asked the witness to forget she had seen him."

"Why are you telling me this, Samuel?" asked Mahmood. "Since Carole mentioned to me her conversation last night, as she mentioned it to you, I've been making no secret of my past relationship with Ojala."

"Where were you at about nine o'clock last night?"

Carole turned to the Superintendent. She thought of asking him the reason for the question, but she and Emmet had undertaken to be silent.

She turned to Mahmood. He studied the Superintendent. Carole studied him.

"I was here," answered Mahmood, "in the library, reading poetry."

"What poet?"

Mahmood continued studying the Superintendent, before answering, "Banjo Paterson."

"What poems?"

Again, Mahmood continued studying him, before answering. "*The Man from Snowy River*," he said.

The Superintendent smiled. "There was movement at the station," he recited, his deep voice suddenly rhythmical, "for the word had passed around."

Carole's and Emmet's eyes turned slowly towards him. The only thing more surprising than Mahmood's answer was the Superintendent's response.

"That the colt from old Regret had got away," continued the Superintendent.

When she knew he had finished, Carole looked back at Mahmood. "Are you testing me, Samuel?" he asked. "Last night was the first time I read Banjo Paterson. I can't remember his poems as well as you can."

The Superintendent turned to Emmet, still watching him. Emmet spoke first. "I am not sufficiently familiar with the poem, Superintendent," he said.

"Can you confirm Mahmood was in this house at nine o'clock last night, Doctor Wynworth?"

"I was with my wife at the Ethnic Communities Council dinner," he answered.

The Superintendent turned towards Carole, who could not

recall words from committee reports and parliamentary papers she had read only an hour beforehand as well as she recalled the only poem she'd learnt in her youth, but that poem wasn't by Banjo Paterson. "I saw the film," she smiled.

The disc player continued recording every spoken word. "Where is your daughter, Mrs Wynworth?"

"Tessa? She was out later than we were last night. She has not yet risen this morning."

"Was Mahmood in the house when you returned home last night, Mrs Wynworth?"

Mahmood's failings did not warrant his every movement being scrutinised. "Where is this leading, Superintendent?"

"Please, Mrs Wynworth."

In the crossfire in which she sat, Carole imagined half-truths she could answer, but none of them would satisfy the Superintendent. "I didn't enter the library," Carole answered. "I don't intrude upon his room."

"Is this necessary, Superintendent?" asked Emmet.

The Superintendent's concentrated stare bore towards Mahmood. "The friend of Ojala Kassab who remembered seeing you with her was named Nadine Westwick. She lived alone in a home unit in Burwood, in a security block." Burwood was inner-western Sydney, another old suburb of single-storey Federation homes and multiple-storey concrete apartment buildings progressively replacing them. "Shortly after nine o'clock last night, a neighbour found her lying in a wide pool of blood at the open door of her home." Carole's body seized within her. "She had been stabbed in the heart, once only, but she was dead."

The room was silent for several long moments, before Mahmood spoke. "I am sorry, Superintendent," he said. "No one should kill or be killed."

"That's where I've been this morning," the Superintendent explained. He looked to Carole. "I will need you to tell me the name of the man with whom you spoke about Ojala Kassab and Mahmood last night," he told her, "when Mahmood isn't with us."

The silence that followed didn't end, until the Superintendent again looked at Mahmood. "Is there anything more you wish to say, Mahmood?" he asked.

"Am I in danger, too?" asked Mahmood.

"I don't believe so," the Superintendent answered, checking his watch. "This interview concluded at ten twenty-three a.m.," he finished, reaching his hand towards the disc recorder and switching it off. The Superintendent again looked long at Mahmood. "We are maintaining a protective officer outside this house, who can accompany you anywhere you wish."

"Will you interview Samina Quresh?"

"Why do you ask?"

"She won't be able to help you. We are no longer together."

"I didn't know."

"You don't know everything," Mahmood told him.

"Nobody does."

"Superintendent," said Carole, "may I come with you when you see her?"

"Why, Mrs Wynworth?"

"I may be able to help."

The Superintendent spent a moment staring at her, before speaking. "We do keep breaching normal protocols with you. Don't we, Mrs Wynworth?"

Carole checked the time on her thin wristwatch. "I'll follow you in my car." She deferred her morning appointments until later that day or that week. She grabbed her beige handbag for daylight informalities and found Zaki Quresh's business card in her purse.

Superintendent Dempsey's car never left Carole's sight from her Mercedes Benz behind him. As a policeman, he could have driven through orange traffic lights becoming red that Carole's car could not have passed, but didn't.

When she stopped at red lights, Carole redialled the number of Zaki's home on her mobile telephone, hidden from outside view on the empty passenger seat beside her. Each time, the line was engaged. Her car satellite navigation system issued directions, but following the police car made it more reassuring than necessary.

Looking out through her windscreen and car windows at the

homes she passed, without people she could see, the Superintendent led her into south-western Sydney for the first time that she recalled. He parked his car outside an occasionally painted grey-fibro cottage and low red-brick wall. Beyond the white-painted low iron gates to the concrete pathway and driveway along the side boundary were lawns of hard grass closely cut, without shrubs or other gardens.

Carole parked her car behind his. Opening the door beside her, the cool air collided with the warm air in her car and warm skin of her face. Leaving nothing visible from outside her car, Carole stepped out and closed the door. The button on her key ring locked tight all the doors and boot. It activated the alarms.

Across the street, a group of swarthy-skinned children watched her, talking feverishly among themselves. One laughed and soon the others laughed too. Walking near them were two dark-skinned young women, wearing scarves around their heads. Along the street, three young men were talking into mobile telephones, leaning against a freshly repainted sedan with thick black spoilers down the rear window and shining silver thick wheels.

Carole waved her hand at each of them, as she did to people around her home. None of them responded.

She looked down at her clothes and shoes, suddenly more elegant than they seemed when she dressed into them. Carole ought to have moderated her appearance.

The Superintendent waited for her, before pushing open a gate and proceeding towards the cottage. Cloud white curtains cloaked the double windows to each side of the door, on which a black ornamental figure of a tall arcing palm tree adorned a small peephole in the middle. The Superintendent knocked, while Carole waited at the foot of the few steps behind him.

Opening the door was Zaki Quresh, dressed in the suit he'd worn in Canberra, Carole felt sure. "Mrs Wynworth," he smiled.

"Zaki," she smiled, climbing the few steps, past the Superintendent. She kissed Zaki's cheek. "May I introduce you to Superintendent Dempsey?"

"Mister Quresh," said the Superintendent. He showed Zaki his identification, which Zaki studied as Carole had not. "Can we come inside?"

"It's not so cold out here," said Zaki, looking around. Carole pulled her hands together.

"You might prefer if I talk with you inside," replied the Superintendent, "away from here."

"My wife is cleaning the house."

"Please, Superintendent," interrupted Carole, "be culturally sensitive."

"I am aware of the cultural issues, Mrs Wynworth. I find this one peculiar to this house."

Zaki took Carole's arm and pulled her inside. "Will he ask about tax returns?" he whispered. "Everything I wrote is true."

"He wants to talk about Mahmood."

Zaki stepped back, letting Carole and then the Superintendent into his home. The hallway through the house stretched longer than strangers seeing the small-faced home from the street would have realised. Above the browning walls, frosted light covers shaped like upturned flowers hung from the ceiling.

"I'm very proud of my home," smiled Zaki, closing and locking the front door, "although the bank is a hungry mortgagee."

"Nice," muttered the Superintendent, his eyes roaming while his face didn't move.

"You won't tell people where we live?" gasped Zaki. "You won't describe our home?"

"God, no!" said the Superintendent.

Zaki proceeded past closed doors on each side of the hallway to an open door. "Samina is here," he said, his open hand inviting the Superintendent through the doorway.

The Superintendent entered the room, stepping from view. Carole started after him, when again Zaki took her aside. "Where will this all lead?" he asked her.

Carole smiled her most reassuring smile, her cheeks rising into the sides of her eyes and her lips stretched far apart, although she was unsure she believed it. "Somewhere better," she said, "I trust."

Zaki's face seemed to hover, before looking down more

resigned than convinced. He stepped back, allowing Carole to pass.

In a small, closely furnished lounge room, the curtains were closed across the window. An array of four lights from the ceiling barely illuminated Samina, wearing a long dark dress and with a scarf around her head. She sat in a dark-cushioned armchair, as indeed all the cushions were dark.

"Lovely to see you," said Carole, reaching down to kiss her as the younger woman offered her long left hand to touch. In Samina's right hand was a white porcelain cup of black coffee, like the two cups on saucers standing on a small round table.

Dominating one wall was a timber-veneer bookcase with several colourfully covered books, along with souvenir ashtrays, teaspoons, and mugs from Coffs Harbour, Tweed Heads, and the Gold Coast. Crowding the wall around the door were two identical tall dark chairs with backs of wooden slats. Filling the floor was an elliptical red and black rug.

The Superintendent looked at Carole. "Nice," he again said, as he sat in the armchair nearest Samina.

Zaki entered the room, carrying a black lacquered round tray on which stood two more white porcelain cups of black coffee and saucers. "My wife prefers to remain in her bedroom," he explained. "She is heavily pregnant."

"Your first?" asked Carole, watching Zaki place the tray on the table.

"My fourth, the children are with her."

That was more children than any family Carole knew. "Congratulations," she smiled, her face brightening as Zaki turned back to face her. She stepped towards him and placed her hand on his. "That's marvellous."

Zaki tendered one cup and saucer to the Superintendent. Without taking the cup, the Superintendent placed them on the little round table.

"I am glad you haven't served us margaritas," smiled Carole, still standing.

Zaki offered a cup and saucer to Carole. "Who is Margarita?" he asked her.

"I was thinking of the cocktails Mahmood likes to drink."

Zaki sat in a chair by the door. "Mahmood drinks coffee, tea, and colas, along with drinks you wouldn't know."

Carole sat in the uneasy chair beside him, holding her saucer with one hand and taking her cup with the other. The wooden slats of the chair were hard on her back and the supposedly cushioned seat was lumpy and rough, but still she smiled.

"My life here is good," said Zaki, "but I keep myself careful. Mahmood, Samina, are young, trying to change a world people like me want to preserve."

"Haven't Mahmood and Samina separated?" asked the Superintendent.

"I didn't know," answered Zaki, looking at his younger sister.

Carole occasionally sipped the sugar-laden black coffee, without admitting it was too sweet for her taste. The Superintendent's cup remained untouched on the table.

"Samina," said the Superintendent, "when did you last see or speak with Mahmood?"

"I've not seen or heard from him since Sunday. We came here, we argued, separated, and he left."

The Superintendent looked back and forth between Samina and her brother. "What can either of you tell me about Mahmood?" he asked. "Do you recall the car he drove, any part of the registration plates? Did he mention a school, or a name?"

Samina shook her head. Zaki shook his.

The Superintendent looked at Samina. "Did you ever meet his family?"

"He mentioned his parents, brothers, and sisters," she answered, "without mentioning their names."

The Superintendent's questions came and went, without eliciting any meaningful information. The slats of the chair and lumpy failing cushion became increasingly sore, but Carole adjusted herself to ease her discomfort.

"Did he ever mention his brother Hamid drowning?" asked the Superintendent.

"He had no reason to mention it," answered Samina.

Finally, the Superintendent stood to leave. "Thank you, Miss Quresh," he said. "Mister Quresh." Carole stood with him.

Stepping from the house, the Superintendent returned his

sunglasses to his eyes. Inside then outside, they'd gone back and forth from his eyes every time Carole saw him.

Preparing to step back into her car, Carole brushed her clothes for any dust and dirt that might have collected there. The Superintendent approached her.

"Mrs Wynworth," he said, "would you mind me checking your telephone records to know what telephone calls Mahmood might have made from your home?"

"Won't you check anyway?"

"No, Mrs Wynworth," he smiled. "Would you object to us inspecting your property for any evidence that Mahmood left and returned unseen last night?"

A peering neighbour might have seen him; there was nothing Yvette Uppley wouldn't tell the police. The Haughtons had several rose bushes on which Mahmood might have torn his clothing.

"By now," continued the Superintendent, "Luke Parmeter will have already spoken with your neighbours without, I assure you, mentioning his reason for wanting to check."

16

MODESTY

Wednesday was unseasonably warm, hot even, for Sydney in winter. That didn't deter Carole from bringing into the drawing room a large silver tray and four mugs of steaming coffee: three with cream and one without for Mahmood. Mahmood already sat in Emmet's favourite armchair, chewing on a muesli bar, when Carole offered him the tray. He took his mug.

Carole rested the tray on the coffee table. She took her mug and sat on the sofa.

Appearing at the door was Tessa, dressed as she and other young women she knew did on hot days, with her blouse brief and shorts briefer. She picked up her mug from the tray.

"Why would you dress like that?" asked Mahmood. His shirt sleeves and trousers remained long on sunny days.

"I know Lebanese call us sluts," Tessa retorted.

"Tessa!" snapped Carole, quickly sitting more upright but slipping, before composing her balance. "Who called you that?"

"I didn't get their names."

"You're imagining it."

"I've never called anyone names, but out there," said Tessa, pointing to the window, "past the houses where your friends live, I'm just another tarty white slut."

"Darling," said Carole, as she stood up and stepped closer to her daughter, gently holding Tessa's hand. "Please don't blame Mahmood for what you think others have done."

Tessa pulled away from her. "You think the world will be fine if only white people put up with everything," she protested, "while everyone else does as he pleases. Well, your generation tried that and it didn't work."

Carole shook her head. "Never have I been more ashamed than I am ashamed of you now," she said. "Never would I have imagined a daughter of mine speaking as you speak."

Tessa returned her mug to the tray. She stormed out of the drawing room, along the hallway, and out of the house. The front door slammed closed behind her.

"You shouldn't indulge her," Mahmood told Carole.

Standing at the door from the hallway was Emmet. "I have some coffee for you before you go, darling," said Carole.

Emmet continued staring at her, the expression on his face unchanging, before slowly stepping back into the hallway. Leaving her mug behind, Carole went to him.

"I want this interloper out of our home, my dear," said Emmet, his voice softened only a little in deference to Mahmood in the drawing room.

Carole's voice was more measured. "He is our guest, darling," she told him.

"No other guest as been interviewed by the police in our drawing room, Carole."

He rarely called her by her name. If doing so was meant to make her feel disciplined, then Carole did not take kindly to being disciplined in her home. "Then I shall ask the Superintendent to conduct his next interview in the sitting room, Emmet," she told him. "Every person is entitled to the presumption of innocence."

"Not when that presumption puts our lives at risk," said Emmet. "We should never have let him stay."

"I think our home is better for Mahmood being here," insisted Carole.

"Why?" asked Emmet.

"We need to hear fresh perspectives, to understand them. A person from another culture can only enrich us."

"Your au pairs from Ireland enriched us, but none of them were like Mahmood. Besides, they all eventually went home. I liked our home as it was, Carole. Why do you believe Tessa was out so late last night?"

Carole scoffed. "Tessa is out late every night."

Emmet scoffed all the more emphatically. "In my home I like to wander freely in my pyjamas and dressing gown, without thinking about who might see me." He had remained longer in his suit the previous evening than he normally did on weekday evenings. "I like to use toothpicks in my home after meals, without someone glaring at me."

"Then our house is already better for Mahmood being here."

"I want Nari to shampoo the rugs and clean the oven to remove the smells of whatever the invader being here meant was cooked in our kitchen last night."

"You like Lebanese food."

"Only sometimes," answered Emmet, "and I only want to smell it when I'm eating it, not all the time."

Mahmood entered the hallway. He passed Emmet and Carole along his way to the library. He closed the library door behind him.

Emmet followed Mahmood. Carole followed Emmet, hurrying to keep up with him. Emmet pushed open the library door, as Carole reached him.

Mahmood stood at an open bookcase door. "I do like that Banjo Paterson poetry," he explained.

"Are you acquainted with any other terrorists, Mahmood?" demanded Emmet.

Mahmood smoothly closed the bookcase door. "I asked the maid to oil the hinges and wood," he explained, facing his host and hostess.

"What more should we know of you?"

"What more would you like to know, Emmet?"

"We could begin with your name and age," replied Emmet, with every sense that it was the first of many questions he would ask without yet knowing what they were.

Mahmood laughed. Emmet's question was senseless, thought Carole.

"Don't trouble yourself," said Emmet. "You'd probably lie."

"I don't lie, Emmet," insisted Mahmood. "You and I, we both like our privacy."

"Is there any reason why the police will again want to interview you?" asked Emmet. "I want facts, not lies."

Mahmood shook his head. Emmet departed, his feet unusually heavy along the hallway floor. Carole soon followed.

Most of Carole's appointments had been set days or even weeks in advance through her office, but not her meeting with Rodney Bayne that afternoon arranged directly with her that morning. Rodney preferred they not meet in her electorate office. Carole preferred they not meet in her home. His first visit to Carole's electorate was to the secluded Swain Gardens along Stanhope Road.

Secreted among houses with their private gardens, hidden behind shrubs and trees, only local people knew those public gardens were there. Rock walls, steps, and paths headed down to and up from a creek, where the air was heaviest, moss covered the rocks, and the treetops were furthest away. Atop the far side of the gardens from the road was the gazebo, with more bench space than ever seemed required.

There, Rodney stood waiting, wearing a suit without a tie, gazing at the variety of flora. He responded to seeing Carole approach by sitting down, out of sight until she reached him. They were the only people in the gardens.

Meeting Rodney, Carole wore taller heels than she normally wore to walk there, climbing the paths and steps up the hill. When she entered the gazebo, Rodney sat among the benches with his legs crossed, facing her. If he was not relaxed, then he at least appeared to be.

"You're a long way from home," said Carole, referring as much to Parliament House, Canberra as Rodney's home in Adelaide. She sat where she faced him, not beside him.

"I'm here to ensure you understand your opportunities, Carole," replied Rodney, stretching a little further along the bench.

"I imagine the spiders in these gardens saying the same to the flies."

Rodney changed his tack in kind. "You know you don't need to achieve anything in Parliament, Carole. Most members don't. Enjoy a few shadow ministerial positions whenever we're in Opposition and not worry about being responsible for them whenever we're in Government. Relax among the backbenches, while your party members and electorate familiar with you from cocktail parties and dinners keep re-electing you."

"I don't need Parliament for cocktail parties and dinners, Rodney."

"The lords and ladies of this party want to win elections, Carole. We want government. There's a place you can do some good without worrying about pesky voters, where you can keep your comfortable little conscience clean. You're the sort of person who, were you to resign from Parliament, then a few months down the track, a lot of people think would be well-suited to a role at the United Nations."

"The seventeen Rohingya are still in our high commission in Dhaka," said Carole. "The United Nations keeps condemning us for our treatment of refugees and you keep disregarding it."

"If you're wrong about Mahmood, then you're gone from the Parliament, anyway."

"If Mahmood were to be any less innocent than I know that he is, then I have living in my home, in a room downstairs from the rooms in which my family sleeps, a man conspiring with killers. My resignation from Parliament will be the least of my problems."

Rodney stood up, arching his back as if that were the reason he stood. Before long, he stood over Carole. "Soon enough, Xavier Talbot or another journalist will learn Mahmood is living in your home."

"Let him," said Carole, her self-assuredness in flight. "My friends will be delighted; they'll be around to drink tea with Mahmood before the day is out. My critics can learn a thing or two about the benefits of being inclusive."

"Armour-plated glass in our windows and deadlocks on the doors won't help us if the criminals are already in the house," said Rodney, "unless you also want security guards outside your room."

Rodney's presence profaned those gardens. Being there was less pleasant in his company.

"Tell me, Carole, if you knew that one of a thousand refugees would rape or murder someone you knew without knowing which refugee that was, would you still admit them all?"

"When does that situation arise, Rodney?"

"It has arisen, Carole, even if the victim isn't someone you know. I worry more about the people who care about my family and friends than people who don't. There is a greater good than the rights of people who would harm us."

Carole turned her head to the side, dropping her gaze into the gardens. She would get no better response from him.

"Other people aren't as eager for appeasement as you are," Rodney told her. "If too many voters in this country stop tolerating terrorism, somebody will want passports and driver licences to identify Muslims, which might just help them know which hostages to release. Somebody else will want us to pay Muslims money to emigrate to Muslim countries, which we can't afford to pay. Somebody will demand we stop paying inducements for immigrants to come and to stay."

Carole looked back towards him, without waiting for his next missive she would nonchalantly deflect. "I'm more worried about this government withdrawing this country from the refugee convention," she told him, "or repealing the legal prohibitions against religious discrimination and vilification."

Rodney smiled. "If you knew we wouldn't, then would you feel more relaxed eating fresh lobster and drinking vintage champagne with the United Nations?"

"I can eat lobster and drink champagne at home, Rodney. If you want them so much, then I can arrange for someone to serve them for you at my gate."

"I envy you," said Rodney. "We're offering you progress to something less demanding, more rewarding, with people with whom you agree, without whips to check when you don't: a sojourn over the sea."

Carole stood up and faced him, still a little taller than she was. "Please thank the PM," she told him, a small self-suffering smile compromising the earnestness in her face, "but I'm too young to retire. I have too much to do."

"This is it, for you Carole," Rodney told her. "Carole Wynworth, MP, with nothing left to value but your vote and no bargain left to chase but your compliance. You could have stepped up, instead of trying to spoil other people's shows. You could have walked the world stage, instead of cowering behind the curtains of a closing matinee."

Carole walked away from him, back down the hill. That day, she wouldn't rest on a bench, beside a little moist lawn.

That evening, Carole returned to her home to see the door to Tessa's bedroom closed, as it so often was since Mahmood arrived. She and Tessa had never enjoyed, or suffered, the sorts of reconciliations the fracas that morning ought to have inspired. If she were to knock on her daughter's bedroom door, they would have fought. Carole did not like to fight.

Mahmood sat alone at the bare dining table, drinking a margarita in one of Carole's new margarita glasses without a coaster on the tabletop. Carole brought him a coaster and placed his glass on it. "Coasters protect the wood," she explained, as she sat in another chair. She had already drunk more wine than she liked to drink of a day.

The next time Mahmood raised his glass to sip from it, he again returned it to the tabletop. "I have asked Tessa not to say her grace before meals," said Mahmood. "I have offered her a Muslim prayer to say."

"Thank you, Mahmood," smiled Carole. "I have tried to teach her to be sensitive to Muslims."

"The Christians on the university campus could be very rude."

"I've been remiss," said Carole, sitting up. "I've so much enjoyed you being here, I've forgotten the rest of this country. We should invite the newspapers and television stations here – we can start with the *North Shore Times* – to see how well you've settled in and how happy we all are. Any home welcoming Rohingya refugees will be just as pleased."

"I don't want the Rohingya disrupting my house," answered Mahmood. "Are they the reason you're out so much?"

"I might have had the chance to represent this country at the United Nations," Carole told him.

"Why must a Christian represent us?" asked Mahmood. "Muslims are alienated from real political power."

"Mahmood," said Carole, her voice hesitating. "The United Nations gives Islam a broad forum."

"The Jews haven't returned Palestine."

"Israel must exist," she insisted.

"When Palestinians are the majority there," said Mahmood, "the Jews will go and there will be peace. In time, you will understand why we yearn for the lands in which we live to be Muslim lands under sharia, without the decadence of democracy and pornography in public places. Asking a man to place his citizenship above his religion is asking him to raise cloth on a pole above Allah, but a Muslim country requires no blasphemy. This country's submission to Islam will be good for you, too."

Sometimes, Carole felt very tired. "Good night, Mahmood," she said, before retiring upstairs.

In her bed, Carole slept soundly, with her dreams of any night, until she woke to a searing scream. Before she could switch on the light at her side of the bed, Emmet had switched on the light at his side. The scream continued: a female scream, in a house in which the only other female was Tessa.

Carole followed Emmet rushing out of their room along the landing to Tessa's room, where her light was shining. Mahmood stood at the open door, wearing tracksuit pants and nothing else.

"What is this?" roared Emmet, continuing towards him. Tessa's scream stopped, breaking into tears. Mahmood stepped back.

Carole rushed past Emmet and then Mahmood, to find Tessa crying in her bed, her blanket pulled up over her chest so that only her face was visible. Carole sat beside her, her arms around her.

Emmet stepped into the open doorway, facing Mahmood, keeping his daughter and Carole behind him. "Explain yourself," demanded Emmet.

"She wanted to see me."

"I did not," cried out Tessa.

"It's all a misunderstanding," pleaded Carole, still holding Tessa. "Mahmood, please go to your room."

"Wait, Mahmood," bellowed Emmet. "If you ever come up those stairs again, I will kill you."

"Emmet!" Carole reprimanded him. "It's a misunderstanding."

"Don't misunderstand me, Mahmood."

Tessa pushed her mother away from her. "I don't want him here," she said.

"Please," said Carole, standing up, "Emmet, Tessa, both of you, can we have some tolerance, some understanding?"

"I am done with tolerance," hollered Emmet. "I understand too well." He turned to Mahmood. "Why are you here, Mahmood?"

"He has nowhere else to go," answered Carole on Mahmood's behalf, stepping towards Emmet and Mahmood.

Emmet turned back to Carole. "He has a home to go to," said Emmet. "He has countries to go to."

"Emmet, please," said Carole. "He doesn't."

Emmet turned back to Mahmood. "Go downstairs now, Mahmood," he ordered.

"I thought you were better than the bigots," complained Mahmood, standing defiantly, "but you're all Islamophobic."

"Mahmood misconstrued Tessa's dress and words," Carole told Emmet. "It's a different culture."

"He was born here."

"His culture doesn't change." Carole turned to Mahmood. "I will teach you how to conduct relations with my daughter."

"Mother!" yelled Tessa, still in her bed. "Don't pimp me for your self-righteousness!"

"Darling," answered Carole, turning back to her. "You both have to learn to engage."

In Tessa's room was a large armchair. Emmet stomped across the room and sat there. "I'll stay here," he said. "The police presence around this house couldn't be anything more if the Archangel Gabriel stood at our gates, but it can't protect our daughter in her bed when the devil is downstairs."

"Daddy," said Tessa.

Carole confronted Emmet. "Mahmood won't come upstairs again," she told him. "You can't sleep properly in a chair."

"I'll sleep better here than I will sleep worrying about our daughter from my bed."

In the silence, Emmet remained in that chair, his face never before so dour. His eyes remained trained upon Mahmood at the door.

Tessa lay back in her bed. She pulled her blanket all over her, her face included.

Finally, Mahmood turned and went downstairs. Carole left Emmet in Tessa's room and returned to her bed.

The darkness was not enough to let Carole sleep; the silence of the house unconvincing. Sometime later, she didn't know how long, the lights to her room switched on again.

Carole looked up to see Emmet passing through her room, making no effort to be quiet. "Tessa and I will take rooms at the Killara Inn tonight," he told her, talking several pairs of clean underpants and socks from his chest of drawers. "Tomorrow, we'll set off holidaying in Canberra until Sunday. I'll be eating bacon and eggs for breakfast, ham sandwiches for lunch, and roast pork for dinner."

"You don't have to sleep away from home to eat what you want," Carole remonstrated, climbing from their bed. "We can go to restaurants."

"We'll stay at the Ainslie," continued Emmet, laying those pairs of underpants and socks on his side of their bed, "or Olims, or whatever that hotel now calls itself where you and I stayed when we were young, without politicians or journalists. I want to remind myself of the lives we once shared, into which we wanted to bring our children rather than other people's children."

Carole's head shook with images of holidays long past, of her and Emmet sitting outdoors by the fountain and indoors by open-hearth fires. "I can't get away now," she told him, as he must have known. Struggling to realise what was happening, she slumped in her antique Queen Anne chair not made for crying.

"Your refugee in residence is not enriching us," said Emmet. "He is replacing us."

"Please, darling," pleaded Carole. "Don't be like this. We can install lockable gates on the stairs to keep Mahmood from Tessa's room. We can install locks on her door."

Night remained outside, while Emmet dressed into clothes and shoes for a day, before leaving the room. His steps headed downstairs were heavier than they needed to be, as they were coming back up again. He returned to their room carrying a suitcase.

Carole's eyes dampened and mouth quivered. "We have the opera this Saturday night," she pleaded. "You enjoy *The Merry Widow*."

"I'm sure Mahmood can escort you," replied Emmet, opening his suitcase on their bed. "Tell him Banjo Paterson wrote it." Emmet stood looking at his pyjamas and the underclothes he was about to pack, before he again spoke. "We might be back by Saturday night."

"We have never parted like this before, darling," continued Carole.

Emmet packed his underclothes into his suitcase. "You may call me when your lodger is leaving," he said, still not looking at her as he walked back to his wardrobe. Emmet carefully selected several clean shirts from those hanging there, pulling them out one at a time with their heavy wooden hangers and placing them in his suitcase. "The surgery requires my presence on Monday."

That commitment calmed Carole. It shouldn't have.

"If Mahmood is still in this house when Tessa and I return, we will take rooms at the Killara Inn until he goes, or until we buy another house that doesn't welcome every leech looking for my blood to suck."

"This is your home," said Carole, "Tessa's home." Carole wavered about in her seat, almost falling, before bringing herself back again. "We could offer Mahmood money for a hotel?"

"This *was* our home," said Emmet, removing a suit from his

wardrobe and slipping it into a suit cover. "This cannot be our home again with this alien here."

Emmet slipped into the bathroom. He returned with his black-leather toiletry pack.

"If I can't protect you from the consequences of your beliefs," said Emmet, as he finished packing his suitcase, "then I can at least protect our daughter."

Tessa appeared at their open bedroom door, dressed for leaving the house. In her hand was the long handle of her suitcase, standing beside her. She and Carole might never have been close, but they had never before been so far apart.

Rolling his suitcase along the floor, Emmet paused near Carole in her chair. "Goodbye, my dear," he said, rather than "*Au Revoir*," reaching down to kiss her.

Carole's body and neck arched up towards him. Her damp eyes flicked between his, inviting him to see her through them, as tears finally gushed from her eyes. Her head fell into her hands.

17

EVIDENCE

Thursday morning, Carole's eyes fell open to the clamouring light of day. From her bed, her weak eyes struggled to focus on the empty space in which she lay. She needed tears to be warm, but her tears had dried exhausted, drained away.

Carole's fingers touched the cushion of her cheek. When the tears had gone, her face was hollow.

The belongings Emmet had left behind assured Carole that he and Tessa would return, if only briefly. The home remained theirs to Carole, even if it no longer did to him and Tessa, but their estrangement was a shadow from which they could never step: the man who left her once would leave again, when next she opened up their home to a wandering story of misfortune. Emmet would not lose his home a second time. He and Tessa had gone, not ostensibly forever, but forever nevertheless.

What might the neighbours say? Yvette Uppley would talk. Had Carole evicted Emmet or Emmet abandoned Carole?

People would say that politics ruined their marriage. Carole knew they would be wrong, that their separation was something nobody could prevent.

Lifting herself from her bed, Carole dressed in clothes for staying at home: a brown blouse, cardigan, and slacks, with low-heeled shoes. Her emotions dried with her tears, she was not sad, not anything, in a house too big for one, or two.

The house and garden, of which she had been the mistress, had become a house and garden just for her, and Mahmood. She might tend to the garden, if she had nothing else to do, and she had nothing else to do, irrespective of Mahmood's absence or presence.

From her second-storey bedroom, looking through the ripples of old window glass, her low-lying lawns and gardens meant so little. Outside the driveway gates, plainly unconcerned about being seen, stood looking at the house what appeared to be Luke Parmeter.

Outside her room, the stairs creaked, with the slow pacing of a person coming up. Carole turned to see standing at the door, Mahmood: a friend in name and form, innocent against a thoughtless world.

He smiled. He was not going anywhere.

No other friend had entered her and Emmet's bedroom – her bedroom. She would not have entered Mahmood's room, unless she'd heard him crying. Emmet's departure was much too personal for her to mention, but Mahmood must have heard him leave.

Carole stepped towards the open door, without the floorboards creaking. Mahmood stepped back to let her pass. She proceeded downstairs to the drawing room, where she sat in the armchair Emmet had called his but presumably no longer did.

Floorboards creaked and footsteps sounded, from upstairs and from down. Her eyes closed, whereby the creaks and steps became indistinguishable from those she used to hear.

A hand, cold, but comforting, rested gently on her shoulder. Carole's face, still warm, fell against the smooth and cooling skin. His hand moved slightly, modestly caressing her flattered fault-lined face. She knew again that she was right in what she did.

Mahmood pulled his hand away. Carole raised her head. He neared the window, until he stopped. "The policeman is standing at the gate," said Mahmood.

"He has stood there for some time," answered Carole.

Mahmood turned and looked at her. He left the room.

Rising to her feet, Carole poured herself a kettleful of water. She took another teabag from the box, lying on the bench. She prepared herself a cup of middling tea to warm her hands.

She telephoned her electorate office to cancel her appointments for the day. "I'm feeling unwell."

"I hope you're feeling better again soon, Carole." Her electorate office staffers only called her Carole when no strangers were there.

Carole's cup of tea became cold before she finished it. Knowing Mahmood might also want a cup, she knocked on the closed door of his room; the house had been silent she'd last seen him. Mahmood, wearing a long coat, opened the door.

"Would you like some tea?" asked Carole.

"I'm going out," he answered.

Looking past him into his room must have been rude, but Carole did. Drawing her attention wasn't simply an open suitcase on the floor; most of his suitcases remained closed. "What is this?" she asked, stepping past him and kneeling down. She drew from his open suitcase a blue cap, marked Canterbury-Bankstown.

"I bought it last week."

"Why buy a cap the police are seeking?"

"Everybody who didn't already have one is buying it, all the Muslims," explained Mahmood. "It's a joke. The store had almost sold out when I bought mine."

"Have you a receipt?"

"Who gets receipts?"

"Did you pay cash?"

"I don't use credit cards."

"Have you any record of the purchase?"

"Do I need one?"

"Would the store have one?"

"Not with a buyer's name on it."

For the first time, Carole imagined Mahmood's face among the terrorists. She shook her head to shake the image away.

"You're proving just as prejudiced against Muslims as everyone else, Carole."

Carole dropped the cap back in the suitcase. "I do trust you, Mahmood," she told him, "but you must understand how this will look to the police."

"If the police arrest every Muslim wearing a Canterbury-Bankstown cap, the government will need to build another gaol."

The confidence that should have consoled Carole only unsettled her; Mahmood was always self-assured. "Is there anything more about you that I would wish that I knew?" she asked him.

Mahmood's eyes drifted from Carole to the space in which people thought. "One thing," he said, "possibly."

"What?"

Mahmood's eyes turned downward, as he reached his right hand into a pocket of the coat he wore as just another feature of his fashion. Carole studied the incomprehensibly deep pocket and Mahmood's hand and wrist up to his forearm burrowed in it. His hand seemed to linger there, as if trying to find something in a big space, or abruptly baulking at revealing it to Carole mesmerised by what she couldn't see. He might have been embarrassed to have brought it, or regretted having mentioned it.

"Show me," said Carole.

Slowly, Mahmood's forearm rose. His wrist, pale and thin, returned from the pocket to view, slowly widening into the back of his hand, concealing what Carole had not imagined required concealment: the object of its journey. His hand remained close to his coat, but protruding from his fingertips was the end of a silver tube, no more than half an inch of it, whatever it was.

Mahmood's hand moved a short way towards Carole, where it stopped. Carole's eyes set fast upon it. "I have a gun," he said.

Carole concealed her astonishment. Australian suburban homes were not places for guns, not merely because laws largely prohibited them. Guns were for farmers and licensed shooting club members, secured behind thick locks and sturdy gates. They were for uniformed police officers, concealed in leather holsters so only criminals knew they were there. Museum glass cases displayed antique heirloom guns from the era of bushrangers or brought home from old wars, with rustic mechanisms never too dangerous but still filed down until they were unable to fire. If there had ever been a gun in the Wynworth family home, then it was before Carole and Emmet bought the house, at a time when gentlemen would not have mentioned it to ladies.

Mahmood's hand slowly turned over, opening as it did. He revealed a small pistol, with a single silver barrel polished bright and a curved pearl-crafted handle.

Carole laughed, discharging all her nervousness in a flurry. Less of a weapon, the pistol could have been an adornment, slipping easily into a ladies' handbag.

"Have you a licence for that?" she asked, struggling to resume the initiative.

"Zaki Quresh has a licence."

"Zaki Quresh is not here."

"Samina insisted he lend it to me. She thought I might need protection."

"Is that lawful?"

"I should give it back to Zaki."

Carole stepped forward. "Please Mahmood," she told him, "allow me to look after it." She reached out her hand with her palm open upward.

Mahmood studied Carole standing before him. His hand did not move, and the pistol remained harmlessly to its side in his palm.

Carole smiled, assuring him he was safe. He too smiled, and laid the pistol on its side in her hand.

The pistol was cold, not warmed for having lain in Mahmood's pocket or his hand. Never before had Carole touched such a thing, and she stared down at the silver and pearl. The pistol was light, weak, like a lock removed from a wardrobe door that a tradesman was preparing to replace.

"Is it loaded?" she asked.

Carole's hand twitched, as her eyes settled upon the small trigger inside a small eye. No part of her skin should inadvertently tweak it, but she turned her hand so the pistol barrel pointed to the window.

Suddenly, that window seemed vulnerable. Carole turned until she and the pistol faced the doorway. She stepped past Mahmood.

Mahmood remained behind her, the hallway of her home with her. Quickly she assessed what might be the safest place to secure it. Under the ground in the garden perhaps, below several feet of soil, but the pistol was Zaki's, to return to him later.

Carole stepped along the hallway, the pistol in the palm of her hand, careful not to jar it and fire a bullet into a wall. Her shoe caught the edge of a rug and she tripped. Her breath jumped, as her hand almost grabbed but could not quite grab the pistol tightly. It remained in her palm, silent and cold.

The pistol might carry only one bullet; she had not thought to ask. One bullet was enough to kill a man, or woman.

The electronic buzzer sounded from the security pad in the hallway. "Mrs Wynworth," said a voice from the small speaker, "Luke Parmeter here. I would like to come to the house."

Carefully, Carole laid the pistol on the table beside the old-styled telephone. Beside it was a David Jones store catalogue, which Carole placed over the pistol.

She pressed the button broadcasting her voice to the person outside the security gates, speaking into the small microphone. "Why?" she asked.

"May I tell you when I see you?"

Carole removed her finger from the button. Behind her in the hallway, where he would have heard Luke's voice, stood Mahmood.

"What time did you return the night that Nadine Westwick died?" Carole asked him quickly.

"Please Carole, trust me." Mahmood's voice was just as rapid.

"I've never seen you reading poetry," continued Carole.

"I return books to the bookcase in the library."

"I have found other books you've left lying around the house."

"You return them before I've finished reading them."

The electronic buzzer again sounded from the security pad. The police were scratching at her door.

"Where did you go the night that Nadine Westwick died?" Carole asked Mahmood.

"I'm trying to protect you."

She turned her head away, from the visitor of whom she knew so little. "I'm trying to protect you, Mahmood, but you make it very hard."

"I walked, thinking, and returned at nine o'clock."

"Would you lie to protect me, Mahmood?" she asked, turning back to face him.

"I would kill to protect you, Carole."

Carole could only afford a moment to stare at him, before turning back to the security pad. She pressed the button to open the front gates.

Mahmood returned to his room. Carole stood inside her closed front door, waiting for the knock.

It came. She opened the door to Luke.

"I'm sorry for troubling you, Mrs Wynworth, but I must see Mahmood."

"I'll bring him to the sitting room."

Carole returned to Mahmood's room, where she found him standing with one hand on the open window latch and the other on the pane. "Getting some air," he smiled. His hands withdrew.

"He wants to see you," said Carole.

Mahmood stepped close to her. He raised his hand and placed it gently on her cheek. "I didn't kill anyone and I was not involved in the bombing," he assured her, "but only I can collect the evidence to prove it."

"Let the police do their work," said Carole. "You have the presumption of innocence."

His smile broadened into the faintest sense of a small laugh, at his expense as much as hers. "For Muslims," he said, pulling his hand away, "ours is the presumption of guilt."

Carole shook her head, unable to believe him but unwilling to deny him. There were no lies in her to tell. There was just the hope Mahmood might yet explain himself and the dread that he could not.

"Muslims will talk to me," he added, "but not the police."

"There are Muslim police officers."

"Oh, Carole," he laughed. "When the suspects are Muslim and victims are not, then they can be Muslims or police, but they cannot be both."

Mahmood stepped past her into the hallway. He turned towards the rear of the house.

"Mahmood!" called out Luke from the front end of the hallway, as Carole heard Mahmood run towards the rear. "I have a gun!"

The running stopped. Luke walked slowly past the open door from Mahmood's room, his thick black gun drawn long in his outstretched arms, plainly pointed towards Mahmood.

Carole stepped back into the hallway to see Mahmood, standing still. "I thought I had refuge here," Mahmood told Carole. "I thought I had sanctuary."

"I want you to leave my home, Luke," said Carole. "You will leave my guest with me."

"Mrs Wynworth," answered Luke. "If you helped Mahmood leave your home unseen and he killed Nadine Westwick, you could be an accessory for murder."

Carole had no answer. Everything she believed, her life, was invested in Mahmood's innocence and his capacity to prove it, against every prejudice she had fought and failed thus far to conquer. The evidence Mahmood found to exonerate himself would also exonerate her and all she believed.

Luke reached Mahmood. He removed a pair of handcuffs from his pocket.

"Are the handcuffs necessary?" asked Carole.

"They're a precaution, Mrs Wynworth. My instructions are to detain him until the Superintendent arrives."

"Not in my house!" Carole told him.

"I can put them on him outside." Luke directed Mahmood back along the hallway, towards the front of the house.

"Don't let them take me, Carole," said Mahmood, as he walked slowly back towards her.

"You be quiet," said Luke.

"This is my home, Mister Parmeter," said Carole. "Let him speak."

"The police won't try to find Nadine's killer," said Mahmood, walking even slower. "Only I will."

Mahmood, with Luke behind him, reached Carole. She stepped back into the doorway of Mahmood's room to let them pass, before stepping back into the hallway.

"The police don't believe Muslims," said Mahmood.

"We believe some," said Luke.

Mahmood turned back to Carole, as he walked. "Please, Carole," he continued, his voice rising, "don't let them torture me."

"Don't be a fool," scoffed Luke.

Mahmood reached the front door. "Only Carole opens her front door," he told Luke.

Luke stood still, his gun still pointed at Mahmood in front of him. Carole remained still.

"Mrs Wynworth," said Luke, without looking back at her. "If you don't open your front door, then I will."

Carole stepped slowly along the hallway. Time gave her a small chance to think.

"What about justice?" asked Mahmood.

"Justice means capturing and punishing criminals," answered Luke.

"Carole," said Mahmood. "Please help me prove my innocence."

She reached the table on which lay hidden the pearl-handled pistol, without looking at it. All choice flashed back and forth across her mind. Suspect terrorists might not receive bail; recognisance to Carole might mean no more to a judge than it meant to police, especially if she stood accused of being his accomplice.

Carole continued past the hidden pistol. When she reached Luke, he stepped back for her. Mahmood did not.

"Luke," she said. "I don't want my neighbours to see my guest leaving my home with a gun pointed at him."

"Would you prefer that I handcuff him inside?"

"I could find my proof of innocence," said Mahmood, slowly turning around to face Carole, "and return."

Mahmood, Carole, and Luke all faced each other, inside the

front door to her home. Luke's gun remained trained on Mahmood.

"Anything you know about the ferry bombing or murder of Nadine Westwick," said Luke, "you can tell the Superintendent."

"Who can trust him to pursue it?" asked Mahmood.

"I can pursue it," answered Carole.

Mahmood looked at Carole, the meek fear in his eyes. "Whatever I need to do and whoever I need to see will be far from here," he told her, "among people you've tried your best to know but can't. You don't have the chance to save us both that I have."

Too many words in recent days thrashed back and forth in Carole's mind; she needed to believe, so much. If Mahmood never had the chance to look for evidence of his innocence, Carole would forever wonder what he might have found. The brown eyes staring expectantly at her would not allow her to be weak.

The front door still closed, Carole stepped back along the hallway. She stopped at the small table. "I want you to let Mahmood go," she told Luke, as she looked down at the store catalogue. Her body began to quiver.

"I won't do that, Mrs Wynworth."

Her back obscuring Luke's view, Carole's right hand reached down to the table, beside the telephone, a small silver notepad holder, and a silver-capped pencil, to the store catalogue she pulled away. Her right hand moved onto the pistol's smooth, succulent pearl handle, less damning to touch a second time than it had been the first, covering it in part. Trembling more than ever, she clasped the handle.

Her less dexterous left hand took hold of her right, trying to steady it, as Carole raised the pistol. Her whole body quaking, she slowly turned around, her eyes set upon Luke. Her palms and all but one of her faltering fingers gripping the pistol handle, she slipped her right index finger onto the trigger. Her arms stretched out until the barrel pointed towards Luke's chest. He was much taller and stronger than she was, but their guns made them equal.

"If you shoot Mahmood," she told him, her chest taut barely able to breathe, "I will shoot you."

"Do you know what you're doing, Mrs Wynworth?" asked Luke, strangely unthreatened by her.

"You must return here when you've found the evidence, Mahmood," she said, looking primarily at Luke. "I'll need you to open the front door this time."

"Stay where you are, Mahmood," said Luke.

Mahmood remained still. Luke's gun, much larger and more lethal than Carole's pistol, remained targeted at Mahmood.

"I don't want to spill blood on your nice floors and rugs," continued Luke, "but I will if I must."

Breathing became easier the longer Carole stood there. "The blood will be yours, Luke," she told him.

"Please give me the gun, Mrs Wynworth," said Luke, offering her his free hand.

"Your job is to protect me," said Carole. "Protecting me means letting Mahmood go."

"The Superintendent will soon arrive," he told her. "You can discuss it with him."

"I am discussing it with you, Luke." She adjusted her grip. Her pistol edged higher and lower. "I don't want to shoot."

"Politicians don't shoot, Mrs Wynworth. They employ policemen and soldiers to shoot."

Carole continued studying the line of her pistol set at Luke. He did not need to study the sight of his gun to keep it set on Mahmood, or to shoot him.

"Leave, Mahmood," said Carole.

Mahmood turned slowly back to the front door, standing where Carole could see the doorknob. Carole's eyes flicked occasionally to him, never leaving Luke for very long. Slowly, as if ready to stop at any time, Mahmood reached one hand onto the doorknob and the other to the deadlock.

"If you step through that door, Mahmood," said Luke, "I will shoot you."

Carole stepped towards Mahmood. Her eyes and pistol remained set upon Luke, as she stepped in front of Mahmood, shielding him. "You might shoot me, Luke."

"You have placed yourself in danger, Mrs Wynworth."

Behind her, Mahmood opened the front door. The cool outdoors air swept in.

Carole and Luke stared at each other, their eyes piercing each other's, save for her last edges of vision for Luke's gun and the pistol in her hands. Luke's gun moved until it pointed past her to a last line of fire at the open door, if Mahmood should head outside.

Again, Carole stepped into what would be the bullet's way. Finally, Luke lowered his gun.

Carole's chest rested and her lungs released their breath. Her grip on the pistol loosened. Her pistol lowered, a little.

Luke's eyes remained trained over Carole's shoulder, upon Mahmood behind her. Suddenly, Luke moved towards her, around her. The pistol in Carole's hands discharged.

18

HELL

A shot exploded from the pistol in Carole's hands. More than she could have imagined, that small silver tube and pearl pounded her palms and wrists like a cannon, smashing through her ears into her frenzied brain.

Luke Parmeter stopped mid-motion, his arms reflectively grabbing his belly. His inflamed eyes bound hers, captured in a shock of pain somewhere, as he fell in front of Carole to the floor.

From her rigor mortis stance, Carole watched him fall, only her eyes and failing face able to move. Her arms outstretched so near to him remained rigid, her elbows and shoulders locked. That pearl-handled pistol remained pointed where it was pointing when somehow her hands seized and it discharged.

A hand, Mahmood's, grabbed the silver barrel and pulled the pistol from Carole's brittle fingers. Her hands wanted to grab something where there was nothing left to grab. Her arms slid to her side.

Mahmood rushed between her and the bleeding figure bent double on her floor, his coat catching a small breeze. Luke's crippled arms held his stomach. Mahmood ran along the hallway into the house.

"Are...?" Carole started to ask Luke. She looked out through the open door for anyone to help, anyone to hear, before clamouring to the small table. She picked up the telephone, momentarily forgetting the number to dial, before dialling triple zero.

"Emergency," answered a woman's voice.

"I need an ambulance at forty-seven Springdale Road, Killara," said Carole quickly. "A man's been shot."

"What is the nearest cross street?"

Carole tried to recall what she had told a hundred drivers. "Kardella Avenue."

"Where on his body was he shot?"

Carole shook her head, grasping for words. "His stomach, I think, his chest."

"Can you apply pressure to the wound?"

Carole dropped the telephone, letting it crash with its cord to the floor. Luke lay motionless, save for the panting of his lungs. Sweat flooded his shrivelled face and forehead.

She looked around, before bounding along her hallway into the kitchen and hauling open a low drawer of folded tea towels. She grabbed those she could and rushed with them back to Luke, where she knelt on the floor beside him and pressed a bundle of the falling cloths against the wound. Luke's arm fell to the floor.

"I am sorry, so sorry, Luke," said Carole. His lungs vented their breath and his eyelids closed a little. "Luke?"

The pungent shining blood continued slipping through the cracks between the towels into Luke's shirt and buttons, filling every reach. Carole's palms persevered, with tea towel images of old Sydney disappearing in the reddening dye of human blood. If the blood smelt sweet, it shouldn't have. Carole's frantic fingers felt through the towels to Luke's poor battered flesh.

He breathed; she didn't need to find a pulse, although she felt him willing his heart to rest to still the flow. Her fingers cramped but she deserved the pain, until she forced her other hand between them and the soaking swaddling towels. Her fingers not yet hurting pressed towels against Luke's stomach cavity. Unaccustomed to kneeling, her knees were tender on the floor.

Carole only needed to tend his wound until the ambulance arrived. The driveway gates should still be open.

"What's that smell?" asked Luke, from his face near the floor.

Continuing to kneel, her hand pressed through heavy towels, Carole raised her head. Her nose drew in the open air. Mixing with the sickly smell of blood was another smell, of smoke perhaps, from somewhere down the hall. The siren of a fire alarm exploded through the house.

Carole turned back to her patient, grimacing again. The screaming siren smothered every thought inside her head.

"You go," said Luke through his clenched jaw, as loudly as his voice allowed. His arm dragged back to the bloodied cloths and wound, his hand pushing Carole's from a patch of cloth he pressed.

Her arm wrapped around his back, Carole strained her crooked arm as best she could, but could not lift him. His knees pulled close to him, Luke's free arm and hand pressed against the floor. He squirmed to roll himself upward with his weight until he too knelt on the floor.

The sirens continued, burning Carole's head within. The cluttered space between her ears where once was thought was only throbbing anguish. The force of fire was very near, burning towards her face.

Carole rushed to her feet and crouched beside Luke, wrapped her arms around him, and mustered any strength and will she could. She tried to spring her feet through leather shoes, but slipped and fell back to the floor. Luke fell with her, against her, holding his hand against the wound, but she leveraged herself and him upright until he held his weight again.

The high ceilings, much higher than the doors, trapped much of the intensifying smoke inside, clouding the hallway while palls of thickening grey and black flowed out. But for being so near the open door, Carole could have choked, with the thumps of her raging heart pounding air into the remnants of her lungs. The heat from the house began to sear.

Again she crouched, setting her arms around Luke's back more for balance than for strength. Still holding the cloths at his wound, Luke drew up one leg until his foot lay squarely on the floor. She helped him climb back to his feet.

Carole coughed, contracting her watery eyes to the last vision she required to flee the fire. Collecting a quick breath, ash burning the rear side of her neck, she led Luke lurching through the open door outside.

Bright lights on a dark day and outside air swept over them, escaping the full loudness of the siren, discharging small clouds of smoke with them. Stumbling down the steps, Luke tripped and almost fell, but Carole supported him enough for him to reach the driveway. Luke's weak legs dragging through the pebbles, Carole drove them further from the fires of hell behind them, over the small ridge of bricks onto the lawn.

They could have fallen there, but Carole dragged them onwards. They trampled through a tiny garden of supple soil and bloomless flowers to another stretch of grass, where they collapsed.

Luke laid there, his arms draped beside him, his eyes closed. Carole held the bloodied tea towels to his stomach, nursing him, watching the fire ravage her home.

Relatively clean air flowed smoothly through her resurrecting lungs. With her newly free hand, she rummaged through her hair, admitting air to try to dry the roots.

"Mahmood!" she called out. Her mouth was dry. "He returned to the house," she told Luke, even if Luke wasn't listening. "I never saw him leave."

Smoke billowed from the few open windows of the house. Like the open front door, those vents fed the fire with air. Trapped behind closed windows, Carole saw more smoke amassed. No light of day could penetrate it. Flames splattered, growing, while the siren blazed. Somewhere in a security centre or fire station, alarm bells had sounded.

Carole looked along her driveway to see the front gates closed. Had Mahmood closed them? She'd not have noticed him at the security pad in the hallway. He might have entered the kitchen.

For a moment, Carole thought of opening the front gates from her car secure in the garage, but she could not leave Luke again. The gates were not as strong as they appeared.

An ember drifted near her, like rain of flames, capturing her fearful gaze with thoughts of where the flame might land. The fire could set upon her bloodied clothes or hands and she'd not feel more than she already felt, or less.

A tint of freshly scalding smoke from a floating raft of ash slipped between her lips onto her tongue. Carole spat it out. She wet her lips and tongue to wash away the taste of hell, but the taste was already there. Smoke stained all her senses.

Luke's eyes had opened, watching the fire. Carole's hand against the cloth against his wound was firm.

A rush of thick black smoke rose from beside the house. Silk curtains, feather cushions, all the pleasures she most adored burnt easily, but nothing in her home she imagined burning as virulently black as was the smoke.

Flames roared from a window to her bedroom, once sacrosanct and intimate with her heirlooms and apparel: the silver brushes her grandmother bequeathed, a tapestry her mother made. The space from which she'd gazed upon her gardens billowed smoke into the clouded sky. The ashes of her life were grey, not black. So too the clouds were grey, like watered forms of smoke erupting. Thundering rain could save her dwelling, but the fire and smoke were burning into clouds before rain clouds could smother them.

A new, distant siren wailed from the streets beyond the hedges. Drawing Carole's eyes away, the siren quickly became louder. Its wail was her relief, whatever was coming; Carole had never learnt to distinguish one siren from another.

Sitting upright was suddenly easy, looking through the shrubs for a fleet of flashing lights. A flashing red light and siren, a majestic red fire engine, appeared beyond the gates. It paused for just a moment, before crashing through the gates, blasting them aside, and careering along the driveway. The siren waned, as the fire engine slowed and stopped.

Firemen in blue uniforms and golden helmets poured from their vehicle. They released long hoses they set upon the flames and smoke.

One man hurried towards Carole and Luke. "Is anyone inside?" he asked, over the unrelenting siren from the house.

"My friend ran inside before the fire," said Carole. "I think he left by the rear of the house." The man glanced at Luke before rushing back to his colleagues.

"Do you know why Mahmood lit the fire?" asked Luke, just loud enough for her to hear him.

"Don't speak," answered Carole, tears again collecting in her eyes. They had rarely left her eyes of late.

A long ladder rose from the fire engine from which another hose sprayed water into the open and broken windows. Carole watched the firemen try to douse the fire, but her century-old house, once sturdy and resolute against summer thunderstorms and winter hail, withered in the flames.

Another siren came, with another rack of red lights flashing. A second fire engine entered the driveway, too late to wrestle back from hell her home.

Its siren slowed and ceased, but a third siren remained audible from the streets. Flashing lights blue and red, that siren also waning, a red and white ambulance bundled into the driveway, paused, and then spun onto the grass near Carole and Luke.

A paramedic leapt from the vehicle to Luke, his hand taking the place of Carole's hand. Carole clamoured to her feet and stepped backward, out of the way.

"Are you hurt?" he asked Carole.

"No," she said.

A second paramedic hurriedly opened the rear door of the ambulance and dragged out a padded gurney, its legs and wheels opening to the ground. The two men helped Luke onto the gurney they slotted back into their vehicle. They drove away.

For all the men trying to extinguish the fire in front of her, Carole stood alone, apart from them, her blood-stained clothes clinging to her skin with perspiration she did not normally incur. Her face was warm against the glow, but the air behind was cool. Without a house to shield her from the storms when finally the bonfire burnt away, winter would surround her.

Her hardened hands gripped the ragged curls amok that was her hair. Confusion consumed her, as her arms fell against her head, holding her cricked neck from tearing from her shoulders. Her eyes closed, her mind began to float. Carole's frailty fell through her, her legs gave way, and she collapsed broken to the ground.

Her twisted tender knees meant Carole was not quite sitting on the grass, for sitting would be comfortable. Her eyes burned behind her lids with nothing left to weep, shielding them from seeing too much and from the fire seeing them.

Her head buried in her bloodied hands, tears could have helped her then. They could have cooled her skin that flames threatened to scorch. They could have washed her and everything about her far away, to a place she'd never before been and needed desperately to go.

The house's siren was constancy, the only one, without the last of Carole's mind to shut it out. The driving decibels insisted that only Mahmood, her former friend and beneficiary, could have begun the fire. No accident, no spark from an electrical connection, had ignited Hades' flames.

Impressions, false as they might have been, cascaded through her brain. Gently he had touched her face, had smiled when she was smiling, and smiled to cheer her when she was not. He had grasped her vision for a world and espoused it with an eloquence that would have pleased the poets. He had caressed her cheeks and let her cheeks caress his hands, like innocents in a garden of dew-dipped flowers and honeysuckle scents.

Her memories were weak: recorded sounds and images on grainy old worn film. She saw nothing too clearly, without believing anything anyway.

The siren blazed and always would: the interminable scream of Satan gloating over the prize he had acquired. Mahmood had offered her up to one in whom he did not believe. Carole could not have sensibly believed, but Carole was not sensible. The screaming holler demanded explanation as to why Mahmood had paused from the escape Carole crafted for him to obliterate the refuge she granted him.

She'd wanted nothing in return: no favour, no indulgence. She would have run barefoot through burning homes to throw water on a fire that threatened him or his home; she almost had. If he had seen the flames she would not have minded him fleeing while she and her home burnt asunder, but what within him could have made him ignite those flames upon her?

Carole Wynworth was a fool, a perfume-drunken fool, with the frocks of her high fashion and a dunce's cap to boot. Her blouse, cardigan, and slacks were stained with a policeman's clotted blood and gnashed by the ground on which she fell, but the dunce's cap atop her head remained bright and tall and crisp. She did not know Mahmood: his mind, fears, or loves. She did not know his wants, aspirations, or desires. If she knew anything of him, her tormentor, then she knew nothing of anyone.

Of all the things that once she preached that she had learned she did not know, of all the people she once was adamant she understood so well, one thing and person rose above all others in the conviction of her ignorance. That person had meant so well to people who had wished ill upon her, and had abandoned those who could have cast their lots with her to keep her safe.

The siren stopped. The silence screamed for a short time, before it quickly waned into the sounds of heavy boots across a pebble driveway.

Still close to the ground, her hands against her face, Carole's eyes opened. They cleared, to see stabs of light between her fingers. Resigned to reality, they were a stranger's hands.

Her fingers fell away. Her hands were bruised and clumsy, with reams of blood and tides of scratches scarred upon her fingers and her palms.

Her hands fell away, revealing the grass on which she sat perplexed. Beside her grubby hands appeared another hand, but this one large and masculine, at the end of a white shirtsleeve and brown jacket. The palm of the new hand opened towards her. "May I help you up, Mrs Wynworth?"

Carole looked up to Superintendent Dempsey, his face solemn and concerned. "You have your job to do, Superintendent," she reminded him, from her place on the ground.

"You're fortunate to be alive, Mrs Wynworth."

"I might be more fortunate to be dead."

"I wouldn't be," he smiled. His opened hand remained inviting her.

Carole would have preferred that he leave her there, but she was too weak to be rude. "Thank you," she said, placing her hand in his.

He hauled her to her feet, her muscles reforming inside her legs and back as her neck stiffened. One of her shoes had slipped off, which Carole replaced to her foot.

She patted down the worst folds in her slacks and tried to brush down her matted hair. "I must look awful," she said.

"Can I get you some water?" asked the Superintendent.

"Superintendent," she said, facing him. The words she needed to confess did not come easily to mind. She might have wanted to couch them so she did not look too bad, or foolish, or perhaps there was too much to say for her to know where to begin. "I shot Luke Parmeter," she told him. "I didn't mean to shoot him."

"Luke will recover," the Superintendent told her. "We're looking for Mahmood."

"He must have left through the Haughtons' property," said Carole, before affording the Superintendent a little more of the much-too-little she could give him. "He did the day that Nadine Westwick died."

"At a quieter time, federal and state investigators will want a detailed statement from you." He smiled. "Don't leave town," he said, repeating a short line from old television programmes.

"I'm not going anywhere," she said. "This is my home, such as it is."

While the Superintendent walked away, Carole remained where she would not impinge upon or be impinged upon by the uniformed inspectors and heavy-booted hose men. Some rushed and others walked about the scene of the event. One carried from the house a clear plastic bag of something charred and black.

The flames and thickest plumes of smoke slowly ceased obscuring her ruined castle in the gardens. Through empty windows was night indoors, while small palls wafted from the chimneys and from the open and broken windows. The clouds of black that had poured from the smouldering timber panes remained impressed upon the smoke-scarred bricks and walls. A single interrupted cloud was scarred against the canopy and wall of brick above what had been a quaintly welcoming front door, through which Carole had stumbled with her life, bringing Luke outside.

Carole's concentration cast upon the desecration piled before her, until the Superintendent returned to her. "Where did we fail, Superintendent?" asked Carole.

"You might want to sleep at a friend's home tonight, Mrs Wynworth."

"Friends, Superintendent?" she asked.

Yvette Uppley would have delighted in calling the emergency services with a fire to report. She would have watched from her windows the rampant spectacle of the Wynworth home alight, ready to pounce if the fire brigade damaged a single tree, until she'd become bored and returned to her glossy magazines.

Around Carole had been and might still be an audience she could not bear to face. Would the spectators granting refuge to strangers grant refuge to their own, or were they much too proud to think their own required it? Would Mahmood's friends, whoever they could be, grant her the refuge she gave him, or was she always better and much the worse than they?

"Superintendent," she said, "I will try the Killara Inn."

19

PURGATORY

With the fire extinguished, firemen inspected Carole's gutted house for embers and to ensure that what remained would not collapse. Inspectors collected evidence of the cause of the fire. In the garden of what had been her home, Carole had become a bystander: a stranger.

In what seemed a pause from his inquiries, Carole approached Superintendent Dempsey. "Will you find Mahmood, Superintendent?" she asked him.

"We don't even know his name," the Superintendent reminded her. "We have no fingerprints or DNA. All we have is the size and shape of his shoes, impressed into the ground of your neighbours' rear garden. Gucci size eight and a half E with neat new leather soles isn't much to assist us."

"You know that he owns a Canterbury-Bankstown cap."

"There are a lot of Canterbury-Bankstown football caps," the Superintendent pointed out. "We don't know that his cap was the cap in the photographs from the day of the ferry bombing, or who wore his cap that day."

"You know that he is carrying a pearl-handled pistol."

"Zaki Quresh has no knowledge of the pistol or Mahmood's whereabouts. We spoke to him at work, where he said his sister was probably at his home, but the front door and telephones aren't answering. We're also watching the mosques and Islamic centres."

Carole couldn't imagine Mahmood running to so public a place. She couldn't imagine Mahmood.

"Among more than three million people in this city, Mrs Wynworth," the Superintendent warned her, "there are men and women who will shelter Mahmood for no greater reason than they liked him when they saw him on television, or they like his style of clothes. More people will insist our efforts to find him are police harassment of Muslims: that he can't have burnt your home. They won't just be Muslims, Mrs Wynworth, getting in our way. They'll be Australians, white Australians, who would rather befriend a man they've never met than suppose a Muslim committed crime. They'll be Europeans who would rather wage war against their own than allow harm or justice to befall others."

"Do you mean people like me, Superintendent," asked Carole, "granting refuge to everyone claiming the right?"

"You invited him, Mrs Wynworth."

Carole had not been very good at understanding the sensitivities of people whose sensitivities she championed. "When the police find him," she told the Superintendent, "I want to go there with you."

"This is a police operation, Mrs Wynworth," he told her. "The world isn't one big garden party, or even a planet of little garden parties, in which you can wander in for a chat with anyone over vol-au-vents."

He left her alone. Carole kept back from the people working.

Her skin in need of washing became irritable. She rubbed one side of her face. She scratched the other.

Among the people to walk through the broken gates along Carole's pebble driveway, having left their cars parked by the road, appeared Emmet and Tessa. Carole thought of calling out and waving her arms to them, but thought better of herself and them.

Looking around the gardens, Emmet soon saw her. He walked towards her, his stride longer than she'd seen for a long time. His and Tessa's holiday clothes were clean and their hair combed and brushed, while Carole meekly felt again the clammy grime in which she stood. Emmet reached her and wrapped his arms around her.

When they'd been young and so tall and strong a man as Emmet hugged her, Carole never felt smaller, without need to feel any bigger. Their home destroyed, another man would scream at her but Emmet's anger, if it was there, remained within him. That day, if ever in her life, she could bear to him berating her.

"Last night," said Emmet, "after leaving you, I stopped to tell the officer watching the house that we were going. This morning, after the Superintendent called me to tell us about the fire, I tried to call you, but couldn't get an answer."

Carole's mobile telephone was in her handbag. Her handbag was in her bedroom, if any of them survived.

"What once seemed true is not so true," she lamented, comfortable in her husband's arms. "What once seemed right was not." Carole mourned a creed she still yearned to have been true and the times before she learned that it was not. "No longer do I assume all people are the same: alike and like us."

Relaxing Carole from his arms, Emmet turned towards the smouldering ruin of his home. He stepped slowly towards it: uneasy animation of a minor character in a drama played without him. The tall man's gaze reached higher, until a fireman in uniform held his thickly padded arm in Emmet's way.

"This is my home," Emmet told him.

"You will need to wait outside the house until we finish inspecting it."

"I live here." Emmet insisted, drawing upon his deep resolve.

"I'm sorry, sir."

Emmet drifted back to Carole, waiting for the strangers to let him go back home. Carole turned towards her daughter.

Tessa stood with her legs apart and hands deep in the pockets of her long blue denim skirt, glaring at her mother as her mother had never before been. Carole smiled; her smile shamefaced. Tessa continued glaring, while firemen and police walked and talked. When might Carole be with her husband and daughter around a family meal or holiday again, not across a space in a public gallery and another person's view?

She stepped towards her daughter. Her step was hesitant, hoping that Tessa might reciprocate. Tessa remained in judgement where she stood.

Carole stepped again, her tattered shoe bending on the shaken grass and ground. The sweat and blood throughout her knotted hair and grimy clothes became heavier with each step. Her sweated brow capped the motions of her eyes, hollowed back upon her daughter's eyes bearing back towards her.

"You did this," said Tessa. Carole stopped. "You did this as surely as if you'd struck the match yourself."

"I didn't know."

"You didn't care."

"I cared, I cared too much."

"Not about us. If you cherish your home and family so little, why should others cherish us at all? You taught them."

"We can make another home…"

"For whom?" asked Tessa. "Your family isn't enough for you."

Carole dipped her eyes towards the grass and gardens. She did not need to say, did not need her daughter to hear, or her to hear, what her daughter already knew. So much she wanted to tell Tessa a truth, but the truth did not come easily to Carole. She knew better what she did not know than she knew anything at all. "Our home," said Carole, her vision lost among the flower beds, "my darling, however grand or not we make it, will be only ours."

She collected her breath to speak again, allowing Tessa to say something. Tessa remained silent.

"There will be no more Mahmoods within our walls," Carole continued, still looking at the ground, "no more causes but us, no more politics to divide us."

"What will there be?" asked Tessa.

"Educate me," said Carole, looking up to face her. The air seemed milder then against her face. "All I know is that I will protect you."

"You never have."

"Please, darling," continued Carole, "judge me by what I do, not what I have done."

Tessa laughed, looking around the open air, high above them. She sighed, and turned away.

Sometimes Tessa and her father stood together. Sometimes they wandered short distances from each other, around and behind their broken home. Conversation appeared easier between them than between either of them and Carole.

Wandering through the broken driveway gates outside her home could be comforting. The road of lovely homes was the same as it had been yesterday, provided Carole didn't look back towards the carcass of her home or think about those extra cars parked nearby. Occasionally one departed. Less often, another came. Luke Parmeter's car remained.

People walking with or without dogs paused to see the attraction. Some smiled at Carole. She smiled at them, sometimes remembering how scrappily she stood.

Slowly passing her was a painfully familiar early-model red Holden, scraped and knocked as was no other car around. Conspicuously out of place, it parked.

"Oh dear," sighed Carole. Without Parliament sitting that week, political journalists as much as politicians were away from Canberra.

Xavier Talbot stepped oafishly out of his car, in his poorly fitting pale shirt and trousers. Standing there, he observed her, as he chewed on a long bread roll over-burdened with filling.

His bread roll eaten, Xavier crossed the road towards her. When he reached her, Xavier tipped his forehead. "Carole," he said.

"I'd have thought you would have brought your camera, Mister Talbot?"

"For this, we have a professional photographer coming," he told her. "Have you any comment to make?"

"Haven't I said enough?"

"The seventeen Rohingya are still in the Australian High Commission in Dhaka," said Xavier. "Any statement by you now, welcoming refugees to the country and to your next home, could be very persuasive."

Silently, Carole looked at him. She turned and walked back along her driveway, through the broken gates, into her property.

He followed her. Around the driveway, Xavier spoke with the Superintendent. Around the lawns and gardens, he approached Emmet and then Tessa. Emmet and Tessa rebuffed him.

Finally, the firemen allowed Carole, Emmet, and Tessa into the remnants of their home. Xavier started to follow them, when the Superintendent intervened. "Not you," he told him.

"Superintendent," Carole intervened. "This is still our home and I'm inviting the press, if my husband and daughter don't mind."

Carole, the Superintendent, and the journalist all looked at Emmet and Tessa. "By all means," said Emmet. Tessa shrugged her shoulders.

Carole looked back at Xavier. "My only condition is that you report the truth."

The Superintendent escorted them inside. Xavier, Emmet, and then Tessa followed him. Carole was the last to enter.

She paused at the front door. Never before, not even in the still wind of night, had her home felt so dark. Without electrical power, the only vestiges of light came from behind her and from windows through open doors. What wasn't burnt to black was singed to something close to it. Smoke had blanketed with coats of soot anything not scorched. Everything in that house was blacker and dirtier even than she was.

Carole stepped inside, into the wreck of her abode. The firemen's water had begun to dry, but dampness remained everywhere. Ash and smoke had gelled in dust-drenched shadows, further clogging Carole's filth-cluttered skin and hair. Any breeze would help clear the air, blowing that bad day away, but there was none.

The house creaked, more than footsteps on wet wood should have creaked. Carole dare not touch anything; nothing felt like hers anyway.

No longer could Carole see floral patterns in the plaster-cast high ceilings, around the shattered crystal lights. Among the silhouettes of black on black were outlines of pictures on the wall, including a blackened oval frame and glass against a blackened wall.

Carole stopped at the burnt door of her burnt drawing room. What had been white was grey. What had been antique brown was something darker, among the cinders. The water-laden rug was a puddle, with dirty imprints from firemen's boots.

She flexed her feet, gripping her uncomfortable shoes, before carefully stepping onto the rug. It squelched, squeezing ashen water to the sides of her shoes and a little more to the floor. Carole pulled her foot back again, the water slowly receding in the rug.

If the house surprised her with something good to say, it was the shell still intact. The inglorious edifice that had survived so long might yet somehow survive that day, if Carole and her family wanted to rebuild.

From along the hallway, the Superintendent interrupted her. "We believe one fire started in this room," he said. Emmet, Tessa, and Xavier stood with him.

Through the dark light of the hallway, Carole followed them to what was surely the blackest and most destroyed of all the rooms, poorly lit by the black-rimmed broken window. The flames had left little to recognise in the furniture. A tall free-standing lamp had become a brittle black spindle. The open suitcases could have been coffins in an unfinished crematorium, without corpses or anything else obvious in them. Only the twisted, broken wires of the shade remained.

"This was Mahmood's room," said Carole.

"Another fire started in the dining room," said the Superintendent.

Carole could not imagine any reason Mahmood returned there. She could not imagine reason for anything.

"Another started in the library." Only Mahmood entered the library.

Carole went to the library door. The burnt-out bookcase doors had been opened and books thrown into a bonfire before being set alight. There was little left to burn.

Tessa turned to her mother. "If we despise our heritage, why shouldn't others despise it?" asked Tessa. "If we abandon our God so readily, why shouldn't others dismiss Him?"

Carole's head began shaking, consciously and subconsciously in her last moments of denial. "So much was done," she muttered, no longer able to refer to him by name, "in the time between him running back along the hallway and Luke smelling smoke."

"Could he have prepared the fire beforehand?" asked the Superintendent.

"He brought so many suitcases," answered Carole. "I never thought to wonder what was in them."

Before leaving the house, Carole paused before that blackened oval picture glass. With her fingers already too dirty from the day ever to be cleaned, Carole wiped a warm small portion of the portal, revealing her father's long-dead watching eyes. She had given him another chance to see.

Stepping from the house back into cold, Carole winced. Outside was a bright sparse open space it hadn't previously seemed. The day remained cloudy nevertheless.

From a gardening shed she and Emmet rarely entered anymore, Emmet took some gardening gloves. Wearing them, he returned to the house of wet shadows. Soon he came outside again, carrying something unidentifiable.

The photographer that Xavier had summoned photographed Emmet dumping that something on the ground, by the driveway. Carole cared no more about the worse photograph ever taken of her.

Years had passed since Carole last donned a mop or forced her hands into rubber gloves. She shortly would again.

Tessa brought some sticks of celery from the kitchen refrigerator, no longer refrigerating, she gave to her father. Emmet offered some celery to Carole.

Carole chewed her celery. It was her first food since before the fire.

"Would you like us to get something more substantial for lunch, my dear," Emmet asked Carole.

"No thank you, darling," she smiled. "You two head off to a restaurant."

"We'll stay together," said Emmet.

In Tessa's hands was a bottle of mineral water. She knew better than to suggest her parents drink directly from a bottle.

By early afternoon, the last fire engine and last of the firemen had gone, leaving behind lawns churned up and broken by their wheels and other tracks. An electrician Carole had summoned using Emmet's telephone came. A plumber and gasfitter soon followed.

The garage was intact and Carole's car parked there undamaged. Emmet drove his car from the street back beside it.

The Superintendent remained, frequently speaking on his mobile telephone where Carole, her family, and Xavier couldn't hear him. In time, he approached Carole. "I am leaving now, Mrs Wynworth," he told her. "I will be in touch."

"Have you information about Mahmood?"

Emmet and Tessa approached them. Xavier soon followed. The photographer had gone.

"After we spoke to Zaki Quresh this morning," the Superintendent told them, "he returned to his home. The front door and telephone still aren't answering and Zaki switched off his mobile telephone, but we believe Samina Quresh is there, along with a man who might be Mahmood."

Carole's right hand dragged her ragged hair from her face. "They might open their door to me," she told him.

"He is a person of interest in a terrorism and murder investigation and a suspect in an arson investigation, Mrs Wynworth," said the Superintendent, repeating his refusal, "not a dinner-party guest."

"What if the dinner party had been yours, Superintendent?" asked Carole. "Look around you. Imagine you'd adopted a son, who wreaked despair upon your home and family. Wouldn't you want to understand him?"

"I don't adopt, Mrs Wynworth."

"What if I can help you?" she begged. "What if I can save someone from being killed?"

"By not coming, Mrs Wynworth, you might be that someone."

Her voice became strident, almost threatening, stressing every slow syllable. "If you do not take me with you,

Superintendent," she insisted, "I won't be making that statement you wanted about Mahmood, his time with me, or his time in this house."

The Superintendent looked at Emmet, before looking back at Carole. "I think I preferred it when politicians just talked," the Superintendent said. "You can't fix bad people with a hug."

Carole softened her voice, to the tone she'd used more often at the garden parties for school parents once convened around her lawn, rather than the corridors of Parliament House. "I need to help you protect my family," she told him.

The Superintendent continued looking at her, without her releasing him by daring to look away. He checked his watch. "You might be useful, Mrs Wynworth," he told her, "but you must comply with my instructions."

A smile formed slowly in her lips, her face dipping away without her eyes leaving him, watching her. It might be a final moment of her influence.

"I don't know whether this makes me want to vote for your party come election time, Mrs Wynworth," said the Superintendent, "or determined never to vote for it."

Xavier spoke up. "I'll follow you in my car," he said.

"This isn't a parade," the Superintendent told him.

Xavier looked at Carole, tilting his head slightly as if to ask for her support. "You wanted me to report the facts," he reminded her.

Carole remained silent. She deferred to the Superintendent.

Xavier turned back to the Superintendent. "You can't keep me from public streets," Xavier told him.

"I can arrest you for obstruction."

"Only, if I obstruct."

The Superintendent removed his keys from his pocket. "Don't speak a peep until I tell you it's over," he told Xavier, "whatever *it* proves to be."

Emmet stepped closer to Carole. "Do you want me to come with you, my dear?"

She shook her head. "You rest," she told him. "You think about what you want us to do."

Emmet placed his hands on Carole's shoulders as he reached

his head down towards her. He kissed her lips, before stepping back.

Carole looked at Tessa. They'd not spoken with each other since Tessa's words at the door of their burnt-out library. They had had no conversation since soon after Tessa and Emmet arrived.

"Be careful, Mummy," said Tessa, before stepping forward to kiss her mother's cheek. She then stepped back to her father's side.

Carole turned to the Superintendent. "Knowing the fool I've been," she told him in her penance, "Mahmood might trust me."

20

REDEMPTION

Unlike other police cars that had parked outside Carole, Emmet, and Tessa's home that day, Superintendent Dempsey's sparkling sedan from the outside wasn't obviously a police car, except that most cars normally in Springdale Road were more luxurious. Inside were a police radio and electronic gadgetry far more complicated than the simple systems in Carole's and Emmet's cars. The vinyl seat in which Carole sat was noticeably hard.

For an hour or so, without his police lights or siren blaring and so confined by all the traffic, Carole sat beside the Superintendent driving back into the south-western suburbs of Sydney, reciting everything she knew about Mahmood, Zaki, and Samina. She recalled items of detail she'd heard, observed, and been told from the exercise of thinking aloud about them. Mahmood filed his fingernails instead of using clippers. Zaki gambled on poker machines and hoped he was not losing much. Samina was learning to play a tambourine. Only the Superintendent's conversations with other police and with his wife, apologising that he might not be home for dinner, interrupted them.

Behind them was Xavier Talbot in his old car. Every time Carole thought he'd been left behind at traffic lights, he soon reappeared.

Houses cast lengthening shadows in the late afternoon, smoke eased from brick chimneys into the air, and cool air prepared to become cold, when the Superintendent slowed his sedan along the street in which Zaki Quresh lived. Daylight prepared to fade, but street lights weren't yet shining. Lights shone in several other homes, while Zaki's single-storey cottage remained dark. To each side of the front door, the cloud-white curtains were tightly drawn across the double windows.

"I expected to see police cars," said Carole.

"Toto," said the Superintendent, "you're not in Killara anymore. In suburbs like this, police must be more cautious."

The Superintendent parked at the side of the road, across and a short way along the street from Zaki's home. Xavier parked behind him.

"Inside the silver car in front of us and the grey car across the street," said the Superintendent, "behind their tinted windows, are policemen trying not to be noticed."

Those men, like the Superintendent and Carole, could observe the frontage and long sides of Zaki's house. In their cars, they were secure and apart.

"If you look up in the sky," said the Superintendent, "you might see a surveillance drone, watching the rear of the house."

Carole leant forward, staring up through the windscreen. She couldn't see anything but the coming dusk. The street lights remained dark, in spite of the gloom settling around.

"Police can take you home anytime you want us to, Mrs Wynworth."

The Superintendent lowered the window beside him. Carole shivered, wishing she had brought a hat and coat from any cupboard in her home that the fire and smoke had failed to permeate.

Along the footpath, two South Asian boys played cricket. The sounds of a willow bat striking a tennis ball back along the footpath reached Carole's ears. The aromas of Middle Eastern spices and Asian curries wafted from the houses, touching Carole's lips. She was hungry, but they weren't the foods she wanted.

From one house came a young woman with a scarf wrapped

around her head, calling out names Carole could not discern to the boys on the footpath. The boys scampered, with one boy following the young woman into her home and the other carrying the bat and ball into the house adjoining it.

The Superintendent had continued studying Zaki's home, to which Carole again looked. A light flickered on. The curtains remained drawn. The Superintendent closed his car window beside him.

The rear passenger-side door of the car opened. Xavier stepped in, sat down, and closed it. "Don't like curries," he muttered. "Prefer steaks, medium rare."

"We're not here to eat," said the Superintendent, adjusting the rear-vision mirror to watch Xavier in the far corner of the car from him.

"Which house is it?" asked Xavier.

"You two stay here," said the Superintendent, looking down to the car door beside him.

"Superintendent," said Carole, "whoever answers Zaki's door will be less alarmed by me than by you."

The Superintendent faced her. "I'll be less alarmed if you're in the car."

"I can talk to Mahmood, Zaki, and Samina. You can't."

"Mahmood might kill you without talking."

"He could have killed me this morning."

"He almost did." The Superintendent turned to the car door beside him. "You're staying here."

"Do you want me to scream?" asked Carole.

Again he faced her, her firm eyes reflecting the resolve within her. "We could go together," he suggested.

"Do you want us to look like a posse? No, Superintendent."

The Superintendent looked back to Zaki's home, with the light shining from a front room. There were no shrubs or trees outside the house behind which the Superintendent could hide. The red brick wall was too low for a person to crouch behind. "I'll be as close to you as I can be," he told Carole. "Mister Talbot, I want you back in your car."

"Don't you trust me, Superintendent?"

"No."

Carole remained quiet, as Xavier opened the door beside him. He returned slowly to his car.

The street lights flickered alight. The streets becoming a little brighter made the sky seem darker.

"Aren't you frightened, Mrs Wynworth?"

"Yes, I am, Superintendent."

"Good. Fear keeps people alive."

Trying to seem ordinary in a street in which she wasn't, Carole stepped from the Superintendent's car to the footpath, where the smells of spices were almost overpowering. Her ears were primed without knowing for what.

Her arms folded and hands grasping her elbows, Carole walked around the Superintendent's car and across the street to Zaki's short letter box, standing like a sentry by the white-painted low gate. She unwrapped her arms and unlocked the gate. As she pushed it open, the gate squeaked.

Carole stopped, trying to still the beast beating within her. She looked up at the silent house, where the front door remained shut. That incongruous black ornamental figure of a palm tree obscured the distant peephole.

She checked the curtains beyond which a light shone for any glimpse of someone peering through. Nobody was. Nor was anybody peering through the curtains to the other side of the front door.

Leaving the gate open, Carole stepped along the concrete pathway. So much had changed since last she had been there, only two days earlier. Gone was all confidence about her reception. Whatever had moved Mahmood to burn her home might move him to harm her. It might move him to apologise profusely and beg her forgiveness, but Carole could not imagine Mahmood begging for anything. With every reason not to, she laughed; he could still make her laugh.

Carole's sore foot rested on the step up to the door, in a last moment of indecision, concentrating her heartbeat to a rhythm slow enough not to matter. Only a few feet away might be Mahmood, the pearl-handled pistol in his hand. He might be alone, without witnesses, or be part of a pack venting anger

Carole could still not comprehend. What of Zaki, or Samina? Carole did not know what they'd do.

She climbed the step. Turning back to the Superintendent watching her from his car, she nodded, so he knew that she was fine. He could not see her heartbeat thumping.

Also watching her from his car was Xavier Talbot. A water bottle was at his lips.

Standing before the black-iron palm tree motif and peephole without a shadow, Carole looked around the door for a knocker or bell. None was there. Had it been moved, taken away? She stopped, calming herself. It had never been there. Her right hand rising trembled before her eyes as she could not have imagined that it would. So too her left hand, until she pressed it to her side. Her right hand hovered, quivering, a short way from the door, before she seized her mind and flicked her knuckles on the wood.

She jarred with the knock they made, louder than any other noise outside her skin. Within moments anyone might come; those moments might be her last. Nobody might come.

A shadow blocked the light through the peephole. The shadow stayed, much too long for anyone wanting only to see who was there.

The shadow departed. A bolt to the far side of the door jostled with the motions of someone preparing to unlock it. Carole looked down at the doorknob fidgeting with the sound, looked up to Mahmood's height, and looked back down to the knob, as the door slowly slipped open. Bright lights from the house rushed at her, before the sight of one man standing before her: Zaki Quresh.

"Mrs Wynworth," he said, holding the door half open. He was wearing a fawn brown jumper over his casual shirt and trousers.

Carole remained silent for a moment, collecting her breath. "Have you seen Mahmood?" she asked, masking her anxiety. "I need to speak with him."

"Are you all right, Mrs Wynworth?"

"Please, Zaki, do you know where he is?"

"The police telephoned me looking for him," answered Zaki. "Why are they always suspecting Muslims of being criminals?"

"They're not, Zaki."

"Mahmood isn't here, Mrs Wynworth."

From the far side of Zaki, from somewhere in his home, came the sound of a door closing. Carole could not see along the hallway. "Is that your wife, Zaki?" she asked.

"My wife and our children are with friends today, Mrs Wynworth."

"Is that Samina?" asked Carole.

"Why do you ask me so many questions?" asked Zaki, starting to close the door. "Please, go home, Mrs Wynworth."

"The police are with me," said Carole.

Zaki stopped closing the door, leaving it part open. He looked past Carole towards the street. "Where are the police?"

Carole turned and pointed towards the Superintendent in his car. Zaki opened the door fully and stepped outside, looking to where she pointed.

The Superintendent's car door opened and he stepped out. Closing and locking the door, he walked towards Carole and Zaki, through the open gate, to the foot of the front steps.

"Mahmood isn't here," said Zaki.

The Superintendent removed a gun from a holster under his jacket. He pointed it at Zaki.

Zaki threw his hands high in the air. "Mahmood's inside," he cried out, his whole body shaking as he leapt around.

The Superintendent lowered his gun. "Why did you lie?" he asked Zaki.

"Mahmood doesn't want to see anyone," answered Zaki, before looking back at Carole, "not even you, Mrs Wynworth."

"Why?" asked Carole.

"He said your husband and daughter were cruel to him, wanting him to leave their home."

"Did he set the fire so that none of us could have our home?"

"What fire is that?"

"I want to see Mahmood," said the Superintendent.

Zaki stood still, his eyes set upon the Superintendent. "Let me talk to him," he said. "I don't want any problems."

"I'll come with you," said the Superintendent.

"He can talk to me more calmly than he can talk to you," said Zaki.

"Mahmood has to understand that we have several policemen watching the house," said the Superintendent. "We're watching from all sides."

Zaki nodded. "I will tell him," he said, before stepping back inside. He closed the door.

Carole climbed back down the steps to the small front lawn. She and the Superintendent waited, listening for nothing to hear. No lights in Zaki's house switched alight or off. There were no visible movements of the curtains or the door.

Xavier remained in his car, watching them. The aromas of dinners persisted.

"I don't like curries either," the Superintendent told Carole. "My wife roasts terrific pork ribs."

"Too many of my meals are in restaurants, Superintendent," answered Carole.

The door to Zaki's home opened. Slowly he stepped out, his face stark white. Without closing the front door behind him, he proceeded carefully down the steps, in a strange, sleep-like, disconnected trance. In the full glare from the street lights Zaki stood upright, sweating, his eyes glazed over.

"Zaki," asked Carole, "what is it?"

"Mahmood is with Samina," he said slowly, his voice colder than the air, without looking at Carole or the Superintendent but straight ahead. "I should have told you."

Carole reached her hand towards him. He pulled away from her.

"Mahmood says Muslims should not suffer Christian justice," Zaki continued. "The police must withdraw. He is holding Samina hostage, threatening to kill her and me."

"We're not withdrawing," said the Superintendent, bundling Zaki and Carole away from the house, through the open gate and along the footpath.

Soon, several police cars with flashing blue lights arrived, without their sirens sounding. Some parked across the nearest intersections, sealing the street from people and cars. Behind the barricades, packs of spectators grew.

Uniformed policemen and women knocked on the doors of homes adjoining Zaki's home and across the street from it. Most occupants returned inside where they remained, away from windows. Some, the smaller children in what looked like their pyjamas, left their homes to hurry along the footpath.

"You'll have to move along," a uniformed policeman instructed Carole, his arms outstretched to shepherd her away.

"I'm with Superintendent Dempsey," Carole explained, pointing to the policeman without uniform but with a radio at his hand.

"Don't move from where you are."

A helicopter hovered overhead. It shone down a light behind Zaki's home.

Black vans arrived. Black-clothed police took up positions facing Zaki's home, just in their lines of sight.

A police barricade admitted two ambulances. They waited.

The street found a new equilibrium. Only the rotating helicopter blades and flashing police lights connoted real activity.

Carole stood where she barely saw Zaki's open front door, waiting patiently for nothing to happen. Zaki stood beside her. "Without Mahmood," Zaki lamented, "Samina would have gone back home, to Jordan." The street lights reflected in his eyes, blurring with his gathering tears.

With nothing she could say, Carole looked back at Zaki's home. The light through the open door fell dark. The light through the closed curtains ceased.

All that remained to light the frontage of the house were the street lights treating all houses without favour. They illuminated the neatly cut front lawn, open door, and closed windows.

Carole hugged her chest from the cold air; her cardigan was inadequate. Inactivity accentuated the discomfort of her clothes.

The Superintendent returned to Carole and Zaki. "To save my sister," Zaki told the Superintendent, "I would let you slay Mahmood. To save her, I think you should let him go." Zaki turned to Carole. "I'm sorry, Mrs Wynworth."

The Superintendent spoke. "We're monitoring all telephone calls to and from your house," he told Zaki. "Samina telephoned your father in Jordan. Our translator says she told him that she loved him and that god is great, before hanging up." The Superintendent turned to Carole. "Mahmood telephoned your husband."

"Emmet?" she asked, stepping forward.

"Mahmood suggested he should come here, with Tessa, to save your life."

"My life?" she asked. "You can't let them come."

"When that conversation finished, I telephoned your husband. I advised him not to come, but he was adamant. Tessa was just as adamant they come."

"You can stop them, Superintendent," said Carole.

"I couldn't stop you, Mrs Wynworth."

"If you'd really wanted to stop me, Superintendent, you would have."

"If I can call your husband again and say you're going home, or to the Killara Inn, then they will see you there."

Zaki moved closer. "You must stay, Mrs Wynworth," he said. "You created this crisis."

She looked at Zaki. "I'm sorry, Zaki." She looked at the Superintendent and nodded.

Behind the Superintendent was Zaki's home and lawn. Suddenly appearing, gliding through the air from the open front door, was a small white shape.

"What is that?" asked Carole.

The Superintendent turned around. Its flight was slow, without a breeze, but the street lights seemed to focus on it, drifting high above the ground before beginning to fall. It was a folded paper dart, like the ones small boys made at school. All eyes watched its failing flight, as it fell on Zaki's path, slipping a short way before stopping.

Nobody moved. It could have been a trap, thought Carole, enticing fools she no longer was.

Watching the house, the Superintendent stepped back along the footpath. He stepped through the gate to the path and letter, which he picked up.

Still watching the house, between glancing back to where he stepped, he returned to the footpath. The paper remained folded.

The Superintendent returned to Carole. "The top of the paper aeroplane is addressed to you, Mrs Wynworth. I want to know what it says."

Tentatively, she held out her hand to take it. Even more tentatively, she unfolded it, revealing a letter.

"Dear Carole," she read aloud, without sense that she was betraying private correspondence any more than she sensed that she was reading it. "We want our freedom and rights," she said, pausing to look up at the Superintendent, "under the protection of our law."

"That is what you've been saying," said Zaki.

Carole glanced at him, the colour restored to his face, before resuming. "We want Muslim holy days to be public holidays."

"This country is multicultural," grinned Zaki.

With every word Carole became increasingly estranged from what she read. "We want days set aside at beaches," she continued, "zoos, and other public attractions for people in proportion to the proportions of their faith. Muslim women should be free to leisure away from male and non-Muslim eyes."

"We do that now for swimming pools," enthused Zaki.

"We want prayer rooms in shopping centres and airports, libraries and workplaces, glorifying god."

Carole knew to whom Mahmood referred. It wasn't God.

"We want stores and supermarkets to cease playing music. We want suburbs, schools, universities, and hospitals where Muslim men and women can live, learn, and receive medical care without blasphemers."

"You can do that!" exclaimed Zaki.

"You are our hope, Carole," she finished reading, "Love Mahmood and Samina."

Holding the message in two timid fingers as if it were diseased, Carole raised her hand. The Superintendent took it from her.

"He's asking for things you can agree," concluded Zaki, his face aglow.

"I could ask Muslim countries to accommodate Christians," replied Carole.

The glow vanished from Zaki's face. "Why would you?" he asked. "You're no longer Christian. You no longer believe."

"We are what we are, Zaki."

"You can save Samina," protested Zaki.

"The government will not agree to this."

"You need only say that you agree," persisted Zaki, his eyes beginning to plead.

"I do not agree."

"Why, Mrs Wynworth?" asked Zaki, his face intense and eyes scrutinising, judging, and condemning her. "You don't value your culture, your God, yourselves. Why can't you do these things for people who value theirs? To be Jordanian is to be Muslim; I am more faithful to Islam than I might appear. You say your country is better for us being here, but don't prove it."

Carole turned to the Superintendent. "Tell Emmet, I'm coming home," she said.

The Superintendent faced Zaki. "We will wait," he said. "We are patient." He returned to other police officers, his back to Carole and Zaki.

"Mrs Wynworth," said Zaki, finding a new firmness in his voice. "Samina, she relies upon you." His angry hand pointed at his dark home, lit only by the street lights, in which Mahmood and Samina were holed together. "You tell them your reply."

Carole clasped her hands, her fingers pressing harder. The police would ultimately apprehend Mahmood and interview him about the ferry bombing, the murder of Nadine Westwick, and the fire to Carole's family home. She would soon be headed to that home, and to conversations she could not yet imagine with her husband and daughter willing to brave a journey against police advice to save her. Never again might she able to say anything to Mahmood.

Her arms hanging by her side, Carole walked slowly along the footpath, towards the open gate to Zaki's house. The muscles in her legs and arms tightened, as she slow marched without music. Her pace quickened, her cardigan and woollen slacks dragging with her and her leather heels beating the footpath.

Zaki behind her, Carole proceeded through the open gate to his still lawn. Ahead of her, Zaki's home remained silent, still, and dark. The front door stood open to the shadowy lit long hallway. Carole stopped. Zaki stood beside her.

Policemen watching Carole would have assumed the Superintendent knew what she was doing, although she was not yet certain what that was. Her response would be to every yearning in Mahmood's flying message they once shared, and to dragging her daughter and husband to her peril.

"Enough," she called out. "We've given up enough!"

The street of hiding eyes was again silent, but for Carole breathing heavily. The cold became bitter.

"Come back," the Superintendent yelled, from the street behind her.

Carole seized a breath and ducked her head. Zaki crouched close to the ground.

Nothing more happened. Carole slowly raised her head again. Zaki stood back up, staring at his home. The Superintendent reached them, his arm outstretched as if about to collect them.

A gunshot blasted from the house. A large red dot punctured Zaki's forehead.

Carole gasped, as Zaki's face and figure froze. The Superintendent stopped.

Zaki's eyes locked open, he toppled backwards. Carole stepped back, as Zaki fell on the grass in front of her. From the house, a second gunshot blasted.

21

RESOLUTION

Black-clothed police brandishing weapons rushed from all sides past Carole into and around Zaki's home, obscuring Carole's vision through the open door. The curtains remained closed across the front windows, while a light from the house began to shine and then another, until all lights were aglow. Near her feet, Zaki's body lay on the lawn; the time had passed for her to run.

A policeman through the open doorway moved a little, revealing to Carole the hallway glaring under lights. Several tall policemen stood over Mahmood, sitting on the floor. Their pointed guns speared down at him, cradling Samina's body in his arms.

"Carole," he cried out, seeing her seeing him, the tears peppering his words. "Please help me."

The Superintendent stepped in front of her, taking her by the side and turning her around. "You must go back, Mrs Wynworth," he said, his arm around her, pushing her towards the open gate.

"Please, Superintendent," asked Carole. "Let me talk to Mahmood."

"I can't allow that, Mrs Wynworth." He pushed her out of Zaki's property.

"I need to know his reasons. I need to understand."

"Need, Mrs Wynworth?" The Superintendent pushed her back along the footpath. "You might be able to read the reports, later."

Out of sight of Zaki's house, Carole shook herself free. "Superintendent," she said, standing before him. "I need to see him speak to me."

The Superintendent grabbed the attention of a blue-uniformed policeman. "This is Carole Wynworth, MP," he instructed him. "Someone take her home."

"Did you speak with Emmet, Superintendent?" asked Carole.

"No, Mrs Wynworth."

"I'm waiting for Emmet."

"Take care of her," the Superintendent told the policeman. "Telephone her husband and daughter to tell them Mrs Wynworth is safe; they should be together in a car." The Superintendent took a piece of paper from his pocket and gave it to him. "If these numbers are busy, interrupt the calls. If you can convince them to head home, take Mrs Wynworth there."

The Superintendent left her. The uniformed policeman sat in the front seat of a police car, from which he watched Carole.

Subtly breaking free from her captor's eyes, Carole edged back along the footpath to where she saw Zaki's home again. Policemen walked in and out or moved around, talking with each other and with the Superintendent, directing operations. Cameras flashed.

Mahmood remained unseen, somewhere inside the house. If he appeared, Carole would call to him, and hope that in that brief moment he might confess a clue to her. She could not imagine what words could convey.

Ambulance men stepped from their ambulances, removing gurneys and empty black body bags. Again, they waited.

Eventually, the Superintendent approached the ambulance men. "The house is secure," he told them.

The first pair rolled their gurney and carried their body bag through the open gate and up the path to Zaki's body. The other left their gurney near the first, stepped around their colleagues, and carried their body bag into the house.

While the Superintendent watched them, Carole stood beside him. "Mahmood might say things to me that he won't say to you," she told him. "I'll tell you anything I learn."

He turned to her momentarily, without reply. He then left her again.

Xavier appeared beside Carole, unscrewing the cap from a small bottle of sparkling mineral water he offered her. "I didn't bring cups," he said.

Carole's mouth was dry and becoming drier, in a place without any other opportunity to wet it. "Thank you, Xavier," she smiled, taking the bottle from him.

Struggling to purse her lips correctly, she spilled a little water on her chin. Quickly, Carole turned around to dry her face where Xavier couldn't see her, before more carefully placing the bottle at her lips. The water washed her mouth a little cleaner. She returned the bottle almost full to him.

"What is happening in there?" asked Xavier.

"I'll let the Superintendent brief you."

"All I know to report is that two Muslims were shot dead during a police operation in Sydney," said Xavier. "Can I quote you calling them victims of Islamophobia?"

Carole laughed. Xavier became uncharacteristically silent. She imagined him memorising everything he saw and heard for an exclusive *Sydney Morning Herald* exposé, with photographs. The aromas from the houses once so pungent had faded a little with their familiarity.

Returning to his car, Xavier rested in the front seat. His legs hung out the open door, ready to rise again.

The first pair of ambulance men soon returned, delivering their filled and sealed body bag aboard their gurney back into their ambulance. They closed the rear doors, sat in their seats, and waited.

The second pair soon followed, doing the same. Both ambulances then drove away.

The Superintendent returned to Carole. "If you come to see Mahmood in the house, you must leave as soon as I instruct you," he told her. "Come along."

Carole stepped towards him. Again loitering nearby, Xavier also stepped forward.

"Not you," the Superintendent told Xavier.

The Superintendent led Carole back through the open gate, between policemen, towards Zaki's familiar front door. On the grass, a cord marked the place where Zaki fell.

In Zaki's home and hallway, adhesive tape marked the place where Samina's body lay. No blood was visible.

The Superintendent led Carole to the lounge room in which they had sat two days earlier. She baulked to see the figure kneeling: his head bowed forward near the floor. His wrists were cuffed behind his back, confining him in bondage, below a black-clothed policeman standing over him, his long gun pointed at him. Footsteps trekked back or forth along the hallway behind Carole.

"You don't have to see her if you don't want to," the Superintendent said to the suspect on the floor. "Mrs Wynworth wants to speak with you."

Mahmood slowly raised his head. His drab eyes slowly shone and the muscles in his face strengthened to a smile. "Carole," he said.

He was not obviously fearful, nor arrogant. Something of his self-assuredness remained.

Catching Carole's eye from a shelf as other items did not was a familiar silver badge, of barbed wire encircling a lighted candle. Carole touched her cardigan and blouse lapels, but they were empty. She had not seen the badge that day. She had not thought to affix it to her clothes that morning, when she expected to remain at home. "You took my Amnesty badge," she told Mahmood.

"I thought you meant it for me," said Mahmood, his voice waif-life in reply, "or was it always for you?"

"I would have given it to you," Carole begged of him. "We opened our home to you."

The black-clothed policeman remained standing over Mahmood, his gun at the ready. The Superintendent remained by Carole.

"Did your brother really drown?" Carole asked Mahmood.

"Did you arrange for the man to grab my handbag to learn my home address, looking like a hero when you ran after him and brought my handbag back? Did you organise those two boys to be playing by the road, to appear to save them?"

Mahmood began shaking his head. "Trust me, Carole," he said.

"Were you destroying evidence of your fingerprints and DNA," asked Carole, "when you destroyed our home?"

"We didn't think you cared about it," Mahmood answered. "Samina burnt your home. I told her how to get there through the Haughtons' property, but didn't expect her to come this morning with a bag and the materials to start a fire. She drove me here."

"Samina?" asked Carole, stepping away. "Why should she hate us?"

"She didn't hate you, Carole," he explained, "but I felt unwelcome." He dipped his head, not looking at her. "I shouldn't have told her about Emmet and Tessa wanting me to leave. I'm sorry Carole, I wish I hadn't."

Carole slumped into the sofa. Her eye level was closer to Mahmood's face now. Past him, under a souvenir of Zaki's holidays, she noticed the pearl-handled pistol lying on its side.

Mahmood looked up again at Carole, his head turned on his neck. "Samina killed Nadine Westwick," he continued. "Samina gave me her Canterbury-Bankstown cap to hide in your home because she said the police wouldn't look for it there. That was her that the cameras photographed before the ferry bombing, with her hair inside her football jersey. Samina wanted me to approach you in Canberra, to become close to you, to come to your home. My crime was loving her: my blessed and beloved."

Carole leant forward. "You told me you'd separated?"

"Samina wanted me to tell you that." He again dipped his head. This time he wept. "I'm so sorry, Carole," he muttered, without facing her. "I shouldn't have done it, but I loved her so much and I knew you lived so well, with your choice of foods and central heating, your chandeliers and garden chairs. I wanted to live as you live, with all that gold and crystal glass." Again, he looked up at Carole. "You wanted us to be like you and, in some ways, we are. Is that so bad?"

Carole shook her head. His words were too many to believe.

"Samina shot Zaki," Mahmood continued. "The medical examiners will confirm she fired the gun."

Carole looked up at the Superintendent, who responded. "Mahmood could have asked her to hold the gun," said the Superintendent, "before putting his hands around hers, pointing the gun at Zaki, and pulling the trigger."

She looked back at Mahmood, who continued. "Samina often worried that her brother would co-operate with Australian security agencies," Mahmood told Carole. "She thought Zaki had become too Western since coming to this country, but you didn't notice because you don't notice the immigrants that haven't."

"Zaki said you held Samina hostage," Carole replied.

"That was Samina's idea," explained Mahmood. "She thought the police might withdraw. She threatened to kill Zaki if he let the police capture her."

Carole again glanced at the Superintendent, hoping he could dismiss or endorse Mahmood's words. He remained still, his face expressionless.

"If I hadn't taken Samina's gun and killed her," Mahmood resumed, "then she would have killed you or the policemen. I saved your life, Carole."

"We were friends," Carole beseeched Mahmood. "Samina was my friend."

A loud cry stumbled from Mahmood's face. "Oh, Carole," he struggled to say.

Her body gripped, her hands grabbed her legs. "Why me?" she asked.

Slowly, Mahmood gathered himself and raised his head higher. "Dear Carole," he sighed, the water in his eyes inescapable. "You never understood how important you are."

With his hands bound behind his back, Mahmood could not dab the tears from his face. Carole looked at the Superintendent. "Can I wipe his cheek, Superintendent?" she asked him.

The Superintendent took a clean handkerchief from his pocket. He leant down and wiped Mahmood's cheeks.

"Thank you," said Mahmood, venturing a smile, "both of you."

Carefully, the Superintendent took the handkerchief, carried it to the door, and stopped a policeman walking through the house. "Bag this," he said, giving the handkerchief to him. The Superintendent returned to the room.

Mahmood remained on the floor. "I am Muslim in a non-Muslim land," he sighed. "I am Lebanese far from Lebanon."

"Nobody sees you as such," said Carole.

"Our souls don't vanish because you can't see them. Australia is my friend. My country, Lebanon, is my parent: my blood, my heart. A child loves his parents more than his friends. Even a child of one of your divorces must love his parents."

"We love Lebanon," said Carole.

"Listen to your daughter feeling estranged from this country of her birth, feeling powerless and insignificant, alone, so alone. I can say that of me. Your daughter and I, we want to belong."

"You belong, Mahmood, you belong."

He shook his head. "Samina belonged," he told her. "Who else among us did?"

Carole rested back in the sofa. "She did belong, didn't she," said Carole. "In Jordan, she belonged." A thousand moments from her time with Mahmood, Samina, and Zaki flooded through her mind. "Why would a visitor take enough interest in this country to harm us?"

"Don't you like people taking interests in our country, Carole?" asked Mahmood.

Carole stood up to flex her muscles, to let the blood flow more freely through her body, through her brain. "Did you think to reveal your name to the woman you loved?" she inquired.

"Samina never asked."

"Zaki thought you were young. Did Samina?"

"Samina knew my age," answered Mahmood. "Arab women want men old enough to protect them and their children. Western men don't protect their women. Western parents don't protect their children."

No longer looking at him, Carole began walking around the

small room, by the small table, near the curtains still drawn. "Did you befriend me to bring Samina my head on a silver plate?" asked Carole, expecting no reply.

"Please, Carole," sighed Mahmood. "You're hurting yourself."

Carole stopped at the open doorway, looking down at the adhesive tape on the hallway floor. "Samina loved you, and you killed her."

"I know you're upset."

She turned around to face him, her eyes slowly lowering towards him. "Was Ojala Kassab your girlfriend upon which you draped bombs, or another of your protégés?"

"Carole, you're so wrong."

"Not now," she said.

"Are you so pure, Carole?" asked Mahmood. "You made me a caricature of what you want Muslims to be, from the clothes I wear and sound of my voice, feeling good about this country whatever I felt. You used me to promote your desires for this country, not my desires. Don't blame me because I keep my old faith as indomitably as you keep your new one. Every time I acted as you wanted me to act, you smiled and fed me biscuits. Every time I didn't, you shut down your fragile senses."

"I know it's our fault, Mahmood," Carole confessed. "We tried so hard to make everybody happy, for whatever irrational reason, but failed."

Mahmood dipped his head, before raising it again. "None of us belong here now, do we Carole?"

"I'm afraid you'll lose your liberty to a gaol cell," she told him.

Again, Mahmood shook his head, this time allowing a smile to creep across his face. "I have told you the truth about Samina and me."

"You can't prove what you say."

"I don't have to prove it, Carole. Samina won't be on trial. I will be. Without anyone to contradict my evidence, I will raise enough reasonable doubt in the secular judge's mind to mean that your laws of liberty prevent him from convicting me of anything. There is no physical evidence tying me to the ferry bombing, murder of Nadine Westwick, or fire at your home. I will be free."

"That isn't true," said Carole, until the errors she had already made dragged her face around to the Superintendent. "Is what Mahmood says true?"

"Your husband will soon be here, Mrs Wynworth."

"I like you, Carole," continued Mahmood, as if the mood were conversational, "but I will then need to think about your daughter being so rude to me, teasing and then smiting me, defiling me and my faith with her prayers. What should I do if she, or Emmet, or you again make me feel unwanted, when you've repaired the home you've got or moved into a new one? You won't let Tessa be cruel to me again, will you Carole?"

Bound and kneeling on the floor, he defied her. Carole had no answer.

"Out there," said Mahmood, pointing his head to the closed curtains, "people care more about me than they do about you and your family. I'm not talking just about the people in this street, but about the people in yours."

Carole fell back onto the sofa, before again studying Mahmood. His face was not quite smiling. His deep brown eyes were intense and determined. The pride she once admired was threatening her.

She looked up at the Superintendent. "I'd like a moment with Mahmood alone," she said to him, "please."

"I can't allow that, Mrs Wynworth."

"How can he hurt me now?"

"It would violate police procedure, Mrs Wynworth."

"Call it a direct order from the federal government if you wish, Superintendent," suggested Carole. She rose from the sofa and stood before him, much shorter than he was. "Treat it as a request if you wish, from a mother to a father."

The Superintendent looked back at the open doorway. Policemen no longer moved along the hall. The house was silent. He turned back to Mahmood. "You can refuse," he told Mahmood.

From his place on the floor, Mahmood shrugged his shoulders the little the handcuffs on his wrists allowed him. He looked again at Carole.

The Superintendent walked back to Mahmood, bent down

behind him, and tugged the cuffs on his wrists. Standing again, the Superintendent nodded at the black-clothed policeman.

"We'll be outside the door, Mrs Wynworth," said the Superintendent. "I'll tell you when your husband and daughter arrive."

The two policemen left the room, closing the door behind them. The curtains to the room were closed, as they always seemed to be.

Mahmood whispered, just loud enough for Carole to hear him. "I knew you would help me, Carole," he smiled.

She walked calmly across the room to a shelf of Zaki's holiday souvenirs, from which she withdrew the pearl-handled pistol that Mahmood first entrusted to her that morning. Slowly, Carole turned around, again looking at Mahmood. Her hands were never more relaxed than they were holding that pistol for the third time that day. She raised the pistol into her line of sight, pointing it at Mahmood's forehead.

"Carole," he whispered, as unfazed as people all seemed to be when Carole pointed that pistol at them.

She also whispered. "Zaki didn't know anything about this pistol," said Carole.

Their voices would remain soft throughout that private conversation. "He thought lying to infidels was justified to advance Islam," Mahmood explained. "I'm not like that."

Carole moved slowly forward, her eyes trained upon his, never letting her line of fire falter from Mahmood's head. "I am guessing you have reloaded this pistol since this morning," she told him. "The police don't know it's here because you used a bigger gun to kill Zaki and then Samina, which the police confiscated from you."

"You want to shoot Samuel," said Mahmood. "You have seen the police harassing me."

"You will not harm my daughter," Carole told Mahmood, as Carole moved the pistol barrel closer to his forehead, "not anymore."

Mahmood's gaze remained with her widening eyes. "We can try again, Carole, forge a new Australia, for everyone."

If the policemen outside the room heard anything of their

whispers, they surely could not decipher them. The door remained closed.

"Politicians don't shoot people, Carole," smiled Mahmood. "You're a Member of Federal Parliament."

The far end of the pistol touched his skin, too close. She looked back at his eyes, one and then the other. "Don't forget, Mahmood," she whispered, almost choking to use that name, "I've resigned."

"You haven't resigned, Carole. You only resigned if I'm found guilty of something, but I won't be. You can stay in the Parliament: the heroine who brought the police to Samina Quresh." For a moment he raised his voice a little, before his whispers again softened. "I will remember everything that happened."

"I too will remember," whispered Carole.

Again Mahmood smiled, this time almost warmly. "Everything I told you is true, Carole."

"I can't take the chance that it's not."

"Will killing me make you feel better, Carole?"

"I've stopped believing things because they make me feel better, Mahmood."

"You're a Christian," whispered Mahmood, the pace of his voice quickening a little. "You're a woman."

The end of the pistol barrel fidgeted on his forehead, but Carole kept it there. It pressed a little harder, then less so, with the pulse of Carole's hand.

"You can't kill me, Carole, without killing yourself."

The pistol tilted a little one way, and then another. It became a little heavier for her to hold.

"What about justice?" asked Mahmood.

"Justice means capturing and punishing criminals," answered Carole.

"Your courts might convict me, Carole."

"Our courts might not."

A smile and then a grin crept out from Mahmood's mouth. "Is this your principle, Carole Wynworth?"

"This is my reality," she lamented, flexing her soft fingers on the calculating trigger.

Mahmood's grin ruptured into a laugh, a chuckling merry laugh that surely the policemen outside the room heard, before his voice resumed its softness. "Are you better than me, Mrs Wynworth?"

She nodded. "My daughter, my husband," she continued whispering, her eyes starting to water, "my blood, my heart."

Carole's father understood that fights for life and peace sometimes required people to kill. Mister Schimmelmann had died. The time had come for Carole to let her gardener go. The Rohingya refugees could stay in Bangladesh.

A knock came from the door. Mahmood glanced towards it, before looking back at Carole. If he thought about calling out, then it wouldn't have helped him.

"Can you hear the bells, Mahmood?" asked Carole, as her finger squeezed the hairline trigger. The pearl-handled pistol popped a single bullet into Mahmood's forehead.

Mahmood's head fell back as the door thrust open. The Superintendent and black-clothed policeman burst into the room.

Mahmood's body fell back and to its side, awkwardly on the floor. Blood trickled from his forehead hole.

Carole withdrew her left hand from the pistol. Her left arm fell to her side.

The Superintendent reached Mahmood, crouched down, and touched Mahmood's neck. He soon looked up and back to her. "He's dead," said the Superintendent, his voice slow and controlled, but the first voice of a normal volume in that room since he'd left Carole and Mahmood alone. Patiently, he stood up, watching Carole as she watched him. "Now, Mrs Wynworth," he asked her, "what should I do?"

Carole lowered the pistol to her right side. "You decide, Superintendent," she said, her voice returned to her customary tone, as her eyes turned back to the body on the floor. "Amen."

ABOUT THE AUTHOR

Simon Lennon has lived, worked, and travelled throughout Europe, America, Australasia, Asia, and the South Pacific. He is married with six children. He is the author of the following books.

Fiction
The King of a Vacant City
Swansong of a Childless People
A Young Man's Tale
The Insubordinate
Mahmood and Mrs Wynworth

Non-Fiction
Western Individualism
The End of Natural Selection
The Need for Nations
People's Identity
Of Whom We're Born
Biological Us
A Land to Belong
The Failure of Multiculturalism
Reclaiming Western Cultures
Christendom Lost
Aiding Islam

www.ingramcontent.com/pod-product-compliance
Lightning Source LLC
Chambersburg PA
CBHW030253200626
46816CB00002BA/622